GALLOWAY'S GAMBLE

GALLOWAY'S GAMBLE

HOWARD WEINSTEIN

FIVE STAR
A part of Gale, a Cengage Company

GALE
A Cengage Company

Farmington Hills, Mich • San Francisco • New York • Waterville, Maine
Meriden, Conn • Mason, Ohio • Chicago

Five Star™ Publishing, a part of Gale, a Cengage Company.

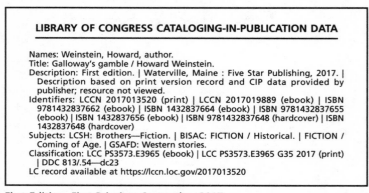

LIBRARY OF CONGRESS CATALOGING-IN-PUBLICATION DATA

Names: Weinstein, Howard, author.
Title: Galloway's gamble / Howard Weinstein.
Description: First edition. | Waterville, Maine : Five Star Publishing, 2017. |
    Description based on print version record and CIP data provided by
    publisher; resource not viewed.
Identifiers: LCCN 2017013520 (print) | LCCN 2017019889 (ebook) | ISBN
    9781432837662 (ebook) | ISBN 1432837664 (ebook) | ISBN 9781432837655
    (ebook) | ISBN 1432837656 (ebook) | ISBN 9781432837648 (hardcover) | ISBN
    1432837648 (hardcover)
Subjects: LCSH: Brothers—Fiction. | BISAC: FICTION / Historical. | FICTION /
    Coming of Age. | GSAFD: Western stories.
Classification: LCC PS3573.E3965 (ebook) | LCC PS3573.E3965 G35 2017 (print)
    | DDC 813/.54—dc23
LC record available at https://lccn.loc.gov/2017013520

First Edition. First Printing: September 2017
Find us on Facebook–https://www.facebook.com/FiveStarCengage
Visit our website–http://www.gale.cengage.com/fivestar/
Contact Five Star™ Publishing at FiveStar@cengage.com

Printed in the United States of America
1 2 3 4 5 6 7 21 20 19 18 17

GALLOWAY'S GAMBLE

ACKNOWLEDGMENTS

Long before *Star Trek* came along and ultimately led me to become a professional writer, I loved watching TV westerns while growing up in the 1950s and '60s. And I remember westerns as both serious and fun—dealing with some significant issues and themes, certainly, but folding those into stories with characters who could also make me laugh. So, *Galloway's Gamble* is gratefully inspired by such classics as *Butch Cassidy and the Sundance Kid, Maverick, Have Gun Will Travel,* and *The Sting* (from a slightly later historical era).

For that inspiration and enjoyment, I thank the following (some living, too many departed): Actors James Garner and Jack Kelly, Paul Newman and Robert Redford, Pete Duel and Ben Murphy. Writers and producers Roy Huggins, Marion Hargrove, William Goldman, David S. Ward, and Gordon Dawson; and directors George Roy Hill and Burt Kennedy.

I'd also like to thank assorted friends, family, and colleagues for encouragement and constructive comments, including: Pat Davis, Diane Lee Baron, Andrew Bergstrom, T.J. Burnside-Clapp, Rick Liftig, Ross Lally, Jim Rhule, Bob Greenberger, Albert Palazzo, Alan Chafin, Leanna Chamish, Paul Balzé, David Tayman, Johnny D. Boggs, Sharon Jarvis, Jonathan Eigen, Thomas Vinciguerra, Victoria Holzrichter, and Susan White (my very patient wife). Thanks, too, to writer pals Dayton Ward and Kevin Dilmore for permission to purloin their names for a con-game moniker; Michael Thomas at Old Tucson Studios in

Arizona; and editors Tiffany Schofield, Erin Bealmear, and Hazel Rumney, and the whole Five Star gang.

Among the many books I read during months of research was *Forty Years a Gambler on the Mississippi,* the now-famous 1887 memoir of actual Mississippi riverboat gambler George H. Devol. This and many other primary source historical books are reprinted (often in original form and format) by publishing company Applewood Books (www.applewoodbooks.com). If you're interested in real-life history, check out Applewood's catalog.

Howard Weinstein
January 2017

ARCHIVIST NOTES: THE MUSIC OF *GALLOWAY'S GAMBLE*

Since Jamey Galloway mentioned specific songs in his memoir, our present-day archivist thought readers might enjoy knowing more about that music, to help you slip into the life and times of the story's characters. Think of it as the book's soundtrack.

Before mass media, people had to provide their own entertainment, and music was a big part of that—in home parlors; churches and meeting houses; saloons, theaters, and concert halls; even around campfires. Songs familiar to mid-nineteenth-century Americans ranged from Negro spirituals to church hymns, to popular tunes by composers like Stephen Foster, whose songs we still know more than 150 years later. Many such songs were printed and sold as inexpensive sheet music, to be sung by one or many human voices, and played on pianos, banjos, guitars, fiddles, mandolins, accordions, and harmonicas.

Jamey noted these seven songs at key moments in his story, so that readers might better share his experience. While our brief archival entries provide context for each song, we hope you'll also want to listen to them. Thanks to the Internet, even obscure music may be available for free listening—often in multiple adaptations. After sampling a variety of options ourselves, we've narrowed down the many choices to a few artists whose arrangements of these songs fit the period and which Jamey would likely recognize.

To find these links, either Google or enter in the YouTube search box the mentioned performer's name and song title, and you should get there without too much trouble. Or feel free to listen to other versions, if you're curious about how these songs evolved and lasted so long in the American songbook.

Camptown Races

This tune by famed composer Stephen Foster was first published in 1850. Like many of Foster's songs, it was written for minstrel shows—sung by white performers in buffoonish blackface—so the original lyrics sound racist and mocking by modern standards. Thanks to catchy melodies and humor, songs like "Camptown Races" stuck around long enough to transcend their origins, and evolve into beloved folk tunes. Listen to folksinger Pete Seeger's traditional arrangement. Close your eyes and imagine you're hearing it in a typical nineteenth-century saloon.

Dixie

You don't have to be a southerner to know this song. But you may be surprised to learn it was written in New York City on a dreary March day in 1859 by Daniel Decatur Emmett for the singing group Bryant's Minstrels. Longing for warmer weather, Emmett came up with the line, "I wish I was in Dixie." Widely performed in northern minstrel shows, "Dixie" was popular there well before southerners adopted it as the Confederacy's unofficial anthem. We suggest folksinger Tom Roush's straight-forward interpretation.

Yellow Rose of Texas

According to legend, this may have originated as a love song during the Texas Revolution in 1836, though it apparently wasn't published until 1858. It did become popular among Texas Confederates during the Civil War, and folksinger John McCutcheon's lively arrangement (from his 1997 album *Sprout*

Wings and Fly) makes it easy to imagine this well-known tune played in many towns, as men marched off to fight.

Oh! Susanna

First published in 1848, this Stephen Foster song was also written for minstrel shows, with original lyrics that were racist and demeaning to African-Americans. As with other Foster songs, this one endured and the lyrics transformed over time into Americana. The version so many of us learned as kids in school and summer camp, more than a century after it was written, is really a love song—a feeling captured well in a sweet, melancholy arrangement by musician Nathan Edwards. James Taylor recorded it with a jazzy lilt on his 1970 album *Sweet Baby James*.

Long Time Traveller

A traditional hymn dating to 1856 or earlier, it was resurrected by the Canadian folk trio The Wailin' Jennys on their 2006 album *Firecracker*. Their harmonies are so mesmerizing that listeners may not realize it's essentially a funeral song—and thus a fitting tune for Juliet and her fellow soiled doves to sing as their graveside tribute to a fallen comrade.

Barbara Allen

This traditional seventeenth-century Scottish ballad would've been very familiar to mid-nineteenth-century Americans. A quick search will turn up many versions and variations in lyrics. We recommend classic arrangements from Pete Seeger and Joan Baez; and Art Garfunkel's lush, heartbreaking interpretation from his *Angel Clare* album (1973).

Down to the River to Pray

As a Negro spiritual, this song could have been well-known to Salem Rhymes and other slaves. Some historians think it may have been one of the songs used to convey key information and direction to slaves trying to escape to the North via the various river and overland routes known as the Underground Railroad. Though less familiar to us today, the song has been recorded numerous times, but nothing beats the crystalline perfection of the performance by Alison Krauss for the soundtrack of the Coen Brothers' 2000 film *O Brother, Where Art Thou?*

Though it's been more than a century since Jamey Galloway wrote his memoirs, we think he would have enjoyed your being able to listen to the same music he heard, songs that played such an important part in his life story.

Howard Weinstein
January 2017

1

"I've always been favored with the mixed blessing of an excellent memory, for the good and the bad."
—Jamey Galloway

February, 1852: Late on a cold Texas night, in a well-tended log cabin, Cara Landry sits still in a rocking chair by the glow of a lone lantern. Pale and pretty, she keeps her hands warm under a blanket across her lap. Her two boys, just shy of four and five years of age, sleep under quilts on a straw mattress in the corner. The steady rhythm of their breathing is the only sound in the room.

Then, outside, footsteps scuff through sand and gravel. Sketched by moonlight, a big man's shadow crosses the drafty window near the front door. After fumbling at the latch, he stumbles in. Drunk. He shoulders the door shut behind him.

The woman's quiet voice sounds as chilly as the night air. "Reuben. I'll be taking the boys and leaving you."

"You be *what*?"

"What you made me do at the saloon—that's the end of this. I'm your wife. Not a whore."

In two strides, swarthy Reuben Landry reaches the bed. When his strong laborer's hands yank both boys out from under their quilts, they wake with a yelp. With one son under each arm, he

15

faces his wife. Drunk as he is, his words are clear. "You ain't takin' nobody. You ain't goin' nowhere. I swear, Cara."

She stands. Her blanket slips to the plank floor, revealing the Colt Dragoon revolver she raises with both hands. Almost as long as her forearm, the black pistol weighs near four pounds. But she aims it steady, elbows braced against her ribs. Her thumb cocks the hammer.

Reuben pouts, not at all taking her seriously. "Now, that's a hell of a thing. I gave you that gun, girl."

"For protection, when you'd be gone. But you're what we need protecting from."

"Is it loaded?"

"Like you taught me."

His smirk softens into a charming, snaggle-toothed smile. "Now, *sha,* set that gun down so we can talk."

"Put the boys back in their bed."

The big Colt doesn't waver. So he lets down the smaller kid, who scuttles to the far side with wide eyes. But Reuben doesn't put the older boy down. Instead, he raises his long knife under the chin of the son thrashing in his grip.

"Let him go," Cara says. "And then get out. Don't come back 'til you can see straight."

Reuben lowers the knife, as if surrendering. He tosses his son onto the bed. A heartbeat later, he lunges blade-first at his wife. Cara squeezes the trigger. Time seems to slow. Stinging smoke and fire explode from the gun.

The shot hits Reuben in the chest. His eyelids flutter in surprise at the sudden flow of his own blood. "Hnnh . . . ain't that a hell of a thing." He falls to his knees and pitches forward. Dead, two yards from Cara's feet.

That dead man was my father. The woman who killed him was my mother. The boy who struggled for his life was my brother,

Jake, older by thirteen months. And I was the tot who cowered. That night is my first vivid memory. I still recall it, right down to the whiskey on his breath, the thunder from her gun, his blood spreading in a ruddy pool on the floor.

But then I've always been favored with the mixed blessing of an excellent memory, for the good and the bad. And, with a new century turned not long ago, I reckoned if that old gunfighter and gambler Bat Masterson could end up a sportswriter in New York City, well, I should write a book myself, before the details blurred into tall tales.

My brother and me rambled through an odyssey that included honor and treachery, tears and laughter, cruelty and kindness. Our journey took us from fighting in the Civil War to escaping from Indians, from the open range to high-stakes poker on grand Mississippi riverboats. Though we rarely looked for trouble, trouble had a way of finding us.

We had no forewarning that we'd someday be forced into a titanic struggle against a formidable enemy, with the very existence of our hometown Serenity Falls hanging in the balance. We learned that Fate rarely nudges us in the right direction— and life, like cards, is a chancy proposition. If you want to win, you've got to be willing to lose.

As William Shakespeare wrote, "Yield not thy neck to fortune's yoke, but let thy dauntless mind still ride in triumph over all mischance."

Everything you will read here I saw with my own eyes, or heard from trustworthy witnesses. It's all pretty much as it happened.

James B. Galloway
September 1905

2

"One woe doth tread upon another's heel, so fast they follow."
—William Shakespeare, *Hamlet*

As my mother used to say, "Good fortune's never a sure thing. And it generally takes its sweet time arriving." She was one to know.

Her parents, Patrick and Rose Galloway, were Scots-Irish newlyweds who left Belfast for Philadelphia in 1825. You could say gambling was in the Galloway blood, since leaving the devil you know for the one you don't—and sailing across a vast sea in a fragile boat—could hardly be called a sure thing. The grandparents I never knew—and all the settlers who came from somewhere else—had to be courageous, or crazy, or both, to literally cast their fate to the wind.

If they were lucky enough to reach the New World, and didn't end up at the bottom of the broad, briny deep, they had no idea what they'd find here. And most arrived without a single friendly face to greet them. They were on their own. If that's not a gamble, I don't know what is.

Cara Galloway was born in Philadelphia on July 4, 1826— exactly a half-century after the Declaration of Independence. Once she was old enough to understand, sharing a birth date with the nation inspired her appreciation of independence in all its forms.

Her father was dashing and amiable, an able carpenter and craftsman who liked his whiskey a bit too much. Her cheerful, determined mother ensured that her only child learned to read, write, and master arithmetic.

But Cara had to fend for herself early. Patrick died when she was eleven, and Rose passed two years later, both taken by the fevers that randomly ravaged the Philadelphia slums. Cara's parents had worked for prosperous lawyer Edwin Everett Eaton and his plump wife, Mildred, Patrick at all sorts of odd jobs and Rose washing floors and laundry at the Eatons' fine brick townhouse.

So the rich family took in the poor orphan and put her to work looking after their two young children, Peter and Mary, as well as doing cleaning chores. To help Cara feel at home, Edwin would show her the many things her father had built or fixed during his employ. Knowing that Patrick Galloway's hands had touched this chair or that door latch helped her feel less alone.

Cara developed a fast fondness for the Eaton children, and a love for teaching them. She discovered a treasury of knowledge and adventure on Edwin's overflowing library shelves. Edwin became a patron of sorts, amused by the bright girl who devoured books in great gulps the way a parched prospector guzzles water. His wife couldn't be troubled by books, so Edwin engaged Cara in lively discussions of history, poetry, and Shakespeare on many an evening after Peter and Mary had been tucked into bed, and Mrs. Eaton retired to her own room.

He also introduced her to the practical and scientific writings of legendary Philadelphian Benjamin Franklin, and she read and reread Franklin's memoir and her mentor's fragile collection of *Poor Richard's Almanack*. As her knowledge grew, so did her confidence, and Edwin gradually stopped regarding her as a child.

For the first time in her short life, Cara even had her own

little slice of paradise: the small garden behind the Eaton home, where she could spend her rare free time reading in the shade of a maple tree, listening to birds, basking in the sweet scent of rose bushes hugging the flagstone path.

Cara learned that sparing the rod didn't necessarily spoil the children, as long as it was replaced by plain and consistent rules. When Mildred Eaton dismissed Cara's theories as poppycock, Cara argued in her own defense—and Mildred slapped her across the face. From then on, her wariness of Mrs. Eaton's temper simmered behind an obedient façade.

But Cara still liked Edwin, and wanted to live up to his high opinion of her potential. To dodge further quarrels with Mildred, Cara simply decided to care for young Peter and Mary her own way when their parents weren't around. This subterfuge worked well enough—until Mildred noticed her children preferred Cara's company to her own. A boiling-over was only a matter of time.

One day, Mildred insisted Cara take a switch to Mary's behind for some paltry misbehavior. Cara refused, and they squabbled. As Mildred raised her hand for a roundhouse slap, Edwin rushed in and banished Cara to her room. When his wife demanded that Cara be thrown out, Edwin convinced her to give the girl another chance.

He came into Cara's room and closed the door behind him. Steeled for a lecture, she was surprised when he complimented her for standing up to Mrs. Eaton. "But then, you're no longer a girl. You've blossomed."

Edwin moved so close she could count the hairs in his nostrils, and his long fingers brushed her face. He kissed her on the cheek and then left her, alone but in the company of multiple terrors—of what he might try next, of feeling powerless, of losing her position and the comforts of a wealthy home.

Over the next few months, Cara fretted: were Mildred's

hostility and Edwin's unwelcome attentions fast outweighing the advantages of life with the Eatons? She tried to lose herself in books about Lewis and Clark's expedition to map the west, longing to see the wilderness for herself.

Her postponed day of reckoning came soon after she turned seventeen in July of '43. Following another squabble with Mildred, Edwin cornered Cara in her room. She expected anger. What she got was worse.

"My wife has become a harsh-tempered, vain cow, and an in-congenial partner in our bed. She knows nothing of literature or history, nor wants to know," he said. "But you and I are kindred spirits. I know your virtues. And I know you are as ready to share your passion as I am to receive such a gift."

How he'd reached *that* conclusion, Cara had no idea. Her frantic eyes darted in search of deliverance. But there was no way out. If she screamed, there was no one to rescue her. Mildred might interrupt, but she'd surely condemn Cara as an ungrateful trollop who'd seduced her husband, and would throw her out into the streets—pausing to beat her first, of course.

So Cara kept her mouth shut. The more she struggled, the tighter Edwin gripped her wrists. She was sure he'd snap her bones before he'd let her go. Then she thought: *What if I just . . . surrender?*

And that's what she did. To her surprise, his grip relaxed. Not enough to wriggle free, but enough to seize the moment of uncertainty.

"My passion and virtue are yours," she whispered, and his face lit up like he was about to take possession of the Promised Land. Amazed at how easily her warm breath in his ear deluded Edwin into mistaking desperation for desire, she decided to play her hand and see where it led. "But not while Mrs. Eaton and the children are in the house."

She murmured that she wanted to give herself to him, but

not rushed. Tomorrow afternoon . . . when it was time for her to take the children to the green for their daily outing, she'd feign illness. Edwin could then suggest that his wife reassert dominion over their children by taking them out herself, and he'd vow to give Cara a stern scolding. "With Mrs. Eaton and the children out, we'll be alone," Cara said, "to do as we please."

Edwin eagerly agreed—and then clung to her, immobilized by his own lust. So she trundled him toward the door. Miraculously, his feet shuffled in the right direction. She urged him on with lines from *Romeo and Juliet:* " 'Good night, good night! Parting is such sweet sorrow—' "

"—'Th-that I shall say . . . g-good night till it be . . . morrow,' " he finished in a red-faced fluster as she opened the door enough to steer him out into the hallway. She shut the door, leaned back against it, and slid to the floor.

It was only a temporary reprieve, and she knew it. As much as she hated to abandon two unspoiled children to the tender mercies of monstrous parents, she stuffed her few essential belongings into her carpetbag.

She took a step toward the door—and then went back for the leather shoulder bag hanging from the mirror over her dresser. Her father had made it for her tenth birthday, with a rose blossom tooled into the closure flap. Its contents were the few other treasured bits of her childhood—an ivory hairbrush, three small carved dolls in dresses her mother had stitched from fabric scraps, and a small mirror with a sculpted handle.

With a sigh, she looked at her growing collection of precious books. They'd weigh her down if she took them all, so she grabbed two she couldn't live without—her mother's King James Bible, and a slender Franklin volume called *The Way to Wealth,* which Edwin had given to her.

Cara crept down the stairs, grateful for knowing every creaky tread and board, and able to evade them all. She slipped out through the kitchen door, bade farewell to her beloved roses, and disappeared into the misty sleeping city beyond the Eatons' garden wall.

Certain Edwin must be hunting for her, she wandered the streets for two days, always looking over her shoulder, wishing she could vanish like a vapor. After narrowly escaping robbery (or worse) at the hands of an alley thug by kicking him in the shins and running, Cara found sanctuary and a meal at Old St. Joseph's Church, a few blocks from the Pennsylvania State House (not yet known as Independence Hall). She learned the church's Sisters of Charity were recruiting teachers willing to establish frontier schools.

Well. She'd survived life with the Eatons, so Cara figured she was qualified to face wilderness savages. There was one catch: the church expected its teachers to be Catholic, which the Galloways of Ulster were not. But she longed to migrate west, and these otherwise perfectly nice Papists offered her a way to do that.

She decided God would forgive her for bearing false witness in His holy church. And if He didn't? Well, she'd deal with that when the time came.

She'd not be pledging to be a nun with perpetual vows. She only had to prove she could read, write, and wrangle numbers; take temporary vows of poverty, chastity, and obedience; and agree to renew those yearly. So she signed up, and the Sisters soon sent her to western Arkansas, to a nub of a town called Turpentine in the piney hills north of Fort Smith.

At her tiny school, she applied her belief that children could thrive under strict but fair rules, without beatings. The parents in town didn't know exactly what she was doing, but their children oddly loved school, learned a great deal, and groaned when they were kept home to toil away at endless chores.

Cara fashioned herself a place in the community, and after

her first year, she thought she might've found a home for good. But she also met Reuben Landry, a bearded, broad-shouldered young Cajun recently moved north from Louisiana.

Intoxicated by the independence to make her own choices, she fell in love with this charming rogue who reminded her of her father. With no heavy heart at all, she wrote to the Sisters of Charity to inform them (and God) she was renouncing her vows. Cara was nineteen when she married Reuben, and she quit teaching—much to the town's disappointment—when my brother, Jacob Patrick, was born on March 12th, 1847.

I came along on April 6th the next year, and they named me James Benjamin (for Benjamin Franklin, my mother's hero), though I was called Jamey from the start. Jake favored Mama's fair face and chestnut hair, but with Daddy's dark eyes. It was easy to tell us apart, since I took after Daddy more, with his darker complexion and wavy black hair, though with Mama's green eyes.

Our strapping daddy was handy with an axe and saw, so he found plenty of work helping settlers clear land and build cabins. Though he had little schooling, he was sly—and could be too clever for his own good. That, coupled with a restless and argumentative nature, started costing him jobs and made it hard to support his family.

Once, he was accused of stealing a chicken from a farmer he'd quarreled with over some fence work. He denied any theft, and we never dined on the evidence. So, either he didn't do it—or he got away with it. Mama never knew for sure.

Soon after the chicken uproar, she discovered mysterious items in the house, including a watch and tools she knew he couldn't afford to buy. Did he trade the stolen chicken for them? He swore they were payment for helping travelers fix a broken wagon wheel. She reckoned the man she loved had lied to her, and that soured her some.

Fact was, she was running out of patience and growing weary of stretching too little food over too many meals. But the day she happened to mention that some neighbors had begged her to resume teaching, his frustration exploded. When she stood up to him (and she barely came up to his chin), he smacked her across the face. Next day, he acted like all was well. But she never looked at him or trusted him the same after that.

Without telling her, Daddy had applied for a homestead—six hundred and forty acres of free land—in the big new state of Texas. When she found out, she was ready to skin him. But he bewitched her with his grand schemes for farming and raising cattle (not that he knew anything about either one).

He might even sell some of his land to newcomers and start his very own town, promising Mama she'd be the queen of Landryville. With her sullen acquiescence, we traded our cabin for a weather-beaten Schuttler prairie schooner and two mules, and set out for Texas.

3

"If I owned Texas and Hell, I'd rent out Texas and live in Hell."
—General Philip H. Sheridan, U.S. Army

If Landryville was Reuben's pipe dream, that land in Texas was real. After a month of travel, through Arkansas and across the Red River, we reached our homestead not far from Serenity Falls, a fledgling one-street town east of Waco, near a broad stream feeding the Brazos River. A hundred or so miles north of Austin and south of Dallas (each of which only had a few hundred residents in those days), it was fair to say Serenity Falls was in the middle of nowhere.

Which described most of Texas in 1849.

Not that he meant to, but Daddy brought us to a place of hills and forests, with plenty of game, and wood for the taking by any man skilled with an axe. The weather could turn cussed hot in summer, but winter was mostly mild, with only an occasional snowfall or ice storm. With plenty of rain for raising crops, the climate had more in common with cotton and tobacco-growing southern states than it did the prairies and deserts to the west and north.

Daddy cut trees and built a log shack as fast as he could, complete with the luxury of a wood-plank floor instead of dirt. He even built an inside wall to provide a small bedroom for the two of them, separate from the main room where Mama cooked and me and Jake slept.

Mama learned that Serenity Falls hadn't been standing long. A young surveyor named Josiah Ford had arrived soon after Texas became a state at the end of '45, looking for a place to start a town. He represented a syndicate of six young men from Memphis, Tennessee, organized by ambitious merchant Silas Atwood. The other four were Atwood's younger brother, Samuel, and three cousins—brothers Louis, Arthur, and Zeb Brewer.

Assisted by Samuel Atwood, Ford staked the group's claim, situated on the southern bank of an uncharted stream he called Pine Cut Run. He named the new town after the waterfall that lullabied them to sleep the first night they camped there.

Starting with six hundred and forty acres, the group filed for five more adjacent homesteads, giving them a total of six square miles to subdivide, develop, and sell to newcomers. That plan faltered when Ford and Samuel were on their way back to Tennessee, and were set upon by robbers. Ford was killed, and Samuel swore he heard Ford curse the town and Texas with his dying breath. So much for serenity.

Still, the surviving partners and some family members moved there in the spring of '47. Between homesickness and death, the founding group soon dwindled to two, with only Silas Atwood and cousin Louis remaining, in charge of the Serenity Falls Bank & Land Company. By the end of '48, enough settlers had arrived for the bank and land company to prosper.

When Louis Brewer's young wife died in childbirth, the grief-stricken cousin decided Josiah Ford really had cursed Serenity Falls, sold his share to Silas Atwood and went home. Now, since Texas in its infinite wisdom had decided to ban the incorporation of banks, Atwood's private bank was unbound by regulation or charter. Eventually, this would prove a bad idea.

I must say this for my daddy. He did give farming a try. Predictably, he failed—and after a year, he hated farming as much as any man ever hated anything. Instead, he worked clearing other farmers' land and helping settlers build houses. Much of the money he earned slipped through his fingers at the ironically named Silver Spoon Saloon, where he spent much of his time drinking and gambling—usually in that order, which didn't improve his odds of winning.

The Silver Spoon hunkered by its lonesome, surrounded by empty lots on both sides and behind, in the center of the town's broad commercial Main Street. Other early merchants and businesses included Duncan's General Store, Stoker's Hardware, the livery, a butcher, and three other even less elegant saloons. Atwood's two-story brick bank stood proud on the highest hill in town.

Main Street intersected at its north end with the literally named North Street, which soon had ten small cabins on neatly divided lots. Optimistic town plans included a grid of twenty new streets beyond that.

The more Daddy drank and gambled, the more he was given to fits of anger aimed at his wife and sons. Mama grew to prefer his absence, no matter what he might be doing out of her sight—at least until the night he came home and announced he'd traded most of our land for the Silver Spoon, keeping only the cabin and two acres. Mama was stunned speechless, but what's done was done.

The saloon's original owner, a Mexican named Diego Cruz de Saltillo, was delighted by the swap. Cruz was a man of medium build, but the corded muscle in his arms hinted at deceptive strength. He had thick black hair with gray nipping at the edges of his mustache.

Born in 1812, he'd migrated north of the border, living among the Anglos and fighting for Texas in the war against Mexico that led to establishment of the Texas Republic in '36. After years of backbreaking work as a *vaquero* for various small cattle ranchers, Cruz left the dust behind and settled in Serenity Falls two weeks after its founding. He rented himself a prime lot, set up a tent, and opened the town's first saloon.

As soon as he was able, he'd bought the lot and built something more permanent, if far from majestic: a log box with a gently pitched roof, six strides wide and forty feet from front to back. The public room had a door flanked by two windows, a wood-plank bar on the left side, and a stone hearth on the right. A door at the back led to a storeroom, and the kitchen, which included a table, four chairs, a corner cot, and a cast-iron stove where Cruz cooked simple meals for saloon patrons.

Though he eked out a passable living running the Silver Spoon, there were times when he hated it. He especially bridled at having to provide whores to compete with the other drinking joints in town. The whores did their work in a low shed out back, divided into a half-dozen cribs bedded with straw and blankets. Not much better than stable stalls, they were drafty and cold in winter, sweltering and swirling with flies in summer.

The swap was Daddy's idea, and Cruz agreed so fast it might've roused Reuben's suspicions, if he hadn't been so drunk. But there was no law against drunks making deals. Daddy got to own the place he spent most of his time anyway, which meant drinking for free. And Cruz had what he wanted— land—so he could do what he preferred, growing and cooking food. But he stayed on at the saloon as bartender, cook, and bookkeeper. Since Daddy was seldom sober, Cruz pretty much still ran the place.

He'd initially regarded Reuben Landry as a harmless drunk, since Daddy rarely got into fights at the saloon. But that opinion changed when Mama, Jake, and me started coming around the Silver Spoon more, and Cruz saw how he treated us—especially Mama.

The Mexican did not take kindly to bullies, which is why

he'd fought for Texas in the first place. Whenever Daddy would curse at Mama, or threaten to hit her, Cruz would be glowering nearby, ready to step in. But Mama always warned him off with a look, and never showed fear.

When Reuben wasn't skunked on whiskey, he had some good days as a father. He'd show us off to folks at the Silver Spoon, calling us his "little men" and bragging on how smart and strong we were. When Jake was four and I was three, Daddy decided he'd teach us to ride.

I took to being on a horse like I was born there. But on Jake's first try riding solo, without anyone holding the reins and guiding him, a hawk shrieked overhead, and the spooked horse took off. They tore down the alley behind the saloon and headed straight for the river, with Jake screaming and clinging to that saddle horn.

A few strides from the water, the horse ran into a little mud flat and skidded to a stop. Jake flew over the horse's head, flipped like a circus acrobat, and landed in the water. Luckily, it was deep enough—with a sandy bottom instead of rocks—that he came up scared and wet, but not hurt.

His hat fared less well, when the horse put his hoof right through the crown as it lay in the mud. That was the start of my brother's lifelong problematic relationship with hats, which often ended badly for the hats. And though he eventually overcame his mortal fear of horses, it was a rare occasion when a horse was his first choice of transportation.

Daddy's drinking grew worse—and so did his abuse. Too many mornings, Mama felt shame as she went about her business in town, knowing people were staring at bruises on her face and neck. She was grateful they couldn't see the worst bruises under her clothing. But she feared less for her own safety than for me and Jake. She couldn't understand how a man could beat his own little sons.

Daddy spent more and more of his time at the Silver Spoon—too drunk to be of much use, or just flat passed out. No surprise that those were the times Mama felt safest. She also wanted to feel useful, so she put in more time helping Cruz manage the saloon. She impressed the Mexican with her skill at keeping the accounts in her meticulous writing, and she worried about the four bedraggled girls serving as whores. Hardly a week went by without her patching up their cuts and bruises inflicted by the men who used them.

Of course, the "soiled doves" would also beat up on each other, and scuffle over alcohol and drugs. Seeing all that degradation up close, Mama understood why Cruz wasn't unhappy to trade the Silver Spoon for our land.

But even though he wasn't the owner anymore, Cruz found it hard to look the other way. Many a night, he'd brandish his butcher knife and escort some roughneck cowhand or traveler off the premises, while Mama tended to another bloodied whore.

Still and all, Cruz never expected what happened between Cara and Reuben that fateful February night. It was a bustling Saturday, with Cruz extra busy dishing out stew and pouring drinks, and the whores working overtime—until they came up one short.

When a rawboned ranch hand insisted on immediate service, Reuben snatched Cara away from the cashbox and dragged her toward the customer. "She's a good'n," he said. "Used her personally. Many a time."

Mama shook herself loose. Daddy backhanded her across the face and shoved her at the cowboy. "He needs a whore. And we need the money."

The scariest thing to Cara was the lack of anger in Reuben's voice. It was just business, and his wife was just another whore. When she saw Cruz and his glinting butcher knife taking a step toward them, she looked him away. The Mexican retreated, though he didn't want to. But he understood this was between Cara and her husband.

So she took that drunken, dusty cowboy out to the cribs and did what she had to. Feeling the prickly straw and scratchy blanket against her bare goose-fleshed legs, she felt as low as a body could get. And she wondered what she'd do next.

Four hours later, Daddy lay dead at Mama's feet. She set the gun down on the supper table he'd built and stepped around his body. She wrapped us each in a quilt and put our shoes on. In silence, Mama walked us the two miles into town, to the dark and empty Silver Spoon.

Cruz emerged from the back room, wearing a nightshirt and carrying a lantern. "So, Reuben . . . he's dead, huh." He said it like he knew.

Mama nodded. Cruz took us kids to the back room and put us to bed. Jake fell asleep almost right away, but I couldn't. I heard Cruz talking low to Mama in the front as he poured drinks for both of them and sat her down at a table. "You okay?"

"I just left him there," she said, her first words since firing the Colt.

"He's dead. Don't matter much now."

"I . . . might've left the door open. What if animals go in?"

"I'll go see." But when Cruz stood, Mama clutched his wrist, so he sat down again. They stayed that way for a couple of hours, until the sun came up.

Cruz went out and came back with Sheriff Huggins, who sat with Mama and asked her about the night before. Francis "Jawbone" Huggins was a mountain of a man, bald as a boulder, with an easy, lopsided smile under a soup-strainer mustache. He was pretty young back then, the first and only sheriff Serenity Falls had up to that time, and for a long while after. He was so big he had to ride a draft horse—folks said he might not ride fast, but he could ride all day.

Some people in town thought he was loco for rarely carrying a gun, but Sheriff Huggins was no fool and this strategy wasn't as dangerous as you might think. Contrary to Wild West melodramas and dime novels, not everybody carried a firearm. Farmers had little need for pistols, and used rifles sparingly for hunting or chasing off coyotes and foxes showing an interest in their livestock. Between low pay and the expense of ammunition, even cowboys needed to be pretty angry to fire at another man.

When tempers were inflamed, Jawbone wasn't the first (or last) lawman to conclude that adding another gun to the fray could be like throwing fuel on a fire. He was proud of the fact that he'd never shot anyone, never had to. With his rumbling velvet voice, he could confabulate all day and into the next, if that's what it took to talk folks out of murderous deliberations. And that's how he'd earned the moniker Jawbone.

The name had a second meaning, too. With his size, he could lay out most any man with one punch to the jaw—something he'd done to Reuben a couple of times, hoping to knock some sense into him.

After breakfast, Mama and Cruz loaded us into the saloon's wagon out back. The sun and a south wind had already melted the overnight chill. We met Jawbone on his big bay mare with the white star between her eyes, and all went out to our cabin.

The sheriff examined Daddy's gray corpse, and rolled him onto his back to check the wound. When he asked Mama to show him what happened, she picked up the gun and blanket and sat in the rocking chair, then directed Cruz to reenact the events that led up to the shooting.

"I got no reason to doubt your account, Miz Cara," Jawbone said. "There's no denyin' the darkness in Reuben's nature. Sad to say, this don't come as a surprise."

That was the consensus around town as the news spread. It was almost like neighbors had been weighing odds which Landry would end up dead first. Most expected that to be Mama. So maybe there was a little surprise after all. Since Serenity Falls had no undertaker then, Cruz and the sheriff cobbled together a pine coffin and brought it back to the cabin.

"Did you want to dress him in something else?" Cruz said to Mama.

"No. No point in burying nice clothes."

She did spread a blanket in the bottom of the coffin. Cruz and Sheriff Huggins placed the body inside and nailed down the lid. They cinched a rope around the box, wrestled it onto the flatbed wagon, and hauled Daddy away.

As Mama dressed us, I kept looking at the bloodstain on the floor.

A few of the saloon regulars had dug a grave by the time we reached the cemetery on a hillside at the edge of town, for what could best be called a burial rather than a funeral. Jawbone, Cruz, and a few other men lowered Daddy's mortal remains and shoveled the dirt back into the hole. We had no preacher, either, and nobody really knew what to say. But folks lingered, as if no man should be buried without a word in his honor.

Jawbone cleared his throat. "Reuben Landry must've had some good in him, since this little lady married him. That bein' said, some men are determined to meet a bad end. Ashes to ashes, dust to dust . . . may the good Lord have mercy on his soul." After the awkward group muttered a ragged "Amen," everyone departed but Cruz and us.

Cruz had put together a wooden cross with Daddy's name chiseled into it. He hammered it into the ground. "Didn't know when he was born. Figured I could cut the dates in later."

"Don't bother," Mama said.

She took me and Jake to the saloon instead of the cabin, and that's where we stayed. Cruz camped out in one of the whores' cribs and gave us the back room, so Mama could have the bed while me and Jake slept on the floor.

Otherwise, Mama and the Mexican pretty much went back to running the Silver Spoon. The only difference was not seeing Daddy playing cards or drinking at his usual table by the window—and us and Mama not living in fear of his sudden storms of temper.

Soon, though, men came to Mama and offered to buy the saloon. Most folks expected her to pack up and take us back east. Banker Silas Atwood said if she wanted to leave sooner rather than later, he'd handle the sale for her and send her the money. Mama listened to the offers, but said little. After a few days, she sat with Cruz. "Do you want it back?"

He snorted. "This place?"

"That's a no?"

"Why? Are you leaving?"

"I don't know. What's back east for me? We have no people there, no home."

He glanced around the room. "Is this home?"

"The saloon? Lord, no. And I can't go back to that cabin."

"Is this town home?"

Cara planted her elbows on the table, rested her chin in her hands, and thought it over. "I reckon it is."

"Then don't sell."

"The town's growing. I could make this place better." She saw his skeptical squint.

"You sure about that?"

"No. But I think I've learned something. I'd like to see if I'm right."

"About what?"

"That most men think with their peckers."

"Can't argue with that."

"There's money in that knowledge."

"This joint already makes money."

"Couldn't it make more? Take those whores' cribs out here. They're basically pig stalls. Hot in the summer, flies and mosquitoes, not to mention snakes and scorpions. On a winter night, cold enough to shrink a man who fancies himself a stallion down to the size of a thimble."

Cruz laughed at the image. "Yeah, but this was the cheapest way for me to build it. And if I had to have whores here, I could be inside serving drinks and didn't have to see 'em at their business out back."

"You ever been with a whore?"

"Now and then."

"I'll wager it was never in one of those cribs, worrying about bugs biting your nethers."

"Some hombres don't care."

"Wouldn't a gentleman like yourself prefer a room with walls and windows? A real bed, with real sheets?"

"I would."

"Would you be willing to pay more for the luxury?"

"Me? Sure. But not everybody's got those extra *dineros.*"

"We'll be selling a higher-class experience. Where every man can feel like a king . . . and won't freeze his Johnson off in January."

"Then you gonna need higher-class whores."

"Part of the plan. So . . . are you with me?"

"Never worked for no woman before."

"Never ran a saloon before. So I can use your help."

Cruz shrugged. "Sure. Why not?"

That prompted Cara's first smile in some time. Then she told of Reuben's forsaken fantasy of starting his own town. She glanced around the dingy confines of the Silver Spoon. "Sad thing is, this is the closest I'll ever get to being queen of Landryville."

Cruz raised his drink. "Long live the queen."

Next morning, Mama and Cruz went back to the cabin, loaded our belongings in the wagon, and we moved into the Silver Spoon's cramped back room. Mama also decided she didn't want to be known as Landry anymore, didn't want her sons cursed by their father's name. We'd all go back to the name she was born with—Galloway.

A few days later, she rode alone back to the cabin.

She walked inside. Emptied of the bits and pieces of our lives, it should have seemed larger. But it didn't. She toed the bloodstain on the floorboards her husband had hewn and planed from forest pines. While no mansion, it was a better home than many had. Kept us warm and dry, and safe—from everything but him.

So it seemed a shame, what Mama was about to do.

She walked outside, struck a match to light a kindling branch, and tossed it in through the front door. With a second torch, she circled the cabin and touched it to the wall in several places. The winter-dry wood caught like tinder. She felt the heat scorch her neck as she retreated to her fidgety horse. The fire grew and sparked and crackled.

She rode a safe distance away, and let her horse drop his head to graze. Then she watched in silence, until the roof collapsed, the walls fell in, and the cabin burned to the ground. Satisfied that she'd purged Reuben from what was now her past, Mama rode back to Serenity Falls, and our future.

4

"The hands that hold the gold rule the world."
—Cara Galloway

Between shooting her husband and burning down a perfectly good cabin, Cara had gained herself an outsized reputation in a town small enough that news—and judgments—spread fast. You might have thought the womenfolk would've been most alarmed by her unladylike behavior. Yet they seemingly understood, even sympathized, though few said so out loud.

It was the men who found such mayhem most threatening to the natural order, in which they could commit violent acts from time to time, while women had to cling to saintly forbearance, never mind the provocation. Cara's actions forced these men to wonder: What if their own wives, ostensibly occupied keeping hearth and home, were similarly incited? What anarchy might *that* lead to?

After Cara decided not to sell the saloon, the men of Serenity Falls had to swallow the presence of the town's first legitimate female business proprietor—with whom they'd have to conduct commerce. What if she was truly addled?

When she first got gossipy wind of such concerns, Cara fretted over townsfolk seeing her as a carnival sideshow freak. But even though she'd have nightmares for years about pulling that trigger, she knew she'd done the right thing to save her sons from a man who'd become a monster. And as a twenty-five-year-old widow, with two boys to feed and a business to run, she couldn't let accusations or pity stand in her way.

As the first order of that business, she discovered Reuben's neglect had left the saloon short on supplies as basic as whiskey and glasses. "I don't understand," Cara said to Cruz. "Why didn't you get him to keep up with this?"

"I tried. But he was the boss. You couldn't tell him nothin'."

With both wondering what they'd gotten themselves into, they put together a list of pressing needs. Cruz volunteered to take it over to Duncan's General Store, but Cara said, "No, I'll go."

She snatched the list off the table and stuffed it into her leather shoulder bag, the one she'd carried with her since Philadelphia. With me in tow, Mama avoided the horse manure among the wagon ruts and crossed the wide dirt street over to Duncan's, catty-corner from the Silver Spoon. I'd been in there a couple of times before, but I was still awed by all the whatnot packed into a single store.

Duncan's was a narrow space with a counter running from front to back on one side, and floor-to-ceiling shelves opposite. On those and other shelves behind the counter, partitioned cubbies were an orderly oasis in a world of chaos.

Foodstuffs—coffee, spices, sugar, oatmeal, honey—grouped together in one section, near dishes, pots and pans, and butter churns. Shirts, trousers, hats, and other clothing along with bolts of fabric and sewing supplies gathered in another. Apothecary items, including bottles and tins of patent medicines, hairbrushes, soaps, and miracle elixirs over here. Firearms, ammunition, and black powder over there.

A place for everything, and everything in its place.

The only exceptions were the candy confections I coveted, glittering like sweet jewels right out on the counter. Visible enough to tempt kids accompanying their parents, yet just beyond the larcenous reach of small fingers.

"Mr. Duncan," Mama said, "we're in need of an assortment of items."

Nate Duncan, bony as a bag of antlers, peered over his ever-present newspaper from behind the counter. "All righty, Miz Landry."

Her jaw tightened. "It's Galloway now."

Duncan's eyebrows rose. "Oh?"

"Is that a problem?"

He flinched as she reached into her leather bag. "Oh, *no,* ma'am. *No* problem."

"Did you think I was pulling a gun?" She looked at him like he was crazy.

He looked at her the same way. "Oh, *no,* ma'am. Why would I think that?"

Mama sighed, took out her list, and placed it on the counter. "I'd like a price."

Duncan pinned the page with one cautious finger and slid it over for a look. His lips twitched as he tallied a total in his head. When he told her, she didn't like what she heard.

"Mr. Duncan, I know how to read. And I know how to add."

"I don't doubt that, Miz Lan—*Galloway.* But them's the prices."

"I plan to do a lot of business here."

"Business ain't done by accusing folks of jewin' you, little lady. Women don't have no head for this. Maybe you should sell that saloon to somebody who does."

Mama decided to test how truly squirrelly Duncan thought she was. She reached back into her bag. He flinched again. She squelched a smile. For good measure, her hand lingered inside the bag. "I'd be ever so grateful if you lowered those prices by, say, ten percent?"

Duncan gave her a wan smile. "I . . . I think I can manage that, Miz Galloway."

"If you'd be so kind as to gather all this together, I'll send Cruz over for it later."

"Yes, ma'am. Thank you."

"Oh, *no,* Mr. Duncan. Thank *you.*"

Back at the Silver Spoon, Cruz found Mama's account amusing. "They tryin' to figure if you're a widow . . . or a murderer. Some of 'em, they think maybe you're loco. Did you really have a gun?"

"No, I had Nate's old bills. But that's for me to know, and them to wonder."

Nate Duncan wasn't the only man in town who turned skittish when Mama walked in to transact business. If their jitters about her erratic disposition made favorable terms more likely? Well, then, she'd take advantage of leverage rarely accorded a woman in a man's world—at least until she could enact plans for the saloon's improvement.

So, rather than allaying fears, she dropped hints that often as not she *did* have a firearm in her bag—the very same Colt that sent her husband to his grave. Sometimes, she'd lug that big gun out for target practice, and didn't mind who knew. As a side benefit, she became a pretty fair shot—and didn't mind if that bit of gossip spread around, too.

Her life to that point had forged Cara Galloway's determination to never again be at the mercy of any man. To assure security for her and her sons, she'd have to capitalize on the common vices of those very same men—gambling, drinking, and lust.

Living according to the Golden Rule, doing unto others as you'd have them do unto you, hadn't worked out so well. She'd been forced to accept that there was an older, more powerful and morally ambiguous truth: *The hands that hold the gold rule the world.*

If she ever hoped to direct her own destiny, she'd have to embrace that verity. She didn't have to hold all the gold, or even a great deal. Just enough.

So Mama jumped feet-first into our new life in town. First thing she did was rename the saloon. It was now the Shamrock, according to the new and prettier sign over the door, with its emerald lettering and three-leaf-clover symbol against a fresh white background. A sign in the window emphatically announced: *Under New Management!*

With help from Cruz and some hired hands, Mama set about cleaning up the place, adding more lamps and whitewashing the walls to brighten up the inside. They overhauled the whores' cribs, sealing up cracks and sealing out the elements, adding floorboards, lamps, and raised beds.

Mama also overhauled the whores themselves. No laudanum or opium, drunkenness or petty crime would be tolerated. Some of the girls found these rules onerous, and left in search of more debauched pastures, which weren't hard to find. They were easily replaced by less-soiled and more wholesome doves from among an unfortunately endless supply of orphans, runaways, and abandoned young wives.

Mama vowed to give her girls fair wages and a safe place to live. She wouldn't stand for them to be knocked around, and established that any man who failed to treat them with respect would be dealt with harshly: "Customers are paying for a poke, not a punching bag."

The first drunken ranch hand who ignored that decree shoved around a new whore with golden curls named Rhody Hassett. Like many prostitutes, Rhody carried a rough and tragic past with her. At eleven, she'd been purchased from a disreputable St. Louis orphanage, by a kindly man claiming he needed a servant girl to help his homesteading family as they headed west.

Only there was no family, and the man was collecting girls to use or sell. After five years of brutality at the hands of men and madams, attested to by a missing tooth and a scar sliced into her pretty chin, Rhody had managed to escape with some stolen cash. Her money ran out at Serenity Falls, where she'd landed with only the clothes on her back that summer of '52.

When Mama had found her foraging for food scraps and customers in an alley, she took the girl in—and she wasn't about to let Rhody's new life turn out the same as her old one. That's how the liquored-up young cowboy found himself staring down the business end of Mama's Colt Dragoon. With a waggle of her gun barrel, she directed him away from the sniffling girl on the bed.

He obediently skittered across the room. As Mama took a closer look at Rhody's bloody lip, he mustered some squeaky voiced bravado. "Hey, I already paid for them whore parts of hers, and I expect my money's worth."

"Those whore parts happen to belong to a girl, and you are not permitted to lay an angry hand on her."

"You wouldn't shoot me over a dumb whore."

Mama cocked the pistol. "I might."

"I'm just leaving."

The cowboy grabbed his gear, brushed by Mama, rushed out—and ran right into Sheriff Jawbone Huggins, who hooked the man's arm, halted his hasty departure, and sized up the situation. "Cara. You gonna bring out that cannon every time there's trouble?"

"Maybe."

Jawbone sighed. "Do us both a favor. Hire a security man."

Then he released the spooked cowboy, and the man fled down the hall and out the door.

By the end of that year of Daddy's killing, Mama and Cruz had the Shamrock running pretty smoothly. Business was good, ratifying the wisdom of her improvements.

One enhancement was purely for her, though—three rose bushes planted right outside the back window. She could see them from the kitchen table while she worked on accounts or ate meals with Jake and me. Nobody would ever mistake the saloon's back alley for the Eatons' gracious Philadelphia garden, but she doted on those roses and they survived their first summer in fine bloom.

Her relationship with Cruz didn't grow quite so well. While he could be courtly, even gallant, he chafed at having a woman in charge. And to be fair, Mama contributed to his vexation. Intent on proving herself, her requests often sounded like orders—and each one irritated the proud Mexican like a burr in his britches. She'd tell him what to do. He'd do it his own way, out of pure spite. He'd go out without notifying her. She'd interrogate him when he came back. And on and on.

He ridiculed the time she wasted pampering her roses. She belittled most of his ideas for the saloon—even when he was right—just because she took issue with his ornery attitude. What he wanted most was to add a real restaurant, where he could serve meals more inventive than stews to customers who might appreciate his cooking artistry. The more he pushed, the more she resisted.

For me and Jake, it was almost like having Mama and Daddy arguing over every little thing. One day, after witnessing a particularly emphatic scrap, I burst into tears, rushed in to hug Mama around her legs, and begged her to *please* not shoot Cruz.

"Even little Chico there knows you are a hell-fired, stubborn *mangoneador,*" he growled.

"What the hell did you call me?"

"Bossy."

"Well, I am the boss. Remember that."

"And you remember, I know how to run a saloon and you don't."

That goaded Mama to move ahead with her plans sooner rather than later. The shabby little saloon was like a pig in a dress—embellishments had their limits. It was time to expand, and for that she'd need a loan. Without a word to Cruz, she went to Silas Atwood's Serenity Falls Bank & Land Company. There, in his opulent office—furnished with a fine Oriental rug, massive desk, and leather chairs—she discovered she didn't own the vacant lots surrounding the Shamrock.

"Well, who the hell does?"

"Mr. Cruz," Atwood said around his cigar.

Mama squinted at the short round banker, whose vest buttons always seemed on the verge of popping. "But he traded the saloon to Reuben."

"He only traded the building and the one lot. Cruz is one shrewd greaser. Instead of some fancy joint, he built himself a hovel. Used the rest of his money to buy up the lots around it. Figured he could build on 'em, or sell 'em for profit. Kept 'em when he swapped with your husband."

Mama returned to the saloon and confronted Cruz. "You proud of yourself, cheating a drunk?"

"I didn't cheat nobody. Reuben wanted the saloon, that's what I gave him. He never asked about nothin' else. It ain't cheating to keep something to yourself. It's just business."

"I want to buy those lots from you."

"Not if I don't wanna sell." The Mexican stalked out, got on his horse, rode away—and stayed away.

Mama spent a week trying to prove she didn't need him.

After long days struggling with simple tasks like moving heavy barrels, and doing everything else Cruz used to do, including cooking and tending bar, she worked herself into a state of exhaustion. Swallowing her considerable stubborn pride, she drove the wagon out to where he was living in a tent and cooking over a fire pit—on the land that used to be ours.

"Hey, Cruz."

"Hey, yourself."

"So, here's the plan. You want to see it?"

"Not really."

She spread out some scrolled architect's drawings in the wagon's cargo box. They showed a new two-story building, much larger than the current Shamrock. "You might like it."

He shrugged and poked at the fire with a long stick.

"It'll have hotel rooms."

Cruz shrugged again.

"I know you have your own ideas."

He snorted, as if that was all he had to say, and all she deserved to hear.

"People can't change?" she teased.

"Not that I seen."

"So what'll it take?"

"To get me back? A kitchen. A real kitchen."

"We don't need a real kitchen."

His hand flapped in a dismissive wave. "Ha! See?"

"Unless we have a real restaurant."

With an indifferent huff, he went back to poking the fire.

"A real restaurant needs a real cook," she said.

"Not a cook. A *chef*."

"Okay. A *chef*. Now where on God's green earth am I going to find a chef?"

Cruz jumped to his feet and stomped toward her. "Shit. Jesús, María, y José!"

She waited until he'd come close enough to jab him in the chest. "Or . . . *you* could be the chef."

"Not so fast. I'm still not selling those lots."

She looked crestfallen and waved at the plans in the back of the wagon. "Then I can't expand the place."

"I didn't say you couldn't *build* on those lots. Just I'm not *sellin'* 'em."

"Then . . . what?"

"Partners. *Equal* partners."

"Partners?" She shook her head and turned away in exasperation. "Well, shit."

5

"The Shamrock Saloon, Gambling Emporium, and Finishing School for Whores."
—Serenity Falls Townsfolk

Mama stalked around the campfire. Kicked the dirt. Muttered and swore. Eventually, she nodded to the Mexican. "Okay. Partners."

So Cruz came back to work. Atwood drew up a simple fifty-fifty partnership agreement, but they couldn't borrow enough to build the entire project at once. Instead, they kept the old building, and connected it to a two-story addition with six hotel rooms, a room for Cruz, a small two-room apartment (barely big enough for me, Jake, and Mama), a kitchen and storeroom in the back, and a small dining room out front.

The actual restaurant would have to wait. But it was enough to keep Cruz happy, and added to the value and utility of what was now the Shamrock Saloon & Hotel.

Mama and Cruz settled into a prickly friendship. He'd sometimes call her Rosalita, half-jokingly comparing her to her beloved roses: beautiful, with thorns. He was fourteen years older, so she'd tease him by calling him Old Man whenever they bickered over business.

He could tell when she was genuinely angry by whether she'd

use his full name, spitting out each syllable through gritted teeth, like she did with me and Jake. On occasion, Cruz would remind us: "There are many theories on arguing with a woman—and they're all wrong."

But he also made certain Jake and me appreciated our mother and everything she'd accomplished. Once, when he caught us complaining about our compulsory chores, he grabbed us each by the collars. "I thought you boys was smart. Now I ain't so sure."

We didn't know what to say, and did know there were times when it didn't pay to sass our elders. Still, when Jake looked like he was about to say something, I elbowed him to shut him up.

"Muchacho," Cruz said to my brother, "you know the lesson your mama teaches you every single day?"

Jake shook his head.

"Then I'm gonna tell you. And don't you *niños* forget it. The good Lord deals your hand. All you can do is decide how to play it."

I knew what he meant. When Mama saw a need for doing something, she did it. Back then, it greatly bothered her that there was no school in Serenity Falls. Once and always a teacher, she started opening the Shamrock as the town school for two hours every weekday morning, before the saloon opened at eleven. Me and Jake were always there.

And attendance was mandatory for her girls, no matter their age. Even though most people ridiculed the notion that a prostitute could ever be redeemed and live in polite society, Mama believed otherwise. She wanted to make sure they knew their reading, writing, and 'rithmetic, so they might have options beyond whoring, if they chose. When neighbors referred to her establishment as "the Shamrock Saloon, Gambling

Emporium, and Finishing School for Whores," Mama just smiled.

Sad thing was, most whores had no education, and whoring was not exactly a long-term career. Many got old before their time, ending up desperate, hungry, and homeless. Too many died from drugs, drink, or beatings.

Mama wanted better for her doves—even if she personally had to drag them out of bed after a hard night's work, and plunk them down in a chair for school. She kept hoping one of those girls would realize there was more future in teaching than whoring, and take over the task.

Any day a peddler's wagon rolled into town was like a holiday for Mama. These men, mostly Jews from Europe, would sometimes have books for sale. In the grand scheme of things, books weren't of much use to most folks. To Mama, they were better than gold, and she bought every one she could.

One time, as she came back to the Shamrock with an armload to add to her library, she ran into Cruz shaking his head. "You know they overcharge you. They all know you pay anything they ask."

"You can't pay too much for a book," Mama said, as she sniffed the magical scent of paper, glue, and knowledge.

Secretly, Cruz admired her devotion to books and learning. He himself had been educated for a few years at a mission school, where he'd developed an affinity for romantic poems and sonnets. Any missing volume of poetry was likely to be found in Cruz's custody.

Her growing classroom library included McGuffey's Readers, history books, biographies, the Bible—and, especially, Shakespeare, to whom Mama had a religious devotion, gradually amassing a nearly complete collection of his works. In school, we'd read the plays aloud and act them out. When we didn't exactly understand the plot or the words, she'd discuss it with us until we did.

Jake and me were amused to find ol' Will Shakespeare was a world champ when it came to cooking up insults. We certainly applied more effort to memorizing those than to any other aspect of our schooling.

Not only did Serenity Falls lack a school building in those days, there was no church or preacher, either. So Mama hosted a Bible service each Sunday at ten. Everyone was welcome, and quite a few locals and travelers would shuffle in each Sabbath. As with school, her girls and her sons were required to attend.

You might think growing up in a saloon, surrounded by gamblers and prostitutes, would be onerous and sinful for young boys like me and Jake. I can tell you, between Cruz, the girls, and the patrons, it was never dull. And the town, growing bit by bit, was right outside our door.

If anything threatened to make life truly oppressive for me and my brother, it was the arrival of the bathtub. While the hotel addition was under construction, Mama had reserved a little ground-floor chamber for the five-foot-long tin tub with a wood bottom. As the first such tub in town, it caused a considerable ruckus when it arrived on the freight wagon.

Now, it was one thing for Mama to insist her girls keep themselves clean. And the truth was, they took to bathing like, well, like ducks to water—even the girls raised so poor the only baths they'd ever had were dunks in a lake or stream. It was all part of Mama's plan, along with nice dresses for them and decent sheets for their beds. The girls became so eager for a bath in hot water straight off the stove, Mama had to draw up a schedule, so they'd each get two baths a week without fighting over the tub.

Unfortunately, so did Jake and me. Oh, we protested like grimy little banshees at first. But being clean wasn't as awful as we'd feared. And it was easy enough to get dirty again. When we were little, the girls took turns bathing us, so we wouldn't run off, or drown. We soon came to like our tub time with the girls. But good things usually come to an end, and this one did when Jake turned seven, and Mama barred the path to the tub.

Jake stood stark naked in the hall. "Why can't Rhody give me a bath no more?"

"Because she enjoys diddling with your li'l pecker in the tub more than she should."

"Well . . . what if I like being diddled in the tub?"

Mama rolled her eyes. "These girls are like your sisters. There are things brothers and sisters should not be doing."

Jake thought about it, as best a seven-year-old could. "So . . . I gotta take baths by myself now?"

"You boys are old enough."

"Well . . . can I diddle myself?"

Mama stifled a laugh. "That's up to you."

Jake nodded, feeling like a grown man trustworthy enough to fend for himself. "Well, as long as that's settled," he said, and off he went for his first solo bath.

In general, the gals of the Shamrock did treat us like little brothers, alternately looking out for us and teasing us. In turn, girls were not foreign creatures to us, and we learned to treat them with respect. This would pay dividends for me and Jake later in life.

Once the hotel rooms were open, and Cruz added to the food menu, Mama took two more big steps toward civilizing the Shamrock. She ruled that all saloon patrons had to surrender their weapons at the door, in exchange for a numbered token. The guns were stowed in cubbies inside the locked cashier cage—a secure and orderly improvement over the "dump 'em in the bucket" arrangement common to many saloons.

And, following the sheriff's suggestion, she hired a tall, rawboned Dutchman named Maarten de Groot to enforce her rules. "Dutch" de Groot had earned his passage to America by successfully bare-knuckle boxing for whatever other men were willing to bet. He rarely spoke above a whisper—and rarely had to. Once the townsfolk knew him, few challenged him.

But alcohol has a way of clouding a man's judgment, and transient strangers sometimes grew belligerent when Dutch tried searching them for hidden weapons. Dutch suggested an alternative: having the girls frisk male patrons. Mama didn't cotton to putting her girls in harm's way more than they already were—but Rhody, who had become a bold leader among the doves, spoke up for Dutch's idea.

It turned out most of the men were tickled (so to speak) to get a free sample of good-humored affection, and they willingly surrendered themselves to a thorough search, at the right hands. Some patrons, in fact, lingered longer than necessary and Dutch had to pull them away so they'd drink, gamble, and pay for more advanced services.

One night, the town's livery owner and blacksmith, Juan Carlos Mexia, came in, evidently laden with an arsenal. Mex was a barrel-chested man with a mustache that drooped below his chin. He seemed to be missing every other tooth, which was easy to see as his grin widened with each weapon Rhody found on him. And with each recovery, he shook his head and challenged her to find another, and yet another—each requiring a more concerted search.

After two guns and three knives, Mex said there was one more, and swore it was the last. But she'd have to dig deep to find it. Rhody kissed him on the cheek and told him she'd make it worth his while if he'd close his eyes while she searched. Of course, he went along—and she motioned Dutch over while she cooed in Mex's ear to keep him distracted.

Dutch took over with a sly grin, and such finesse that the blacksmith remained none the wiser. Somehow, the growing pack of spectators held their sniggers and waited for the payoff. Finally, Dutch fished a stubby Philadelphia Deringer out of Mex's drawers—and gave the blacksmith's nethers a hearty squeeze while he was in there. Mex yelped. His eyes popped open. When he saw it wasn't Rhody groping him, he yelped again, jumped back, tripped, and fell on his ass. For a few tense seconds, it looked like there'd be a fight—until Mex burst out laughing. Dutch hauled him to his feet. The blacksmith cackled all the way to the bar, and bought a round for his friends.

Though Jake and me grew up without a father, we had Cruz. He never made a fuss about it, never pretended he was our daddy. He just taught us things boys should know about fishing, shooting, hunting, riding—and life. He almost always called me "Chico" and Jake "Muchacho," only using our Christian names when he caught us squabbling. Then he'd snatch us by our collars and remind us that family had to look out for each other: "Don't you forget—blood is thicker'n water."

He was also the only person who could tell Mama when she was working too hard—or driving others too hard. Sometimes, when she seemed especially careworn, he'd sneak up behind her, hum a tune, and waltz her around the room. She'd end up laughing, and ask where he'd learned to dance so well. From princesses in Europe, he claimed.

He might've been lying. But he could make Mama feel like the Queen of Landryville, if only for a little while.

Jake and me loved living in town. There was more activity, and more kids to play with, especially as Serenity Falls grew. But the town didn't grow so big that we couldn't hear Mama's loud and distinctive whistle calling us home. She'd pucker up and trumpet the beginning of "Camptown Races" and by the time she came to the "doo-dah" notes, we'd have headed back to the Shamrock.

We Galloway boys became well-known by our neighbors, for

both mischief ("James Benjamin Galloway, did you ride through Miz Stoker's freshly hung laundry?") and good deeds, like the time we rescued Nate Duncan's hound dog, Andy Jackson, when he got himself stuck in the mud by the river.

Jake wasn't much given to contemplation. Even when he appeared deep in thought, it was barely knee-deep. He was the kid who'd leap into rivers and lakes, without a care. To Jake, life was one grand adventure and competition. He was always challenging me to contests—which I rarely won, reinforcing my natural caution and lack of confidence. Jake never knew when he was in over his head, and I always thought I was—with horses as the exception, for both of us.

While Jake did learn to ride after a fashion, he never looked steady in a saddle. As Cruz once muttered of Jake's horsemanship, "That boy'd have some trouble riding a hilltop without holding onto a tree."

I felt the same about shooting, much to Cruz's consternation. I could never tell anyone, but every time I pulled the trigger, the thunder, flash, and smoke took me right back to the night Mama shot Daddy.

Jake always had deft hands, and taught himself to juggle at age six, with a touch pliant enough to juggle eggs without breaking them. Once, to test himself, he had me drop eggs from the upstairs balcony. He caught six in a row without cracking a single one, and we returned them to the larder without Cruz ever knowing they'd been "borrowed" for our unauthorized experiment.

With his ever-present itch to keep busy, Jake would entertain himself (and others) by juggling almost anything at hand when he had nothing better to do. Considering his proven dexterity, it came as no surprise when he also showed a real marksman's talent, and he worked hard honing his skills, learning to draw and fire a gun faster than most grown men. When he'd show off, Cruz would remind him, "Good to be quick. Better to be accurate."

In the end, Jake would ride, if he had to. And I could shoot, if it couldn't be avoided. Put the two of us together, you'd have one whole cowboy. Separate us, and we might have trouble simply surviving.

By the time I was six, Cruz had me tending visitors' horses at the Shamrock. He also convinced blacksmith Mex to find odd jobs for me at the livery. While Mex wasn't much for teaching, I learned an awful lot about taking care of horses just by watching, and coincidentally gained an education in swearing.

For my seventh birthday, Mama decided it was time I had my own horse and we went to Mex's big corral on the edge of town, where he had twenty horses for sale. At first, I sat on the fence rail looking over the herd. It didn't take long for one to catch my eye—a wiry little gray colt who ambled over to size me up. I reckon you could say we chose each other. His dappled color darkened from light gray at his muzzle to charcoal by his hocks, like he was emerging from shadows. So Shadow seemed like the right name.

With years of horse sense earned during his younger days as a *vaquero*, Cruz commenced my formal education in horse training. "Chico, a horse knows you better'n you know yourself. He knows when you're happy or sad, when you know what you're doing and when you don't . . . and he *always* knows when you got carrots."

Training Shadow was the most fun I've ever had in my entire life, before or since—though I must say that horse did make it easy. He was smarter than most people, gentle by nature but fiery when asked to run. Pony and boy were bonded pals in no time. I even appropriated Mama's "Camptown Races" whistle to teach Shadow to come when I called.

As we kids grew up, Serenity Falls grew out, little by little.

And Jake and me learned we didn't always have to look for trouble—sometimes it just walked up, all on its own. All you had to do was nod and strike up a conversation.

One day, when he was eleven, Jake had been passing idle time juggling four crab apples out in front of the Shamrock, when he spotted a boy waiting by a loaded cargo wagon outside Duncan's General Store. Taller and likely three years older than Jake, this kid had blond hair so bleached it was almost white. He had a box of matches in his hand, and Jake watched him carelessly lighting one after another. Each time, the kid waited until the flame burned almost to his fingertips before throwing it in the dirt.

"Hey," Jake said as he walked over, still juggling, "what're you up to?"

The bigger kid squinted. "What's it look like?"

"Tryin' to burn your fingers?"

"I'm fixin' to burn something, awright. Maybe this shitty little town."

I'd been out riding Shadow through the hills, and we loped up in time to hear the kid's threat as he struck one more match, watched it for a second—and then flicked it at Jake's face. Jake yelped, and jumped back. The crab apples hit the ground.

You might've expected the other kid to laugh at the high-pitched fear in Jake's voice, but his expression stayed blank and hard as stone. He had the palest blue eyes I've ever seen. Poets say the eyes are the window to the soul. If that's so, then I could see down into a pit so deep and dark it chilled me to the bone.

A bully was one thing. This boy was something way worse.

And this wasn't the first time, and certainly would not be the last, that my headstrong brother refused to back away from a foolish fight. As they squared at each other like a couple of rams ready to lock horns, I shimmied down off Shadow to help.

But a man came stomping out of the store, whacked the other kid across the back of his head, and snatched the box of matches. "Wolf! This is the last time your daddy sends you into town with me. I'm a goddam ranch foreman, not a goddam nursemaid."

"You can't hit me, Bulldog. I'm gonna tell my poppa!"

"Tell 'im any goddam thing you want."

But the kid didn't look so big or tough anymore, as this Bulldog grabbed him by the scruff of his britches and threw him up to the seat of their wagon. The kid scrambled in, as much to wriggle free as anything else. The man climbed up beside him, and the kid gave him a sullen glare.

"Keep this up," Bulldog said, "you are gonna meet a bad end, boy."

The kid folded himself into the corner of the seat, as far away from the man as possible. Jake and me watched the wagon roll away. Skinny ol' Nate Duncan stood in the doorway of his store.

"Who're they?" Jake asked.

"Bulldog Quill's foreman of the Krieg ranch, 'bout twenty miles thataway. The kid is Wilhelm Krieg's boy, Wolf. His mama used to bring him to the store when he was a blue-eyed button." Nate shook his head. "Something turned in that boy after she died."

He went back inside, leaving me to wonder what people had said about me and Jake after our daddy was killed. I could not even imagine life without our mother.

But I *could* imagine this Wolf Krieg kid burning down Serenity Falls someday.

6

"You get to decide who you are . . . and what you're going to be."
—Cara Galloway

"Hey, Mama . . . do I look like Daddy?"

Carrying a tray of washed glasses, Mama noticed me looking in the mirror behind the Shamrock's fancy new mahogany bar. She busied herself putting the glasses away under the bar, a sure sign she'd rather not be talking about Reuben Landry.

But I persisted. "People say I'm the spittin' image of him."

"So what?"

"What if I end up *being* like him? Everybody says he was a drunk, and a gambler."

"Jamey, are you a drunk and a gambler?"

"I'm only eleven!"

"You worry too much. Your daddy didn't worry at all . . . even when he should've." She put away the last glass and stood next to me, so we could look in the mirror together. "What do you see?"

"You and me."

"Anything look the same?"

Not really, since Jake looked much more like Mama than I did.

"What do we know?" Mama would use that question as a

way of cutting through the clutter of a situation. It worked with me, not so much with Jake. "Use your *eyes.*"

"Ohh. We both have green eyes."

She gave me a hug. "You're a mixture of me and your daddy. But *you* get to decide who you are . . . and what you're going to be."

Well. I was already pretty sure I'd stay away from drink. I remembered whiskey on my father's breath, and how getting drunk turned him mean and stupid. I didn't want to be either one. Gambling, though, might be another story. I was drawn almost as much to cards as to horses. At first, I just liked the brightly colored pictures and symbols printed on the cards, and I'd imagine my own tales of medieval derring-do using the kings, queens, and jacks as heroes, damsels, and villains.

Back when I was six, I'd discovered that the balcony at the top of the stairs leading to the new hotel rooms overlooked two tables often used by the town's better poker players. Sitting up there, my skinny legs dangling through the turned-wood railing spindles, I had a bird's-eye view of the players—and their cards. The more I watched, the more my curiosity grew.

There weren't any books on the game yet. Though men (and a few ladies) had been playing stud poker for years, the rules wouldn't be written up in *American Hoyle* until 1864. So I'd asked Cruz, and he and his compadre, Mex, patiently taught me and Jake all about the different hands and strategies.

One morning, as we ate Cruz's delicious fried eggs, I said, "Mama, I see lots of card players cheating."

"Do you think that's okay?"

I knew what she wanted me to say—that it was wrong—but Jake answered first. "Why not? If everybody else is cheating."

"Does that make it right?" Mama asked.

"Well," Jake said, "wouldn't I be stupid if I let everybody else cheat me?"

"What if you didn't play cards with cheaters?"

"How would I know they were cheaters before I played 'em?"

I banged my fork down like a gavel. "All I'm hearing is questions. I want answers."

Cruz scraped fresh egg onto our plates. "Life's got more questions than answers, Chico. Get used to it."

"I got an answer," Jake said. "Cheat!"

"Maybe Chico's got a different answer."

Fact was, I didn't. So I asked another question: "Do you cheat, Cruz?"

"Good players don't have to cheat. And we can tell when somebody else is."

"How do you become that good?"

"Practice."

"Ha," Jake said, "cheatin' sounds easier."

"Not if you want to be a *good* cheater, Muchacho. Takes as much practice to be a good cheater as a good honest player."

Jake shrugged. "Does it matter?"

"Good cheaters sometimes win," Cruz said with a sinister smile, "but bad cheaters get caught . . . and killed."

Though that cooled Jake's interest in cheating, he still just went and played the game, with anybody of any age. But I took my newfound knowledge, and mulled it for a spell while I continued to watch and learn—about poker, and people. Some played well, some so poorly they couldn't beat an eight-year-old. Some cheated regularly, while others never did, as if they thought only honorable folk played cards.

But I noticed a common thread. No matter what the stakes—fortunes or pocket change—even honest players believe they're better gamblers than they really are. And cheaters are rarely as slick as they think.

★ ★ ★ ★ ★

Time for a confession: That same summer, when I was eleven, I fell in love with Juliet Rivard the first day I saw her. She was fifteen when she walked alone into town, thin and threadbare, carrying an unaccountably sunny outlook on life, and not much else.

Soft-spoken, with raven hair and sky-blue eyes, she came to the Shamrock looking for work of any kind. Mama thought she was too young to be whoring, but Juliet said she'd done her share and didn't mind, so long as nobody got rough with her, and she had food in her belly and a warm bed under a dry roof. When Mama tried to dissuade her, Juliet thanked her and said she'd try the other joints in town.

That my mother refused to allow, fearing how this fair child would be treated elsewhere. Even a year after Juliet moved into the Shamrock, though, we still didn't know the circumstances that brought her to Serenity Falls, since she never talked about her previous life.

Now, you might be thinking that boys around that age are starting to fall in love with pretty girls on a regular basis. And you'd be correct. But Juliet was different. If Rhody proved to be a stray who never felt she belonged even where she was wanted, then Juliet was like a solitary sparrow who could weave herself a temperate nest no matter where the winds took her. Her blue eyes radiated good cheer, she was playful without being frivolous, and as polite as if she'd been to a genuine finishing school. If Juliet ever had harsh words, I rarely heard them.

Once Cruz's cooking put some meat on her bones, she could fluff up in a fine dress for a night of working at the saloon, and look older than her age. But when she'd come to school in the morning, wearing a plain skirt and modest blouse, her hair pulled back in a ponytail, she looked young enough to be our friend, which she was.

Speaking of friends, Jake and me had met the little girl who'd become our best friend when Rebecca Shaw and her family came to Serenity Falls in '57 to start a small farm, and she enrolled in Mama's school at the Shamrock. Becky was a bossy, wiry little thing with strawberry-blonde hair and a splash of freckles across her nose. She fell almost exactly between me and Jake in age, and preferred to play with us boys rather than the other girls. She never cried, and gave as good as she got, no matter how rough-and-tumble the enterprise.

Not long after our run-in with Wolf Krieg and his matches, Becky, Jake, and me marched out to our favorite place in the woods. Becky needed these occasional escapes from her chores—mostly looking after her little brother and sisters, Davey, Abigail, and Sarah, so her parents could work their farm. Our shady sanctuary was on the edge of the biggest cotton plantation for miles around—Riverside, owned by a cruel man named Burdett Montgomery, known around town as Bird.

We had everything there kids could want, including Big Bug Creek, where beaver had dammed up the stream, forming a swimming hole and a fine place for catching frogs and turtles. And there was a small clearing, with a big fat tree stump exactly the right size and height to serve as a tabletop for picnics and card games, or for setting up tin cans as targets for rock-throwing contests. Canned foods weren't so common yet, but Cruz saved all the Shamrock's empties for us. Since they didn't break like glass bottles did, we could use cans over and over.

Jake and me were about equal in our rock-throwing skills, but Becky's aim was best of all. I could live with my deficiency, but my brother hated losing to a girl. Poor Jake never seemed to notice Becky was toying with him, like a smart cat with a dim-witted mouse.

I suppose I was complicit in Jake's regular fleecing at Becky's hands. All I had to do was line up the cans, and Jake would not only challenge her, he'd bet on the outcome with whatever coins or trinkets he might have.

That particular morning, I was referee, as usual, taking custody of the collected betting stakes. While they scoured the ground for suitable rocks, I set up nine cans. The contestants would alternate and the first to knock down five would win. Jake won the coin toss to see who'd go first.

"That's an omen," he said to Becky.

"Could be your lucky day," she said.

"Luck's got nothin' to do with it, honey."

"If you say so."

They took turns, one throw after another. I was convinced Becky missed on purpose a couple of times, just to keep it close. Jake took the lead, four cans to three. Then Becky tied the score. But it was Jake's turn to throw at the lone can left standing. He had victory within his grasp as he casually juggled his last two rocks.

Becky looked crestfallen. Maybe she wasn't toying with him. Maybe she'd actually outsmarted herself. Maybe Jake would really win. But then he turned gallant and said, "You first."

I stared at my dumb brother, overconfidence personified. Becky could practically hit those cans with her eyes closed. There was no way she'd miss.

But she did. For the first time since we'd known her, she looked like she wanted to cry. "Your turn," she said, with a whimper in her voice.

Now victory really *was* within Jake's reach. He chose his best rock. Gazed across the clearing at the last can. And waited too long.

Becky's lower lip quivered. "I can't believe it. I'm going to lose. This is your big chance, Jake."

Yep, Jake had her right where she wanted him.

Instead of just winging that rock, he closed one eye, drew his arm back *slooowly,* aiming, aiming, aiming . . . and missed by a foot. Jake stomped in frustration. I almost felt sorry for him. Becky gave him a sad little smile, picked up a random rock, flung it . . . and there went the last can. Sore-loser Jake stormed off into the woods.

Becky looked worried, for real. "Should we go after him?"

"Nahh, he should be used to losing by now."

"You can give him back his share of the bet."

"That'll make him feel worse."

"I'll give him another chance to beat me, at something."

"He'll take it."

"I know." She sighed, as we started back toward town. "Sometimes I wish he wouldn't."

"How'd you know you'd win?"

"I didn't, silly."

I thought for a second. "Ohhh. You were sure Jake would *lose.*"

"Yep."

"But what if he didn't?"

"So what? If you wanna win, you can't be afraid to lose."

"You weren't really going to cry, were you?"

She laughed. "No. But I wanted Jake to think I was. Sometimes boys are just too easy. Y'know, I used to wonder if you boys let me win 'cuz I'm a girl."

"I sure don't."

She tossed me a little sideways smile. And I don't know what came over me, but I tried to kiss her on the cheek. I barely grazed her, as she darted away like a spooked fawn. But she stopped, cast a glance over her shoulder, and held out her hand. I was confused, but I grabbed it anyway.

We walked halfway back to town like that, not saying anything at all. But I was smiling the whole time. While I was trying to figure it out, Becky startled me with a real kiss, right on my lips.

It's funny, when you're that close to another person's face, the distance of two little noses, it looks like there's one big eye right in the middle, staring back at you. When Becky's eye—*eyes*—closed, I was ready for the second kiss. It was softer than the first, and lasted longer. I could taste salty sweetness from the sweat that had trickled down her face.

As we walked for a while longer, I felt like I'd won a lottery jackpot—until Becky slipped her hand out of mine. She looked me in the eyes—considerably more than two noses apart—and I felt doom all the way down to the pit of my stomach.

"I'm sorry, Jamey."

"For what?"

"For leadin' you on. I think you're too young for me." She sighed real deep, as if *her* heart was the one being broken.

"*What?* You're only six months older than me!"

But she turned and walked away, leaving me befuddled. That was the first time I learned a lesson I'd have to learn many times over: no matter how much you want something, sometimes you have to wait and let it come to you. And then, sometimes, it just gets up and walks away again, *for no good reason.*

We thought Jake had run home to lick his wounds, but he'd been shadowing us from the wooded ridgeline above the trail, spying on our kisses and our walk. Once he saw Becky by herself, he intercepted her. As is often the case with men, Jake thought he was in charge, swooping in to soothe a lovelorn little girl. Poor Jake.

They came face to face. She gave him that same enchanting sideways smile I'd fallen for. And she kissed him on the mouth before he knew what was happening. She took him by the hand and led him along for a while. At the outskirts of Serenity Falls, she heaved that same great sigh, took him by the shoulders, and broke the news: "Jake, I think you're too old for me. I'm real sorry."

She left him there and walked on alone.

Same as Jake had, I'd been following and saw the whole thing. I ambled up to my brother and we traded baffled shrugs. Shoulders slumped, we shuffled toward home. But I couldn't resist summing up what I saw as the day's news: "*I* got my first kiss before *you* did."

Jake shoved me. I called him a sore loser. He wrapped me in a headlock, wrestled me to the ground, and pummeled me for a while. I twisted my face out of the weeds long enough to yelp, "Hey! Remember? Blood's thicker'n water?"

"I'll think on that—after I see some blood."

But I could tell his heart wasn't in it when he left me flat on my back, and trudged off.

Despite a torn shirt and skinned knuckles, I thought I scored the best of the day's meager rewards. They say you never forget your first crush, first kiss, or first broken heart. Becky had taken care of all three of those milestones in a single afternoon . . . for *both* of us. For that alone, she'd have stuck in our memories forever.

After all that, you might think Jake and me wouldn't have minded never seeing Becky Shaw again. But she was our best friend. And what're a few kisses among friends, anyway? Maybe it was simply a case of hope springing eternal, as poet Alexander Pope wrote. Or maybe, like Tennyson said, 'tis better to have loved and lost than never to have loved at all. Whatever the reason, the odd truth was we actually felt closer to Becky than before.

Late that August, we three were trudging back to town from Big Bug Creek, on the road passing by the edge of Riverside. We paused in the shade to watch some of Bird Montgomery's slaves slowly harvesting cotton under a broiling sun. As I wondered how they could survive that heat, one man collapsed in a dead faint.

A skinny boy working nearby shouted, "Daddy!" He rushed over to the man and tried to lift him up. We could see the boy growing frantic, cradling his daddy's limp head in his arms. Jake and me just stood there—but Becky ran over to help. Scared of what might happen for trespassing on Montgomery land, we followed her anyway.

Becky didn't have her own canteen, so she grabbed for Jake's. Jake yanked the canteen back. "You can't let it touch a black man's lips!"

Becky looked at him like he was an idiot. "Says who?"

"I don't know. *People.*"

She took my canteen instead. She knelt next to the man and the skinny, scared boy. At first, the water trickled over the slave's parched lips like he was a dead man. Then he started coming around, and gulped that water down.

When his eyes opened, they grew big with terror as he realized it was a white girl tending to him—along with two weak-kneed white boys. The man tried to scrabble away from us, but he still couldn't stand. His son calmed him down. Becky gave the canteen to the boy, who helped his father drink slowly, until it was empty.

Then she handed it to me. "Run back to the creek and fill it up."

Like an automaton, I did as I was told. I hadn't ever seen a black man up so close before. He and the boy weren't really black, more different shades of brown. Then again, white people are really more pink or tan. Chinese aren't yellow. And Indians aren't red. So the whole notion of separating people by color seemed fishy.

Growing up in Philadelphia, Mama had known quite a few free blacks—shopkeepers, maids, street-sweepers, bums, leading lives no different from whites. That experience shaped her opinions on Negroes and slavery. She didn't allow her sons to call them niggers, like many whites did. Most people said that word full of disdain and hate. Some said it all humdrum, like talking about a plow horse.

But this man and his son were just plain people in need. So what if they had darker skin? Mama had taught us to call them Negroes or blacks, or even Africans, all words with some dignity—something every man, woman, and child was given by God. And while folks sometimes surrendered their own dignity, nobody had a right to take it from you. That's what Mama believed, so that's what I believed, now that I actually had a reason to think about it.

When I came back with the water, Becky introduced me to Henry and his son, Salem—"Short for Jerusalem," the boy explained in his froggy voice. By then, Henry had recovered some, and he passed the replenished canteen to his son. That's when I noticed the insides of their lips and mouths were pink, like a white person. And the palms of Henry's work-scarred hands weren't much darker than my own.

Salem drank his fill and handed the canteen back to Becky.

"Keep it," she said.

"Much obliged," Henry said, as he struggled to his feet. "Y'all better go, before the overseer thinks we shirkin'."

As we backed away, a fat man on a horse was already riding down the row of cotton, with fury on his face and a long quirt in his hand. I didn't know if he was about to whip the horse, the slaves, or us. But when he shouted, his voice sounded more pleading than angry. "You two niggahs . . . back to pickin'. You little white pissants, git!"

We saw him wheel the horse in a tight circle around the father and son. "Henry, I don't wanna whip you again." Instead, he used his quirt to prod the slaves back to work. They never looked him in the eye.

Before we knew it, Becky had found a rock and thrown it

with her usual skill. It hit the overseer above his right ear and staggered him. But he stayed in his saddle, cursed, and rode his horse right toward us. We froze with fear. Would he beat us? Capture us and make us slaves? Kill us and bury us in the swamps?

He reined his horse to a halt and loomed over us, looking bone-tired as he wiped the blood away where Becky's rock cut his head. "You think I like whuppin' them niggahs? It's my job. I got kids like you, they go hungry if I don't. That's just the way it is." Then he turned his horse away at a weary walk.

So we escaped with our lives and freedom. As we scurried back to town, I thought about all the ways people try to control others: What Mama had to do to get herself free of Reuben. How she still had to fight for respect from the men in Serenity Falls. How some folks looked down on the whores like they were hardly human at all.

In the grand order of things, slaves had it the worst. But I wondered: Does anybody really control their own lives? Or is everybody at the mercy of one overseer or another?

7

"I didn't start tossing the monte 'til I was almost nine, so I pretty much wasted those first eight years."
—Jake Galloway

While rarely disagreeable, brother Jake reveled in disagreement—the sort of difference of opinion that made horse races, as Mark Twain has said. Most days, Jake would start an argument at the drop of a hat—and he'd even drop the hat himself. Always on the prowl for a contest, he'd challenge other kids to arm wrestling, foot races, even bug races—and bet on anything and everything.

I generally steered clear of his competitive schemes. But that changed after I got my little colt, Shadow. Shadow was real fast, and not only for his size. Though barely fourteen hands, he had a miraculous stride longer than most horses of any size. He could outrun and outlast pert near any horse I ever saw.

Jake took advantage of this by organizing horse races whenever he could. Afraid of losing, I resisted at first, but once I realized I usually won, I became an eager partner. I liked knowing that riding was something I could do better than Jake, and he couldn't win these contests without me.

At some point, though, Jake started to worry that Shadow's renown would scare off rivals. So he came up with a plan we first tried one mild April day, around my twelfth birthday, when I raced Ted Whitney, an optimistic fellow in his mid-twenties who rode a regal buckskin mare I'd beaten once before.

Townsfolk heard us coming and scattered as we raced neck and neck up Main Street, and out the other end of town. Following the stage road, we rushed by the roaring falls to the north.

I was at my happiest when riding. The percussion of Shadow's hooves, the steady rhythm of his breathing, my own heartbeat, and the whistling wind in my ears blended into a symphony of speed and power. I was the conductor—but Shadow was the orchestra.

We left the road and cut across an open field. Whitney and his mare took the lead, and stretched it out as we veered back to the road where it curved through the woods.

A mile away, Juliet and Jake waited in the roadside shade, at the crumbling stone wall that served as our start-finish line. She paced and peered down the road, toward the bend where she knew we'd appear soon. Jake calmly chomped a perfect, juicy apple (which he was supposed to be saving for my horse).

Juliet heard us before she saw us. "Jake! Here they come!" The horses sprinted into view. When she saw Whitney held a three-length lead, Juliet pummeled Jake's shoulder. "No! No, no, no! Jamey's losing!"

Jake wiped apple juice off his chin with a big blue bandanna. "You worry too much."

She wasn't the only one. Ted Whitney tossed a nervous glance over his shoulder.

It was time. Nobody could tell but me and my pony when I eased up on the reins, let him stretch out, and put his head down. I barely touched his flanks with my heels, and he surged as if fired from a slingshot. He didn't care about winning, stakes, or glory. He ran for the pure pleasure of running, what he knew and loved and did best. With each ground-gobbling stride, Shadow closed on the buckskin mare. Once he took the lead, he glided so smooth I felt like I was soaring on the back of a hawk.

Shadow nipped ahead to win by a neck. As the horses loped by, Jake waved the bandanna every which way. Juliet jumped for joy, and gave Jake a hug and a peck on the cheek. They both rushed to Shadow as I hopped down. Juliet gave me a bigger hug, and a longer kiss. Shadow turned his head to nuzzle Jake, but decided to snatch the half-eaten apple instead.

Jake surrendered the apple, flinched, and skittered away. "Whoa, Shadow. No grabbin'!"

He felt better when Whitney leaned down from his saddle and handed him four dollars. "Gosh, you almost won this time, Mr. Whitney."

"Rematch, next time I'm in town."

"Sure thing. Orrr—win your money back now." Jake's voice cracked—normally a random prank played by nature to embarrass growing boys. In Jake's case, a tool of deception he deployed at will, knowing it led folks to judge him as callow and comical, and they'd tend to drop their guard, without even realizing it.

The offer tickled Whitney's interest. "How?"

"Maybe a . . . shooting contest?"

"Who with?"

"Me?"

"Nuhh-uhh. Heard about you."

Jake batted his eyes. "I'm just a kid." This time, the cracking voice cast no spell.

"A kid who never misses."

"Got yourself a reputation there, Mr. Gunfighter," Juliet whispered in Jake's ear.

Jake pulled a deck of cards out of his pocket and squinted up at Whitney. "Then how 'bout three-card monte?"

Whitney snorted. "I was born at night, but not last night."

He wheeled and rode off, calling back, "But I will be racing you again, Jamey."

"Well, I gotta get back," Juliet said after Whitney had gone. "Your mama does not like when I'm late for work."

We started walking toward town, three amigos and a horse—Juliet in the middle, her arms over our shoulders.

"Mama says you're always losing track of time," I said, "getting lost in a book."

"Or daydreams," Jake said.

"Or singing while you're hanging the laundry."

Juliet laughed. "All true." Then she kissed us each on the cheek.

"Jamey," Jake said, "I'm your big brother."

"So you keep telling me."

"Then do what I tell ya."

"I did! I cut it close."

"Not that close."

"You think it's so easy, you ride the horse."

Juliet looked from Jake to me and back again. "Wait. You—you fixed the race?"

"No!" I said. "Shadow always wins."

"Problem is," Jake said, "he wins too easy."

Juliet cocked her head. "So?"

Jake said, "Word spreads that Shadow beats every horse by a mile—"

"—nobody wants to race 'im," I said.

"And we don't win any money," Jake finished.

Juliet scowled. "Seems a little shady to me."

"Jake's idea," I said.

"Yeah," Jake said, "I'm full of 'em."

Juliet rolled her eyes. "You're fulla something, all right."

Now, I can honestly stipulate most of Jake's betting propositions were fair trials of skill or strength. Sure, he liked to win, but usually engaged for the pure sporting pleasure. He couldn't help it if Shadow's challengers preferred to emphasize how close they'd come to winning while overlooking the fact they'd lost.

Not that Jake had forsaken all interest in cheating. While our exposure to card players at the Shamrock had inspired me to learn how the games were played, Jake was more fascinated by how the cards themselves could be manipulated. He never tired of watching crackerjack players shuffle, cut, and deal. He begged them to teach him what they knew, practiced perpetually, and polished his card-handling skills.

But learning to excel at something and finding a suitable application are two different things. For a time, Jake was a bit like a Michelangelo in search of a canvas grand enough for his talents. He found it when he was nine—after an obliging gambler schooled him in the game that most lent itself to undetectable cheating: three-card monte.

Monte is just the old shell game, with cards. The dealer slaps three down on a table, naming one—often the queen of hearts—as the money card. With dealer and player each risking an equal bet, the dealer turns the cards facedown. Then he shuffles them, with the object of causing the other player to lose track of the queen. When the fast-shuffle is done, if the player knows where that queen landed, he wins the money. If not, he loses.

How hard could that be? It's only three cards—but those three cards are always under the dealer's control. If he's honest, you'd have a fighting chance. But simplicity doesn't preclude bedevilment. It might even make it easier, since players convince themselves any sharp-eyed fool can follow one little queen.

The main prerequisites for mastering the art of shady monte-dealing were fast and sure fingers, guts, and confidence. Jake had 'em all. The secret was the dealer's ability to make it look like he's tossed down the *bottom* of two cards held in the fingers of one hand, when he's actually tossed the *top* card. Or vice versa. Once the cards are mixed up, only the dealer knows where the queen is hiding.

Other means of misdirection included the dealer "accidentally" dropping the queen, causing a crimp in one corner—which the dealer pretends not to notice. But once the other player sees it, he's convinced he'll be able to spot that bent card every time, so he bets with brazen overconfidence. In the course of play, the dealer can smooth that marked queen and even add an identical bend to another card. When the player gets had, he can hardly complain, since he'd intended to cheat the dealer all along.

As it turned out, monte was ideally a team activity. The dealer needed a shill to play a few rounds in order to lure prospective gamblers into the game, by showing how easy it was to win. When Jake said he couldn't do it without me . . . well, I joined in, even though I knew I was helping with a deception. Maybe I just needed to feel needed.

Now, if you're thinking it wouldn't take long for even an inexperienced monte player to figure out he was never going to win, you'd generally be correct. And in a small town, the novelty of a kid being such a sly dealer would wear off pretty fast, which it did. A reasonably smart person—Ted Whitney, for example—would seek other amusement.

Fortunately for Jake, not everyone was smart.

One day, Jake and me were about to head home after a morning of futile frog hunting down at Big Bug Creek, when the five Montgomery brothers found us at our clearing near their daddy's plantation. Three of them sat on their ponies, blocking our path.

They ranged in age from Arnold, at fourteen a year older than Jake, down to the runt of the litter, nine-year-old Ebenezer.

Second oldest was Barnabas at thirteen—and Arney and Barney could pass for twins—followed by twelve-year-old Cole, and Del, who was ten. Arney, Barney, Cole, Del, and Eb, bullies all.

We didn't know them well, since their school attendance was spotty. But we knew the skinny middle one, Cole, was the ringleader. "If it ain't the Galloway boys," he said, chomping a cheekful of tobacco. "Y'know, your ma's a whore schoolteacher."

"Y'know," Jake said, "everybody says *your* mama and daddy stopped at five kids 'cuz they didn't know the alphabet past the letter E."

Cole puffed up his bony chest. "This here land belongs to our daddy's plantation."

"Montgomery land ends at the road," I said, with a helpful smile. "In case you didn't notice, this is the other side of the road."

"Five of us say it ain't," Cole said, as his brothers hopped off their ponies.

Jake nudged me. "Does that surprise you?"

"What—that a Montgomery can count to five?"

They spread out and surrounded us. Jake and me stood shoulder to shoulder. "Five against two," Jake said. "Not good odds."

"We're doomed."

"Probably."

"We're fixin' to kick yer teeth out," Cole said with a grin. "Go cryin' all toothless, back to your ma, the whore school-teacher."

Jake eyed me. "Got any bright ideas?"

"We could run . . ."

Jake shook his head, like it was against his religion.

"Better than getting our asses kicked." I frowned, thinking fast, until an idea popped into my head. "Monte . . . ?"

Jake brightened, and turned toward Cole. "You could kick

our teeth out. But we wouldn't make it easy. Or, you could take all our money and worldly goods by beating us at the world's simplest card game—three-card monte. So easy, even you could win."

Cole was intrigued. "Just three cards."

"And we already know you can count to five." Jake reached into his pocket and took out his deck, then gestured toward the big tree stump. "I'll show you."

"I know how to play monte." Cole smiled when he spied Jake giving me a scared-rabbit glance. "Do you?"

"Jake, don't be an idiot," I said. "I just got paid for workin' at the livery. And you got all that money you were gonna bring to the bank. Cole knows how to play, and you barely learned."

Jake punched me in the shoulder. "You're the idiot! You just told 'em we got a lotta money on us." Ahh, and there it was—Jake's magical cracking voice.

Cole (whose voice hadn't changed at all yet) couldn't stop grinning at Jake's jitters. "One way or 'nother, we gonna take yer money. Cards is less tirin'. And maybe you get to keep yer teeth."

"Well . . . okay," Jake said with a nervous swallow. "Can we play a couple of rounds for small bets, 'til my fingers start working?"

"I'm feelin' generous. Start with a dime."

Cole and me each put a coin on the tree stump. With a deep breath, Jake tried to limber up by shuffling the deck—and clumsily flipped the cards all over the ground. I closed my eyes and shook my head.

Jake gathered the cards, then laid out the queen of hearts and kings of spades and clubs, face up. "Now, umm . . . follow the queen."

That would be the queen with the visible crimp on her corner, which, of course, Cole had no trouble tracking. Moving at half-speed, Jake switched the cards back and forth, 'round and 'round. When he stopped, Cole pointed at the card on the left. Jake turned it up. Queen of hearts.

Cole took both dimes.

I glared at Jake.

"Two bits this time," Cole ordered in a tone that discouraged debate. He put his quarter-dollar down. I grimly placed our coin next to his. Jake set up the cards and shuffled them around. Once again, Cole knew exactly where the queen stopped. "Yer not real good at this game, are you, boy."

Jake hung his head. "I . . . I reckon not."

Cole patted the top of the stump. "Dollar bet this time." He and Jake put their money down. 'Round and 'round went the cards. Cole won again. And again. And again, after that. Crowing about his gambling skill, Cole Montgomery now had over three dollars of our money. "You can quit now and take yer beatin'," he offered. He dribbled some muddy tobacco juice, then wiped his chin with his sleeve.

Jake picked up the three cards, shuffling them from one hand to the other. "Barney, you are so ugly I hear your mama takes you everywhere she goes—just so she don't have to kiss you goodbye."

My jaw dropped. "Jake! Don't get 'em mad."

He ignored me. "Arney, you look like something the dog's been hidin' under the porch. And you, Cole? If dumb was dirt? You'd cover at least ten acres."

"Bold talk for a loser," Cole said, failing to notice Jake smoothing the corner of the queen, and adding an identical bend to the king of spades. "How much you Galloway whore-suckers got left?"

We dug into our pockets, and scrounged up five dollars between us. Cole put his hand out toward his brothers, who obediently emptied their own pockets and matched our five.

Cole and Jake placed all that money down. Only this round, Cole discovered that the bent card he followed so carefully was not the queen. Now *we* had ten dollars. And Cole wasn't smiling.

"Let's finish this," he said, putting his last ten dollars into the pot.

We matched it, and the twenty-dollar assortment of paper and coin was a princely sum. Looking dead serious, Jake showed the red queen in the middle of the three cards. Cole nodded, and Jake flipped them facedown. He began to slip them around, slow at first—slow enough for Cole to see that *two* cards now had bent corners. Jake started picking up two at a time and tossing them down again, too fast to follow. When he stopped, Cole's beady eyeballs bounced from card to card.

"Gotta pick one," Jake said with a half-smile. Now, Cole still had a one-in-three chance of guessing right. This time, though, the card he chose turned out to be the king of clubs.

"You cheated," Cole muttered. He reached for the twenty dollars—but I was faster. I clamped his hand, while Jake snapped up the money. Cole yanked free of my grip, and the five Montgomery boys circled us. Me and my brother stood back to back, wheeling slowly.

"Say goodbye to your teeth," Cole said, and they charged.

No sooner had they rammed us when we all heard a blood-curdling howl come tearing through the trees. The three Montgomery ponies spooked and scattered.

Jake and me hit the dirt to avoid being clobbered by a big tree limb swinging our way, smiting our enemies like the jawbone Samson brandished to slay a thousand Philistines. Montgomery brothers fell every which way, yipping like whipped dogs as the branch-wielder kept thrashing them. Cole scrambled away, leading a hasty retreat to the safe haven of Riverside across the road.

After they'd skedaddled, me and Jake got our first good look at our savior. He had his loose shirt pulled up over the top of his head, like a monk's hood. When he slipped it down, we realized it was that slave boy Salem we'd met a year before, when we'd shared our canteen with him and his daddy. We almost didn't recognize him, since all that field work had made him broader and stronger. But the froggy voice was familiar: "You boys okay?"

"Pretty much," Jake said as we brushed ourselves off. "Thanks for helpin'."

"You sure needed it."

"I reckon we're even now."

"I ain't keeping score," Salem said as he tossed the big branch aside. It looked so heavy, I doubted Jake or me could've lifted it, much less swung it like a scythe.

"You still a slave over there?" I asked.

"What else?"

"Aren't you worried those Montgomery boys're gonna tell on you?"

"I know them boys. They bullies. They also cowards. They won't never admit they been run off by a slave and two skinny white boys." Then his voice got all low and mysterious. "They also scared of the African hoodoo."

Jake cocked his head. "Awww, there's no such thing."

"Maybe there ain't." Salem let out a surprise hoot and flashed his hands at us. We nearly jumped right out of our boots, and he fell down laughing. We laughed, sheepishly—both because he fooled us, and because we didn't know if there really was African hoodoo, or not.

"Your daddy okay?" Jake asked.

"Yep."

"You got other kin?"

"I did. But Mama and Sister got sold."

What he said, and the tranquil way he said it, chilled my blood. I knew slaves were bought and sold like farm animals, but I'd never thought much about it because I'd never known one by name before. "You know where they are?"

"Nope."

I couldn't understand making peace with that.

"You got kin?" Salem asked.

"We live in town with our mama," Jake said. "She owns the Shamrock Saloon."

"Never been to town. You got a daddy?"

"He's dead," Jake said.

"How'd he die?"

"Mama shot him. When we were little."

It struck me that Jake and Salem had used the same temperate tone in relating horrors no child should've known. By the way Salem squinted, it was likely he couldn't grasp what happened in our family any more than I could imagine having kin sold away.

"How old're you?" I asked him.

"Slaves not supposed to know."

"Why not?"

Salem shrugged. He figured he'd better get back over to the plantation, and we watched him go. From time to time after that, we'd see him working in the fields. We'd wave and he'd wave back.

Had Salem not been a slave, we might've grown up friends. But the narrow lane that separated Riverside's cotton fields from our clearing in the woods might well have been as wide as an ocean. Becky, Jake, and me had crossed it once, to lend a hand. Now Salem had done the same for us.

Still, those events couldn't diminish the difference and distance between our lives. No matter how I tried, I'd never be able to understand how it felt to wake up each morning not knowing how old I was, but knowing I was owned by another human being.

8

"Whoring's what she does, not who she is. Whereas I suspect a lying bully is who and what you are."
—Cara Galloway

Even southerners referred to slavery as "that peculiar institution," and it (and their agricultural economy) rested upon the bedrock belief that whip-scarred Negroes were less than human. By 1860, southerners owned four million slaves—outnumbering their white masters in some states. There'd already been a few failed slave rebellions: How could white southerners be certain there wouldn't be a successful one someday? Or maybe they preferred not thinking about it.

Meanwhile, northern abolitionists whipped up an angry storm. The more sermons rang out against slavery, the more southerners dug in their heels against what they saw as Yankee hypocrisy. By harvest time in '60, with a momentous presidential election looming, the southern clamor for secession had grown unyielding.

One man's revolution being another man's treason, northerners regarded such belligerence as rank sedition. But, either way, it looked more and more like the Union would not survive to see its centennial.

Mama was dealing with her own form of rebellion in the

person of Rhody Hassett. When Mama had first taken her in eight years earlier, Rhody was like a feral cat who didn't cotton to being cornered. It had taken considerable time and patience, but her wildness did even out and she proved sly and quick-witted, with a fine singing voice often called into service at the Shamrock's piano. In time, she became like an older sister to the other girls.

Even so, the demons buried in her heart eventually clawed their way out. After she'd turned twenty-one, her moodiness began to set others on edge, including Mama, who dithered between forbearance and rectitude. Deep in her soul, Rhody must have thought herself unworthy of love. The more it was offered, the more she deflected it, and the more likely it became that her nightmare would come true—that she'd be cast out of the only safe home she'd known, unless she mended her ways.

Unable to swim free of her own bleak depths, she turned to alcohol and laudanum to level her disposition. The other girls tried to cover for her. But that sisterhood—and Mama's tolerance—expired when Rhody tempted some of the girls into drugs and drink, against Mama's explicit rules. Confrontation loomed like a thundercloud. Who would unleash the storm—Mama or Rhody?

Juliet Rivard, soft-spoken though she was, had assumed leadership among the younger whores. She and three others decided to risk Mama's wrath by begging her to give their friend and sister another chance. They found Mama at her desk in the back office and made their stand.

Juliet shook her dark hair back over her shoulders and squared her chin. "The Bible says, 'their sins and iniquities will I remember no more.' "

Mama pursed her lips. "The Bible does invite forgiveness."

"It tells us to forgive others, so the Lord may forgive us. We all have our sins, Mama," Juliet said. At Cara's invitation, the girls almost all called her Mama. Most of them had never known a mother's real love, so the ones who stayed were eager to claim the closest thing to it. "This one, too. 'Forbearing one another, and forgiving one another, if any man have a quarrel against any: even as Christ forgave you, so also do ye.' "

"Honey, it's one thing to forgive. It's another to be worthy of forgiveness. You agree?"

"I reckon."

"So, if I forgive Rhody, doesn't she have to *do* something with that forgiveness?"

"Stop the sinning that got her in trouble?"

"Do you think you can soften her heart, and get her to swear she's done with drugs and whiskey?"

"I . . . I can try."

"If you can do that, Rhody can stay for as long as she abides by her promise. Now, you girls scoot so I can get my work done."

With Rhody's fate hanging in the balance, Juliet left Mama's office and found me out back doing barn chores. She took me by the hand and pulled me up to the loft, where we plopped ourselves down in some straw and she told me what had transpired. "Why'd your mama put this on me?"

"Because you spoke up."

"I don't know what to tell Rhody."

"You'll think of something."

But nothing Juliet said mattered. Rhody had no repentance in her, and she ripped into Mama. "Cara thinks she's so holy? Y'know, she killed her own husband? Like that's not a sin!" Rhody paced the floor in her room. "You and me? This is all we'll ever be. Shunned by decent folks. Long as we walk this earth, we're gonna walk it alone."

"But we're *not* alone here."

"We are condemned. Good for nothin' but whorin'."

"Mama's trying to change that. Giving us some hope."

"We're *hopeless,* girl. So I'm gonna take the little pleasure I can in drugs and drink, before I go the rest of the way to Hell."

Juliet knew Rhody's heart was hardened, like Pharaoh's had been against the Hebrews. At least Moses had the wrath of God to call down the ten plagues. Juliet had nothing but words. So she left Rhody and tearfully told Mama she'd failed.

"It's not your failure, child. It's Rhody's choice."

And that left Mama with only one choice. But by the time she went to banish Rhody, she was already gone.

Mama sat on Rhody's bed. She'd had a taste of the life Rhody had lived, what with Reuben's abuse, even finding herself lying under a stranger in the whore's straw that one time. She knew the odds against these girls building any other life for themselves: *Who am I to say Rhody's wrong? Who am I to tell anybody else how to live?*

Juliet retreated to the hayloft, and that's where I found her crying. This time, we didn't talk. We just sat together, holding hands. After a while, her breathing settled and I realized she'd fallen asleep against my shoulder, which was wet from her tears. Knowing I'd helped quiet her troubled heart made me feel at peace, and I also fell asleep.

When we woke a couple of hours later, it was almost dark. Juliet gave me a peck on the cheek—and then kissed me softly on the mouth. But it was only a moment, and Mama would be wondering where we were.

A week later, Sheriff Huggins found Rhody's body in an alley. She'd been beaten, stabbed, and left to die. When he came to tell Mama, she just closed her eyes, shrouded by grief—and guilt over not giving that poor girl another chance. She paid for the burial, and we were all at the grave as they lowered Rhody's coffin.

Juliet stepped forward. "Y'all need to know, Rhody had good in her. Lord, that girl could sing. She helped me feel at home. She may even have saved a soul or two among us girls. But not all souls can be saved hereabouts. Some have to serve their time in this world, and leave their own salvation in the hands of Jesus. Rhody taught us this song. We'd like to sing it for her."

As four other doves gathered around, Juliet started in a shy, sweet voice that broke every heart at that graveside. One by one, the other girls joined in to weave the most delicate harmony I've ever heard:

> *Ye fleeting charms of earth, farewell, your springs of*
> *joy are dry.*
> *My soul now seeks a better home, a brighter world on*
> *high.*
>
> *I'm a long time travelling here below, I'm a long time*
> *travelling away from home.*
> *I'm a long time travelling here below, To lay this body*
> *down.*
>
> *Farewell my friends whose tender care has long*
> *engaged my love.*
> *Your fond embrace I now exchange for better friends*
> *above.*
>
> *I'm a long time travelling here below, I'm a long time*
> *travelling away from home.*
> *I'm a long time travelling here below, To lay this body*
> *down . . .*
> *To lay this body down.*

Juliet and the girls stepped back to surround Mama. Pretty near everyone had to wipe away a tear. We all murmured,

"Amen." And that's how we said farewell to Rhody, a girl who deserved a better hand than life dealt her.

Lincoln, of course, won the election that November. South Carolina was the first state to secede, followed by five more in January.

Texas became the seventh member of the Confederate States of America on February 1st, though not without an uproar. Our beloved governor and founding hero Sam Houston shocked many a Texan when he spoke out against secession. When called upon to pledge allegiance to the Confederacy, they say he just sat in his chair down in the capitol basement and whittled. He knew this was a road to ruin, and refused to lead us there.

"After the sacrifice of countless millions of treasure and hundreds of thousands of lives . . . you may win southern independence, but I doubt it," Sam Houston warned. ". . . The North is determined to preserve this Union. They are not a fiery, impulsive people as you are, for they live in colder climates. But when they begin to move in a given direction, they move with the steady momentum and perseverance of a mighty avalanche."

So the people of Texas took this great man—who'd fought the British in the War of 1812; got elected governor of Tennessee in '27; commanded the ragtag Texian army fighting for independence from Mexico in '36; defeated General Santa Anna, the butcher of the Alamo, in an eighteen-minute battle in which Houston himself was wounded; twice got elected president of the Republic of Texas, then led the drive to statehood in '45; served as the first U.S. senator from Texas and then as governor, becoming the only American ever elected governor in two different states—and booted him from office in disgrace.

That's when I learned that people who put heroes up on

pedestals can just as easily knock them down.

By the time Confederate cannons fired on the Federals at Fort Sumter on April 12, 1861, there'd been plenty of time for southerners to get riled up. Texans joined their brethren from other states and strutted off to war. Jake and me were too young to serve the dubious Confederate cause and, like our hero Sam Houston, our family had no kind words for secession, or slavery.

I couldn't figure it out then, and still can't years later. But every new war seems to be eagerly embraced by the populace as a golden opportunity for righteous glory—at least until the dead and maimed start collecting in considerable numbers. This war was no exception.

The first Confederate company to march into Serenity Falls, recruiting locals with the promise of swift victory bearing God's own blessing, was greeted with a patriotic passion like I'd never seen, this being my first war and all. A day later, when those proud soldiers—fortified by the recruitment of some of our own young men—marched off in their crisp gray uniforms, waving the Confederate battle flag, with their drummer and two pipers playing "Dixie" and "Yellow Rose of Texas," why, it was like a combination revival meeting and circus.

With most early fighting centered around Washington and Richmond far to the northeast, Texas wasn't a primary battleground. So we had to find our war-related excitement where we could. In mid-summer, that included a dusty surprise—a cattle drive heading right for the heart of Serenity Falls.

This small herd of a hundred head belonged to Wilhelm Krieg. His Bar KR outfit (with a distinctive backwards K on its brand) was one of the biggest ranches in Texas, and growing. Coming from open rangeland to the southwest, the herd stopped for the night on the outskirts of town. Krieg's foreman,

Bulldog Quill, had determined that our stretch of Pine Cut Run offered the easiest crossing for miles around. So Krieg's outfit pointed their cattle in our direction, with the intent of driving them straight through town—a plan unknown to us, until a hundred beeves showed up on our doorstep.

While the Bar KR trail hands camped outside town with the cattle, Krieg and Bulldog came in with a supply wagon. After stocking up on provisions from Duncan's General Store, they came to the Shamrock for a room and a hot meal, during which Sheriff Huggins ambled up to their supper table at the saloon. "Bulldog. Mr. Krieg."

Krieg was a short, barrel-chested man in his early forties. Like that ornery son of his, who Jake and me had met a couple of years before, Krieg had blond hair, blue eyes, and a pugnacious set to his jaw. He spoke with a slight German accent. "Sheriff. You have a reason for interrupting my meal?"

"A hundred reasons, on the hoof."

"They will be gone in the morning."

"Gone where?"

"Through your little town, across Pine Cut Run, and on to the Confederate quartermaster."

"Did it occur to you to ask permission to run your cattle through our little town?"

"And if I had?"

"We might've said no."

"There is a war on, you see. They need meat, I have cattle. I take the fastest, most direct route to delivery."

"What if we stop you from taking this particular direct route?"

"Would you like for the Confederate government to know you and your little town impeded their war effort?"

"Big supporter of the Confederacy, sir?"

"I am a businessman. I do not care one way or the other for the cause. Only about getting paid."

Jawbone tapped the six-pointed star pinned to his vest. "This badge and me suggest you go around town, like always."

"No one says no to a Krieg."

"The law might differ."

"The only law that matters is supply and demand. Only a fool stands in its way."

I'll say this for Wilhelm Krieg: he stuck to his guns. Next morning, at sunup, Krieg's drovers calmly paraded their herd down Main Street, and across Pine Cut Run. The whole town came out to watch, and it was easy to see that our section of the river, situated as it was between our thundering namesake falls to the north and rocky rapids to the south, really was the ideal spot for cattle crossing.

A week later, some of Krieg's men and one of their wagons came rattling back into town. Bulldog Quill strode into the Shamrock, wanting a ground-floor room. When Mama explained the guest rooms were upstairs, the foreman snapped: "We got an injury needs treatin' and we don't want to have to carry Mr. Krieg upstairs."

Mama agreed, and they brought Wilhelm Krieg in on a litter. He grimaced in pain, his right leg immobilized by a makeshift splint. Mama took them to a room under the stairs, normally occupied by the whores, who loitered with me and Jake up on the steps, hanging at the rail, watching and overhearing.

"What happened?" Mama asked the foreman.

"Storm spooked the herd. Mr. Krieg got thrown. Got his leg stomped bad."

"See?" Jake whispered to me. "His horse darn near killed him."

Mama came back with the doctor a short time later. He was a thin, flinty fellow with chinstrap whiskers. His black leather bag under one arm, he found his patient sitting up in bed, drinking whiskey to dull his pain.

"Mr. Krieg," Mama said, "this is Dr. Stump."

Krieg's eyebrows arched. "Dr. *Stump?*"

"Calvin Stump," Doc said. "Unfortunate name for a physician, isn't it? And yet, in my years of practice, I've never had the occasion to lop off anybody's limb. Yet."

"I will keep my leg."

"I'll be the judge of that." Doc put his bag down, and glared at the trail hands hovering behind him. "Everybody but Miz Cara, out—*now.*"

The cowboys shuffled out, and Doc regarded the injured leg. "Thrown from your horse and trampled, I'd wager."

"Three days ago."

"You westerners are crazier than a soup sandwich riding on those beasts. You're lucky it didn't stomp the living snot right out of you."

"You're not from Texas."

"No, sir. New York. Educated at Rush Medical College in Chicago."

"How did you end up here?"

"God only knows. Maybe it's the year I served in prison for killing a patient with a morphine overdose. He was dying anyway, and I saw no purpose in prolonging it."

Doc touched the mangled leg, and Krieg swiped his hand away. "I have no need of your services."

"My little assistant disagrees," Doc said, pointing a pocket pistol at Krieg's nose.

"He rarely shoots his patients," Mama said.

"Rarely?"

"Most are coaxed into compliance," Doc said.

Krieg shook his head and settled down, for the moment. "The sheriff carries no gun, but the doctor does."

"Jawbone Huggins is a big man, with a great deal of patience," Doc said as he slipped the gun back into his coat pocket, then carefully removed the splint. "As a small impatient man, I find this a helpful means of persuasion. You have two fractures. The fibula, near the ankle, when you were thrown. Then your horse stepped on your leg closer to your knee, and splintered your tibia. You ended up on ground which was either sandy, wet, or both."

"How did you know?"

"Because soft ground under you is the only reason this leg's not a shattered mess, with an open fracture and sheared bones sticking out through your muscle and skin, leading to a deep bone infection."

"So this is not that serious."

"Don't count your chickens. Infection and gangrene could still kill you in a week. Even if it heals, you'll be hobbled for life. And pain'll be your constant companion."

"So, what now?"

"Set those bones. Watch and wait."

As that watching and waiting commenced, Bulldog Quill stayed on, with a couple of other men to serve as couriers between town and the Bar KR ranch, if needed. The others returned to the cattle drive.

Mama served Krieg a tray of afternoon tea and fresh-baked cookies to distract him from fretting too much about what his cowboys might be up to without his supervision. His restlessness seemed relieved by company, so she poured herself a cup and sat with him.

"I am obliged for your hospitality, Miss Cara."

"You're something of a ghost, Mr. Krieg."

"How so?"

"Out there on the range, rarely in town."

"I come only for business, and only when I must."

"Never just for a drink? A game of cards?"

"Frivolities I ended after my wife died giving birth to my

daughter, some years ago."

"All work and no play?"

"I had a ranch to build. A baby girl and son to raise, alone."

"I know what that's like."

His eyebrows went up. "Ahh . . . yes. You are the one who shot her husband."

"Ten years ago," she said, as if she'd expected that event to be long forgotten.

"People remember. What could drive you to such an act?"

Mama's eyes narrowed as she sifted miserable memories that seemed distant yet fresh. "Reuben got to be a mean drunk. Hit me and my boys. The night he forced me to work here as a whore—well, I reckon that was one of those last straws people always talk about, but rarely experience firsthand."

"Yet you built this place into something better."

"I did. So, I know how easy it is to lose yourself in work."

"Work makes us free. Prosperity is power. Power is security."

"Isn't there more to life than money?"

"This land is harsh, you see. Women and children are frail. They need protection."

"Is your daughter frail?"

"Victoria?" Simply saying her name brought a rare smile to his face. "No, she is not. It surprises me. But still I think I shall send her back to Philadelphia to live with Felicity's family."

"Philadelphia's where I was born."

"That is where I first came to this country. Where I met my Felicity."

"What about your boy?"

"Wolfgang?" Krieg's smile faded. "He has learned to . . . protect himself."

Wolf Krieg was no longer a boy, but a husky eighteen-year-old who looked very much like his father. He'd been working on the cattle drive and was one of the drovers who remained in town. When Jake and me saw him at the Shamrock, we recognized his flaxen hair and pale dead eyes right away. And, unlike the city hats or wide-brimmed Stetsons most common in that place and time, he wore a distinctive low-crowned John Bull top hat with a narrow brim fashioned in a tight kettle curl, and a twisted brass chain for a hatband.

The third day of Krieg's stay, when Doc Stump concluded his patient was out of mortal danger, and likely to keep his leg, that's when Wolf made his presence known. He'd been drinking the afternoon away, and I saw Juliet take him to a room in the back. I decided to stay close, just in case. It wasn't long before I heard the crash of a shattering bottle from inside, and Wolf snarling, "Get over here."

I shouted out to Jake sweeping the floor near the bar: "Get Mama—and her gun!"

I heard a thud and a shriek, furniture skidding and feet skittering. I wanted to rush in and rescue Juliet, I truly did. But I was a skinny thirteen, I'd hardly be a momentary obstacle—and maybe the mere contemplation of such self-sacrifice was all it took for the good Lord to deliver salvation since, a few palpitations later, Mama and her big revolver reached the door and barged in.

The bed was skewed away from the wall, and terrified Juliet in her frilly underthings kept it between her and Wolf as she dodged out of his reach. Her nose oozed blood beneath the start of a shiner under her left eye.

Wolf feinted as if to chase her, but he was hobbled by his britches down around his knees. He froze when he saw Mama's gun pointed in his direction.

As Juliet scooted over to her side, Mama leveled her gaze at Wolf's ice-blue eyes, and her voice came out calm as an April breeze. "Problem?"

"She ain't doing what I want."

Juliet whispered in Mama's ear.

Mama shook her head at Wolf. "Oh, you'd have to pay her a lot more for that. And nobody threatens my girls."

"If I don't get her," Wolf said with his ever-present smirk, "you don't keep my money."

Broken bottle in one hand, pants held up with the other, he took a reckless step toward Mama.

She blasted a hole in the floor, an inch from his right boot.

He leapt sideways like a man with a hot-foot and toppled onto his ass. "N-never met a gal was that good a shot."

"I'm not. I was aiming for your pecker. Next shot'll be aimed at your toes. So there's no telling what I might hit."

Wolf thought better of rash conduct, lurched to his feet, and hiked up his pants. "Lady, I'm Wolf Krieg—"

"I don't care if you're the Prince of Wales." Mama gestured toward the door with her gun barrel. "Let's go see your father."

Wolf grudgingly picked up his hat and gunbelt, and we all paraded to Krieg's room down the hall. The three of them entered, while Jake and me hovered outside the door.

"Your son's handiwork," Mama said, pointing at Juliet's face.

Wolf protested, "All I did was try and get what I paid for. She fell."

"The hell I did!" Juliet said.

"Nobody's gonna take a whore's word over mine."

"My girls are honest," Mama said. "Whoring's what she does, not who she is. Whereas I suspect a lying bully is who and what you are."

Krieg sat up straight. "I will not abide such insolence."

"I hope not," Mama said.

"You misunderstand. No woman speaks to my son this way."

Mama stared at him. "Then I don't know which one of you is a bigger idiot."

"These insults will not be forgotten. Or forgiven."

"You have twenty minutes to haul his carcass and yours out of my joint." Mama turned and left, taking Juliet with her.

Twenty minutes later, Dutch de Groot and the sheriff ushered the Kriegs and their men out of the Shamrock—and out of town.

"Aren't you afraid of Krieg?" I asked Mama at the bar later.

"Hombres like Krieg think they run the world," Cruz said.

"And hombres like us disagree," Mama said.

Maybe *one* Wilhelm Krieg couldn't run the world. But I had the feeling there were an awful lot of people just like him strutting around.

9

"If you go to war with the United States, you will never conquer her . . . If she does not whip you by guns, powder, and steel, she will starve you to death. It will take the flower of the country—the young men."
—Sam Houston

George Rhymes was a burly, scary-looking young fellow with wild hair and a bushy bird's-nest beard. A printer's apprentice in Ohio, he'd set out with his wife and two little boys, hoping to find a growing town in need of a print shop and a newspaper. Serenity Falls happened to be such a place when George arrived in April 1862.

By then, his printing venture was pretty much all he had. His wife and sons had died on their journey, and he'd buried them along the way. So he threw himself into his new enterprise, if only to fend off the madness of grief.

Other than conducting business, though, this kindly soul kept mostly to himself—until unforeseen events turned Serenity Falls upside down at the end of that year. That's when banker Silas Atwood decided to foreclose on most of the mortgages in town—including all the best farm land on the river side, where our friend Becky Shaw and her family lived.

Since nobody could pay off an entire mortgage within thirty

days, townsfolk were essentially evicted from property they thought they were on their way to owning. When George Rhymes wrote the news on this upheaval for his *Serenity Falls Mercury* paper, he asked fat Silas Atwood why.

Atwood's only comment: "It's nothing personal, just business."

The crux of that business was kicking farmers off their land in order to resell it to Bird Montgomery, the greedy plantation owner—and Atwood's dear friend and drinking companion.

After more than a year of war, with no end in sight, northern naval blockades were already strangling the southern economy by cutting off agricultural exports to England and the rest of Europe.

Montgomery seized on hard times to snatch up bountiful bottomland cheaply and expand his beloved Riverside. Like many deluded southerners, he believed Confederate persistence would triumph. When it did, he'd be ready to cash in on postwar demand for cotton, tobacco, rice, corn, and other crops.

As George tried to report fairly on all this, he learned about the people and politics embedded in the short history of Serenity Falls, and his *Mercury* editorials grew increasingly critical of Montgomery and Atwood. But that didn't sully Atwood's pleasure over selling to a speculator. From the banker's perch, it was more convenient dealing with one large landowner, instead of a whole bunch of itty-bitty farmers and merchants.

One secret George hadn't discovered was Bird Montgomery's covert leverage: the planter knew from one too many drunken confessions, lubricated by the banker's weakness for bourbon, that Atwood had squandered much of his bank's assets on risky investments.

Meanwhile, Atwood was comforted by knowing if the Confederacy failed, and Montgomery went broke, his land would revert to the bank—and Atwood could sell it all over again. As Bird Montgomery said, celebrating all that fertile soil filched from small farmers, "God ain't makin' no more land."

Not all the town's merchants were caught up in the mass foreclosure. But they wouldn't survive long without homestead farmers partaking of their various goods and services.

Serenity Falls had no real government yet in those days, just an informal council of community leaders, including my mother. They conferred, and decided the only way to strike back against Atwood was for the entire town to up and walk away from their mortgages. If the banker wanted the land, he could have it—all of it. Almost everyone in town agreed, so that's what they did.

This injustice at the hands of the rich infuriated me, Jake, and Becky. Wasn't the South supposedly fighting for "states' rights" against the federal government—David versus Goliath? It seemed what they were really fighting for was the right to keep human beings in chains, while cutthroat bankers and landowners robbed plain folk blind.

But there wasn't much anybody could do about it, including our sheriff. Much as he hated it, it fell to Jawbone Huggins to enforce the mortgage call, since it was legal. But he had no intention of lifting a finger against townsfolk who chose to default on their mortgages.

For some residents, this was too much to bear. They pulled up stakes entirely and headed north or west, as far from the war as possible. Those who stayed dismantled Serenity Falls, nail by nail, log by log, board by board. One wagonload after another, they transported all that raw material to the northwest. Squatting on hardscrabble land nobody owned or wanted on the fringes of hill country, they spent that winter and spring rebuilding.

The relocated town was christened Serenity, though that proved to be wishful thinking. Miles from what had been home, the town withered. The population dwindled to little more than half of what it had been. If Wolf Krieg followed through on his childish threat and burned down *this* incarnation of town, nobody would've much cared.

To me, Jake, and Becky, there was only one good thing about the new location—more pockets of antislavery Unionist sentiment, especially among German immigrants (who also brewed some fine beer). We kids had lost our old favorite haunts, and we weren't really kids anymore, either. As her parents struggled to farm less forgiving soil, Becky took on more chores and spent more time looking after her little brother and sisters.

The reconstituted Shamrock was smaller than before, but I seemed to have more work than ever. Mama had fewer girls, and they worked harder, too.

Jake, who'd turned sixteen, was surly more often than not. He spent more time shooting and gun cleaning, and less honing his cardsharp skills. Instead of juggling for fun, he mastered the art of swapping out a spent revolver cylinder for a loaded one without looking, under Cruz's tutelage. Even I reluctantly worked on improving my own shooting in case of invasion, or conscription by the foundering Confederacy.

During that dark time, I began to grasp how the world seemed to work: When it came to the gleeful greed and corruption of titans of commerce, money was their means and power was their end. And if they saw you as an obstacle, the good Lord himself couldn't save your sorry hide.

In the middle of '63, the Union navy and army forces commanded by Major General Ulysses S. Grant laid siege to the fortified city of Vicksburg, Mississippi, on the great river. Confederate troops under Lieutenant General John Pemberton held out for more than forty days and forty nights, longer than the Lord drenched Noah and his ark.

But Noah had a better outcome.

Without reinforcements or supplies, Pemberton surrendered, with unintended symbolism, on July 4th. That gave the Federals control of the Mississippi, effectively cutting off what was known as the Trans-Mississippi Department of the war—including Texas—from the rest of the Confederacy. As Grant wrote years later, "The fate of the Confederacy was sealed when Vicksburg fell."

By the fall of '64, despite scattered southern victories, the eventual outcome appeared inevitable. As Sam Houston had predicted, the North's military and industrial might were too much for the Confederacy, and Texas remained largely separated from the wilting war effort.

That's when my restless brother concluded this could be his last chance to join that war. One morning, during a half-hearted rock-throwing contest with Becky at the Shaw farm, he revealed his decision. Becky had a succinct response: "Jake, you are loco."

Looking to me for fraternal solidarity, all I gave him was a shrug. "Hard to argue with her."

Though Becky hated the Confederacy with more venom than me or my brother could muster, Jake plainly did not care for the southern cause. Still, he was seventeen now, and war was a challenge he felt he had to face to be a man.

"That makes you loco," Becky said, "and an idiot."

"It's an adventure. Hell, there's so little fighting hereabouts, I'll probably never even get to fire a shot in anger. It's just something I gotta do, is all."

"Then you are loco, an idiot . . . *and* lame-brained." Becky stalked away.

When Jake announced his intention to Mama, she was dead-set against it. But it's hard to pound a rational dent into an irrational proposition, so she appealed to Cruz. She hoped he'd use his own war experiences to talk Jake out of any desire to risk life and limb for a cause he didn't even believe in.

Cruz weighed the dilemma. "I been to war. And I've read poetry. Me? I learn more about being a man from poetry. But every man needs to choose for himself."

Furious at both Jake and Cruz, Mama stomped into her office and slammed the door. Still, as much as she wanted to tie down her headstrong son, she knew she couldn't.

As word spread around town, I decided I couldn't let Jake go alone. When I told Mama I was going, too, she shoved my behind into the nearest chair: "Oh, no, you don't. I will not lose both my sons for no good reason."

"But, Mama, blood is thicker'n water."

"What in hell is that supposed to mean?"

"We'll be safer looking out for each other."

"James Benjamin Galloway, you are barely sixteen. You are too young, too skinny, and too gentle to go to war. Your brother has it in him, you don't. That's the end of this."

Everybody in the whole saloon heard my own mother declare I wasn't man enough to fight alongside Jake. Worst of all, Juliet heard the whole mess. My face blazed with embarrassment, and I bolted outside.

Later, Becky found me scuffing the dirt as I walked along the road. "Hey," she said.

"Hey, yourself."

"Did you say what they're sayin' you said?"

I wanted to crawl into a hole. But there wasn't one handy, and I was too woebegone to dig one. "Yeah, I said it."

"Why?"

I shrugged.

"Don't follow Jake's foolishness." Then she squeezed my face in both her hands and kissed me. Not like when we were kids—for real. At first, I was too dumbfounded to kiss her back. When she unlocked our lips, she whispered, "You don't have to get yourself killed to prove anything."

"You mean . . . I'm not too young for you anymore?"

She kissed me again, for a whole lot longer. "Does that change your mind about joining Jake's big adventure?"

I let out the longest sigh of my life. "I wish it did. But if he's going . . ."

She shook her head. "Then maybe you're too stupid for *any* girl to marry."

I couldn't bear the hurt on her face, so I trudged back to town—where Jake intercepted me . . . and swatted the back of my head.

"Oww! What's that for?"

"Saying you wanna go with me. Is that your dumb way of tryin' to convince me to stay?"

"No! If you're going, I'm going."

"Well, all right then. Let's tell Mama."

We found her back at the Shamrock and, first thing, Jake said, "You're right. Jamey's not tough enough."

"Hey!" I squawked.

But Jake shut me up with a glare. "I say Jamey can't lick me in a fair fight. But if he can, that's proof we're wrong about him."

"I'll lick you, no problem."

"You're doomed."

Over Mama's objections, we marched out to the alley between the Shamrock and our barn. All the girls and customers from the saloon gathered, and soon other townsfolk joined the jumble of spectators. The war was often said to pit brother against brother, and there we were.

Seeing all the doves out to watch us, Jake peeled out of his shirt to show off his muscles. I was too self-conscious about my skinny frame, and kept my shirt on.

As we circled each other like a couple of roosters, Mama muttered to Cruz, "I have raised two all-fired idiots."

Jake heard her and laughed. "Mama—take bets! Make some money on this!"

As we commenced grappling, I heard Becky rooting for Jake to knock my block off, plainly hoping Mama would keep me home safe. I felt like everyone was against me. But even though I had a lot to prove, I couldn't bring myself to fight my own brother all-out.

Jake seized on my hesitation and taunted me, waving insults like a bullfighter's red cape. "Hey, Jamey-boy . . . 'thou lump of foul deformity! Out of my sight—thou dost infect my eyes.' "

It took me a second to realize . . . he was hurling Shakespearean slander my way. Well, two could play that game. " 'Thou sodden-witted lord! Thou hast no more brain than I have in mine elbows.' "

With a dismissive wave at me, Jake addressed the crowd. "Ha! 'He is white-livered and red-faced.' "

"Ha! '*You* have a plentiful lack of wit.' "

Most folks had no idea what we were doing, but Mama knew. As appalled as she was at our brawling, she couldn't help feeling a little proud of our scholarship. The crowd, however, was there to see a fight, not two jabbering knaves. Mex the blacksmith catcalled, "*Ay dios mio.* Somebody throw a punch!"

So I took a roundhouse swing, and missed clean. Jake skipped aside. I spun and fell on my behind.

" 'You had measured how long a fool you were upon the ground,' " Jake jeered.

I scrambled to my feet. " 'Such antics do not amount to a man.' " And then I charged at him again. That time, he sidestepped, stuck his foot out, and sent me tumbling ass over teakettle.

Jake snickered. " 'Your abilities are too infant-like for doing much alone.' "

As my pitiful stumbling continued, I grew madder and madder. Jake landed a few shoves and punches, but he barely broke a sweat. I was dripping and dusty, with a bloody nose. Back on my feet after a tumble, ready to charge again, I realized the angrier I got, the more Jake used it against me. Not only was I not beating him, I was beating myself.

I took a deep breath, and started seeing our fight like a game of poker or chess. Jake looked a little surprised when I reeled back instead of lunging forward. As soon as I stopped rushing him, he'd have to come at me, if he wanted to finish me off. And he had to—as big brother, his pride was at stake. No way he could let me off the hook.

Taking my time, I spotted weaknesses I'd missed in my initial fury—and the tables turned, with Jake now desperate and off-balance. I threw everything into one lucky punch to his gut that knocked all the wind out of him. He staggered and fell on his ass, with me sneering down at him. " 'I scorn you, scurvy companion.' "

He gasped for breath. "You're tougher'n you look, little brother."

"I've been wrangling horses since I was six. They're stronger than you. Smarter, too."

Flat on his back, Jake reached for a hand up. But I walked away, wiping my bloody nose on my sleeve. Then he called out, "That kid can whip his weight in wildcats."

Savoring Jake's public surrender, I turned back and yanked him to his feet.

Forced to concede she couldn't keep us home, Mama saw to it we were well-equipped, including a pair of new Remington revolvers for each of us. The Remingtons were easier to reload than the popular Colt pistols—no small thing when somebody's shooting at you. Mama had purchased the guns for us before the war made them scarce, and hidden them away for a special occasion. This was not the occasion she'd had in mind.

She also provided us with spare cylinders, ammunition and percussion caps, new boots, and packs stuffed with as much food as we could carry. We were as ready for Jake's grand adventure as we'd ever be, and we'd leave to seek our destiny—or doom—the following morning.

That night, after everyone had gone to sleep, I padded past Juliet's bedroom door. The door opened, her hand snaked out, grabbed me, and pulled me inside. I figured she just wanted to talk—until she shut the door, wrapped her arms around me, and kissed me.

"Should we be doing this?" I whispered.

"Why not?"

"Mama's rules."

"I know. You boys aren't fair game for us whores."

"I never liked that rule much."

Juliet shushed me with a finger to my lips. "You ever screwed?"

I hoped it was too dark for her to see me blush, while I thought about fibbing. "W-with a girl?"

"No . . . a farm critter."

I told the truth. "Nope."

"Nope to girls? Or farm critters?"

"Both."

"But you're leavin' tomorrow." She kissed me again and steered me to the bed.

"Juliet . . . I . . . I don't have any money on me."

She smiled in the moonlight coming through the curtains. "I just . . . I want you to remember me."

Well, I'd have remembered Juliet anyway. But that night removed any doubt. I was nervous, because I knew she knew a whole lot more about what we were up to than I did. Truth was, I didn't know much. And she was a whore, after all.

But not then, she wasn't. She was my teacher, and she made

the first time easy and sweet. It couldn't have been perfect—no first time ever is. But it felt that way to me. The second and third times, I could tell by the way she did less teaching, I must've been a good student.

I should've crept back to my own room. But we fell asleep instead, like we had in the hayloft that afternoon when Rhody left, four years earlier. At daybreak, I woke up in a hurry. Juliet stayed in bed, propped up on one elbow, watching me. I put on some of my clothes, grabbed the rest, and kissed her. I opened the door, careful and quiet, backing out so I could catch one more glimpse of her smile. But the smile disappeared.

"Don't worry," I said. "Mama'll never know."

Juliet grimaced. "She might."

"She's . . . standing right behind me, isn't she?" I turned, face to face with Mama in the hall. She backed me into the room. Juliet flopped down and hid under the sheet.

"You know the rules," Mama scolded. "You both know them."

"Mama, listen—"

Juliet cut me off. "Jamey, this is between your mama and me."

And they went on talking about me like I wasn't there. I had mixed feelings: proud for spending the night with Juliet, ashamed for letting Mama down—and for getting caught. I felt more like a man, ready to go off to war—but wondered whether leaving Juliet behind might not be the *dumbest* thing I could possibly do.

Juliet hung her head. "This was my fault, not Jamey's."

"These boys're like your brothers."

"I know," Juliet said. Then she looked Mama straight in the eye. "But he's not my brother. And he's not a boy."

"And I'm the fool for thinking this wouldn't happen with one of you girls, sooner or later."

Juliet gathered the sheet around her and stood up. "I guess

you'll want me gone."

"No more than I want my boys gone."

"It won't happen again."

"Ohhh, it might," Mama said with a philosophical sigh.

Before we could go out and find Confederate troops to join, they found us. I was in the barn, saying goodbye to Shadow before leaving him in Cruz's care, when a platoon of thirty thin and raggedy soldiers trudged into town. Most were from Company C of the Texas Volunteers 6th Infantry, but there were survivors of other companies among them. In tattered piecemeal uniforms, they were a far cry from the spit-and-shine troops bound for glory a few short years earlier.

In fact, only their soft-spoken commander, Captain Patrick Henry Mercier, wore a whole uniform—complete with shiny buttons. Mercier was grateful to welcome two new recruits. But their supply wagon carried only the most basic equipment, so Jake and me were each issued an Enfield rifle, some ammunition, and nothing else.

We marched out with those ill-provisioned rebels the next morning, following Mercier on his haggard horse. Our only musical accompaniment came from one inexperienced drummer boy doing his best to rap out a somber, wobbly cadence.

10

"Sound trumpets! Let our bloody colours wave! And either victory, or else a grave."
—William Shakespeare, *Henry VI*

If you think you know how you'd react when somebody shoots at you, think again.

The ragtag remainder of Company C spent that autumn of '64 searching half-heartedly for some Yankees to engage, roaming East Texas and western Louisiana, back and forth across the Sabine River. Shaggy cypress trees, with branches draped in pale Spanish moss, reminded me of gaunt old women wearing shawls to ward off an evening chill.

With flagging energy devoted mostly to foraging, many of our comrades seemed ready to go home. Though few said it out loud, they'd come to see the holy southern cause as a lost cause. And speaking of flags, nobody much cared about carrying the battle flag anymore. But Captain Patrick Henry Mercier insisted on it.

Mercier had no patience for defeatism. He was named for Revolutionary War hero and fellow Virginian Patrick Henry, the firebrand who famously said, "Give me liberty, or give me death!" This quietly fervent Yankee-hater proudly carried the nickname "No Mercy" Mercier—which, as far as anybody knew, he'd bestowed upon himself.

Bespectacled and bookish, he appeared younger than his twenty-eight years, and like he'd be more at home behind a clerk's desk than leading men into battle. But Mercier had studied history at The College of William & Mary before moving to Texas, and he'd acquired a vast collection of quotes on the subject of warfare, which he'd dispense in nightly campfire sermons.

"If we have faith in God and fear of his almighty wrath, our righteous cause cannot be lost," he preached one chilly November night.

I swallowed a sip of bitter coffee. "Captain, are you saying this is a divine mission?"

"It is, son. We're fightin' for nothing less than sacred individual liberty."

"We're spending most of our time scrounging for food."

"You know what the great General Napoleon Bonaparte said."

"No, sir . . ."

"Hardship, poverty, and want are the best school for a soldier."

"I'm pretty sure Napoleon lost," Jake mumbled in my ear.

"Men," Mercier said, "let's get some rest. If we're to face a battle tomorrow, remember: death before dishonor."

He'd end each day with that motto. But here's the thing—you can recover from dishonor, whereas death tends to be a permanent state of affairs.

The wellspring of Captain Mercier's optimism was the Battle of Mansfield back in April of '64, in DeSoto Parish, Louisiana. That was the start of the Union Army's blunderous Red River Campaign, aiming to capture the key city of Shreveport in northwest Louisiana, and then invade Texas. It resulted in a rare Confederate victory, which eventually led the Federals to scrap the campaign altogether. That rebel triumph was a fading memory to most, but not to our captain.

As fall turned into a mild winter, our army life consisted mostly of marching and boredom. Oh, we'd fired a few shots in the general direction of what we reckoned to be Federal troops. But we were never close enough to be sure. You might think I'd have welcomed such a low level of danger. But it left me with lots of time to fret over theoretical mortal dreads, such as how we were supposed to load our muskets in the heat of battle. Those old Enfield rifles, of course, only fired one shot at a time. You had to stand up to reload, not a smart thing if somebody was shooting back at you.

On the bright side, boredom left ample time for playing cards wherever we made camp. Not that underpaid soldiers had much to lose. But, like most gamblers we'd observed, these men also believed they were better poker players than they really were. Me and Jake weren't looking to leave any man skint down to his empty pockets, but we won more than we lost.

By far, the worst gambler was First Sergeant Ike Frizzell, who had boundless faith that his next hand would be a winner. That matched his boundless faith in the good Lord, and every morning before we broke camp, Frizzell would bow his head and lead us in a mumbled group recitation of the 23rd Psalm:

" 'The Lord is my Shepherd, I shall not want. He maketh me to lie down in green pastures, he leadeth me beside still waters. He restoreth my soul. He leadeth me in the paths of righteousness for His name's sake. Yea, though I walk through the valley of the shadow of death, I will fear no evil, for thou art with me. Thy rod and thy staff comfort me. Thou preparest a table before me in the presence of mine enemies. Thou anointest my head with oil. My cup runneth over. Surely, goodness and mercy shall follow me all the days of my life, and I will dwell in the House of the Lord forever. *Amen!*' "

Other than the drummer boy, Jake and me were the youngest members of the company. That didn't stop us from becoming friends with the second oldest, John Kirby. All of twenty-six and hailing from South Carolina, he'd been visiting kin in Texas when the war broke out. Rather than go all the way back home to enlist, he joined the Texas Volunteers and he'd been with Company C ever since.

Kirby was an affable soul, regarded as the company's big brother. He was also a good-luck charm of considerable potency, owing to his knack for survival. He'd been wounded four times, and he'd show his scars when asked. Any one of those wounds could have been fatal, had the bullets struck an inch in one direction or another.

He'd served long enough that he could've left for home. But he felt compelled by loyalty to his men to stay. He could sing in a sweet Irish tenor and played his harmonica pretty well. With Frizzell strumming his battered banjo, we had some rousing sing-alongs 'round the campfire.

Kirby had a sharpshooter's skill, and he'd surely earned his field promotion to lieutenant. The best meal we had during our time in the army was a big 'gator we'd spotted napping in the sun one morning. Kirby nailed it with one shot. Once we'd hacked through that hide, the roasted meat tasted very much like chicken.

Something else about Johnny Kirby: he had this letter tucked into his breast pocket, addressed to his wife and daughters back in Charleston, and carefully wrapped in canvas to protect it from the rain. Kirby also had a small notebook he'd take out whenever he could, and he'd draw meticulous pencil sketches, which he never shared with the men. Instead, each time he finished one, he'd tear it out, fold it, and slip it into the envelope containing his letter.

It wasn't uncommon among soldiers to have last words written and addressed, to be sent to their families if they were killed. But Kirby's letter had taken on the status of talisman. Soon after we'd joined up, Sergeant Frizzell took us aside and gave us the queerest order: "If Johnny Kirby asks you to take his letter and send it home if he croaks, tell him you won't."

Jake squinted. "Why?"

"Because Johnny's our luck. If we find ourselves a fight, he'll be the last man standin' anyways. So it don't matter. But it's a tradition. So long as Johnny worries nobody'll send his letter home, he won't die. And if he don't die, we'll escape any scrapes with those Yankee bastards."

Who were we to upend a comforting superstition? Sure enough, it wasn't long before Kirby asked, even though he knew we'd say no. "I hope y'all are right about me being such a lucky charm," he said with a sigh.

Considering the question at the heart of the war—whether slavery would continue and spread—I was surprised to learn that most of these southern soldiers didn't own a single slave. When I asked Kirby about it, he gave me a patient smile. "We're not fightin' for slavery. Only doing our Christian duty to protect our homes and families."

I tugged my hat brim down to my eyebrows, which I tended to do when I was confused. It helped me focus on the matter at hand. "But didn't the South fire the first shots?"

"Doesn't matter who fires first, if he's provoked."

"It doesn't?"

"If northerners can tell us how to work our farms, then maybe they'd start tellin' me how to run my dry goods store back home, sayin' what I can or can't sell."

"Why would they?"

"They wouldn't need a reason. But I believe in my heart the good Lord's blessed our struggle. It's not about the slaves. It's about Yankees tryin' to step on us, and tell us our way of life is sinful."

"What if it *is* sinful?"

"Well, then the good Lord'll tell us that, I reckon."

"What if all this suffering *is* Him telling us, and we ain't listening?"

"The Israelites suffered on their way to the Promised Land. I don't expect we're immune." Kirby shook his head with a wry grin. "Y'all ask too many questions, Jamey. Anybody ever tell you that?"

And then he took out his harmonica and played the old ballad "Barb'ry Allen." Some of the men started singing along. I didn't know all the words, so I didn't join in. But it sure was pretty and sad.

Once, I asked Kirby to teach me to play the harmonica. He did try, and it would be kind to say I was not a natural. But when he saw my determination, he wanted me to have his harmonica if anything happened to him.

"Aww, that's like asking me to say I'll send your letter."

Kirby just chuckled.

Right after the new year, though, even shiny John Kirby turned gloomy. He pleaded with anybody who couldn't escape to *please* promise to mail his letter, like he believed his luck was running out. Still, nobody would tempt fate. I could see this weighed heavy on Kirby, but Jake warned me not to rock the boat. So, I didn't.

One dewy March morning, with a hint of spring on the breeze and birds chirping, we came across bodies at the edge of some woods. Five Confederates in their piecemeal uniforms, looking a lot like us, but all shot up and sprawled on their deathbed of damp leaves. They'd been stripped of their weapons, but the Federals who'd taken their lives and rifles had deemed the rest of their shabby clothing and equipment unworthy of scavenging.

We stood back, sober as deacons, as Mercier and Sergeant Frizzell toed all those corpses face up. Mercier looked closely at one, as if familiar. But he wasn't looking at that soldier's face. He crouched down to inspect the dead man's frayed gray jacket. Then Mercier took out his knife, carefully cut off seven brass buttons, and tucked them into his vest pocket. "These'll polish up. Sergeant, have these men buried proper."

Frizzell nodded at us, and Kirby handed out shovels from the supply wagon. When the job was finished, we moved on. For the rest of that day, nobody was in the mood for joshing or singing, or even talking.

The next late afternoon, we spied a wagon up the road, pulled by a lone mule and carrying one man. At Frizzell's order, the company hid in the bushes and trees on either side of the road, rifles ready. As the wagon drew closer, we could see the driver was a black man dressed in a clean white shirt and a brown vest and trousers. The wagon's cargo box was empty.

"Let'm pass, sir?" Frizzell said.

Mercier shook his head. "Could be an escaped slave."

"Ridin' by hisself in broad daylight?"

Mercier drew his revolver and stepped out of hiding. The startled man in the wagon hauled his mule to a stop. He pulled his hat off as a sign of respect, showing the gray in his hair.

"What's your name and destination, sir?" Mercier asked. His genteel voice had none of the contempt I'd expected.

"Name's Tuck, sir," the black man said with jittery dignity. "I work at the Collins farm, five mile thataway."

"What's your business on this road?" When Tuck reached inside his vest, Mercier cocked and pointed his gun. "Nice and slow."

Tuck carefully pulled out an envelope and handed it down. "Jus' delivered cotton to the mill."

As the rest of the company emerged from the bushes, Mercier examined Tuck's documents. "You're a special Nigrah to be allowed out on your own."

"Massa Collins trusts me, Cap'n. I ain't never let 'm down."

"Says here you got paid for that cotton." Tuck reached under the seat, pulled out a sack heavy with coins, and handed it to Mercier, who jingled the money inside. "I don't see any letters of permission here among these papers."

"Ever'body know me here, between the farm and the mill. I make this run all the time."

"I don't know you."

"Not bein' from here."

"Y'all wouldn't be fixin' to rob your master."

Tuck looked at the sack of money in Mercier's hand. "Are you fixin' to rob *me*?"

"Was that a little Nigrah joke?"

"If you ride with me back to the Collins farm, jus' down the road, they'll tell you."

"I don't think we'll be doing that. Now, y'all come down here."

It wasn't a request, and Tuck knew it. By the dread in his eyes, he also knew nothing good could come from his stepping down from that wagon. But if he shook those reins to rouse his mule and run for it, Mercier would've shot him. So, the slave set his hat on the seat and climbed down.

Mercier had this poor Tuck fella bound hand and foot, then dragged over to a tall tree. As if he'd done this before, Frizzell tied the noose, and tossed the rope over a sturdy branch. Then he let the noose down, and Mercier slipped it around the slave's neck.

I'd have been begging for mercy. But Tuck held his head high, dignity edging out fear.

"You're not pleadin' for your life," Mercier said, with some consternation.

"Figure it wouldn't do me no good, Cap'n. If it's all the same, let's be done."

"If all you had to do to save your black neck would be to admit you are a slave aimin' to escape . . ."

"I don't expect you be showin' no mercy to no runaway."

"I might surprise you."

"An' I might sprout wings and fly. But I don't think you'd wager much on that."

"You're not afraid of dyin'?"

"I been whupped bloody and a whisper away from Jesus' sweet embrace. You treated me polite during our short time knowin' each other. So, I think you won't leave me kickin'."

"Well, then . . . would you rather be hoisted? Or fall from a height?"

"I expect a fall would be better. Maybe bring my wagon over, set me standin' on the back, and give that ol' mule a slap. Minnie can step lively when she's prodded."

"Then that's what we'll do, Tuck."

Mercier ordered me and Jake to get the wagon. We wanted no part of this lynching, but we didn't have a choice. With me in the driver's seat and Jake alongside Minnie with a grip on her harness, we backed the wagon under the tree.

Two men lifted Tuck like a potato sack and stood him upright on what amounted to a wheeled gallows. Frizzell tightened the noose and adjusted the rope around the tree branch, leaving enough slack for a body to drop. Tuck looked over his shoulder at me. "Minnie's well broke. Jus' take that whip under the seat, tell her to git up, and slap her on the rump. I'd be obliged for that favor."

I couldn't talk around the lump in my throat, so I nodded.

Mercier stood behind the wagon. "You a Christian, Tuck?"

"I am, Cap'n."

"Then may God have mercy on your nigger black soul. Private Galloway, you ready?"

I wanted to shout, "*No,* sir!" But before I could answer, a rifle ball whistled over our heads, followed by a volley of shots from unseen enemies on the wooded hillside above us.

With a briskness borne of experience, Frizzell shouted orders.

With a briskness borne of pants-pissing fear, I abandoned my sitting-duck position on the wagon seat. As we all scurried for cover, Jake and I dove into a gulley behind a big toppled tree. Dead branches and a tangle of vines created a blind, from which we could see without anybody seeing us.

The enemy threw at least a dozen more shots our way. But that helped us locate them, and our men fired back. Except me. I didn't want to have to stand up and come out of hiding to reload that damned rifle. Jake fired his rifle, then laid it aside in favor of his revolvers.

Up on the wagon, his life literally hanging by a thread, Tuck knew if the mule moved, he was done for. So he murmured re-assurance to Minnie, hoping to keep her from bolting as gunfire boomed around her.

The Yankees advanced slowly through the woods and down the hill. Johnny Kirby, on his belly, claimed the first kill by shooting a bluecoat straight through the heart. And then he had to reload. The exact instant he stood up, half-crouched behind a tree, the enemy unleashed a barrage. With a short cry, Kirby fell backwards. *Dead.*

The rifle reports faded. The breeze blew choking smoke into our faces. The startling silence of those bloodied woods seemed to last forever.

But it was no more than a few seconds until the next furious volley came our way.

Mercier ordered a charge.

Nobody moved.

Every man in our company was thinking the same thing: *If Kirby's dead, so are we.*

11

"Better a live coward than a dead hero."
—Jamey Galloway

"Fire at them, God damn you!" Mercier shouted.

A few of our men did. The Yankees answered. Three more of our company fell.

Tuck sang softly to Minnie. She seemed remarkably unperturbed. It said something about our predicament that a slave with a noose around his neck might've had a brighter immediate future than we did.

Our boys fired random rounds at the Yankees, and they shot right back. I turned to see Jake reloading his Remingtons. He had a look on his face I knew well, and didn't like. He was about to try something, even if it was something dumb.

"Jake, we're doomed."

"Probably. Maybe we should charge."

"What? Why would you even *think* that?"

Jake frowned. "I'm your big brother."

"So?"

"You look up to me."

"You being humble and all."

"I stay here hidin', what kind of example would I be settin' for you?"

"I don't know."

"I'll tell you. I'd be a coward."

"And if you run out there?"

"Well, that'd be an example of being brave." A dubious pause. "Wouldn't it?"

"Or *stupid.*"

Jake snorted. "Well, now you got me conflicted."

"Better a live coward than a dead hero."

" 'Cowards die many times before their deaths,' " Jake said, quoting Shakespeare's *Julius Caesar.* " 'The valiant never taste of death but once.' "

"I can live with that."

"Frizzell!" Mercier called.

"Yes, sir."

"Stand ready."

As he hunched against a twisted tree, I heard Frizzell start muttering his psalm. Was he begging for salvation in this life, or the next? "The Lord is my Shepherd . . . I shall not want. He maketh me to lie down in green pastures . . ."

"This ain't gonna end well," Jake said. "Gimme your rifle."

"What're you gonna do?"

"Just shut up and give it."

I did both. Through the smoke, I saw the sergeant worm his way back to his feet, continuing his prayer: "He leadeth me in the paths of righteousness for His name's sake. Yea, though I walk through the valley of the shadow of death—"

That's when they shot Frizzell dead.

Jake ignored the gunfire all around us. He braced my rifle on the fallen tree trunk and took aim—but not at the enemy.

"Jake, what're you doing?"

"That mule's not gonna stand still forever."

"You're gonna shoot the mule?"

"I'm not gonna shoot the mule."

"Why would you shoot the mule?"

"I'm not—"

"Don't shoot the mule!"

"I'm *not* shooting the damn mule—but I might shoot you."

Mercier popped up, trying to figure how many men he had left—and a bullet struck him right between the eyes. With that, the dregs of our company tried to scatter. Under thundering enemy fire, a few got away, most got killed.

During all that shooting, that's when Jake pulled the trigger. His shot grazed the rope above Tuck's head—but failed to cut it clean. Half the rope's woven strands held together, still smoking from the heat of the bullet.

Jake's jaw clenched. "Dammit!" He set the rifle down and drew his Remington.

"Maybe you should've shot the mule."

"Maybe you should shut up."

Minnie wasn't standing still any more. She twitched her ears, brayed her displeasure—and took a step.

Jake cocked the pistol.

"You'll never hit that rope again in a million years."

"Thanks for your vote of confidence. But I'm aiming for the mule."

Minnie took another step. And another strand of the singed rope snapped.

Jake held his fire.

Minnie moved again. The final two strands broke.

"Good thing you didn't shoot the mule."

Jake gave me a peevish squint.

"I would not have bet on that shot," I said with admiration.

"Me, neither," said the fellow known to bet on pert near anything.

The smoke cleared in the wind. With our side gone, or dead, their side had nobody left to shoot at—except Jake and me, if they found us. As the Union soldiers came down the hillside, we hunkered in that gulley like petrified field mice hiding from a hawk.

The Yankees came over to Tuck, still standing on the wagon. The sergeant gazed up at the severed rope and shook his head. "You are one lucky bastard, boy."

Tuck nodded.

The sergeant cut the ropes binding Tuck's hands and feet. "If I was you, I'd be on my way."

Tuck nodded again. With the floppy noose still around his neck, he clambered into the wagon seat, took up the reins, and got Minnie moving. *Fast.*

The sergeant barked orders; his men formed up and marched down the road.

Jake and me waited a good hour, in case those Union troops returned. It was near dusk when we finally crawled out of our hidey-hole. We surveyed the killing ground before us, and weighed our next step. Even if we could find scattered survivors of Company C, we'd had our fill of this particular adventure.

However, our choices were few, and none were promising. For starters, most of what little money we had was nearly worthless Confederate scrip. If rebels found us first, we could be shot as deserters—but we didn't fancy a future as Federal prisoners either. It was just as well our dirty clothing resembled nobody's uniform. If chanced upon by either side, we might be able to talk our way out of trouble.

We considered trying for a night's sleep, but we were too jumpy to rest. So we decided to use the cover of darkness to slog as far from this miserable, meaningless battlefield as possible. I couldn't help looking at the bodies in the fading daylight. "Should we bury 'em?"

"It'll take too long. And we'll be dog-tired." Jake groaned when I went to Kirby's body. "Aww, c'mon, Jamey. He's dead. It's not like it matters to him anymore."

"Well, it matters to me." I crouched and found the letter in

Kirby's pocket, along with his harmonica. The envelope wasn't sealed, and I slid the pages out.

"It's private. Leave it be."

He was right—but I *had* to know: What would a man choose to say to his wife and kids from beyond the grave? I found not only his letter but a score of his folded sketches. They were delicately wrought pencil drawings not of war, but of the countryside, and of his comrades engaged in life's daily details: shaving, cooking, drinking coffee around the campfire, playing cards, laughing.

Nestled in the center was one more sketch—of his two precious little girls, drawn from memories war couldn't dim, and only death could erase. I held the letter like a sacred scroll, and read it out loud:

My Dearest Companion,

If you receive this letter, then you will know I have gone to my Heavenly reward. Though I wanted to return to your embrace more than anything, know that my last Earthly thoughts were of you and our Dear Girls, and so will be my eternal thoughts. Certainty that we will someday reunite in the loving arms of Jesus has tamed my fear of Death's cold grip.

But I also weep with the pain of knowing that you and our dear little Molly and Grace shall grieve that this loving Husband and doting Father could not be with you for a natural lifetime. Though I cannot touch thy hands, dance at their weddings, or hold our grandchildren, know that I shall always watch over thee, Dear Claire.

My breath will be the cooling breeze of a summer evening. My heart will soar with the harbor gulls over your heads. My tears of joy shall fall in every spring shower. Though my body be gone to dust, my spirit will never leave thee lonely.

In my time at war, I have known some good men and some harsh. I shared with them the songs you and I have loved so well. And in these humble drawings, I share with you some of the daily joys I have seen. Being apart from thee has been my trial, the promise of reunion my Salvation. I leave this life with a prayer for your happiness.

Please give a Father's lost and belated kisses to our Dear Little Girls. Tell them that in the eyes of their now departed Father, their faces have always put the sun to shame, and lit even my darkest days.

Your loving Husband and Father,
Johnny Kirby

With a sigh for their love and loss, I wrapped the letter back in its protective canvas. Jake favored mailing it first chance we got. With the war on, I argued, the odds of it safely crossing the South were slim. I planned to hold onto it for a while.

"What if you do and *we* get killed?" Jake said with a nod toward the dead around us. "But you wanna keep it? Suit yourself."

We couldn't bury everyone. But we agreed to bury Johnny Kirby.

As we dug a shallow grave, I wondered whether I could ever write a letter like his. I tried to conjure something like the poetic simplicity thoughts of his wife and daughters inspired in Kirby, but I couldn't. And if by some miracle the words came to me, who would I even write to? Becky? Juliet? I liked them both, but was that enough?

Kirby loved his wife and girls with a devotion he believed strong enough to transcend death. I'd never known that kind of love, and didn't know if I ever would.

It was dark by the time we were done. I bowed my head to

the fresh mound of damp dirt. "Johnny, I swear . . . we'll get this letter to your family, even if we have to deliver it ourselves." Then I glanced at Jake. "Kinda wish we'd told him that while he was still alive."

"Aww, shut up."

Though the Union troops had looted the bodies of most usable supplies (including Tuck's sack of coins), we took whatever remained—some hardtack, matches, canteens, some ammunition, and a couple of knives. When our packs were stuffed, Jake addressed Captain Mercier's corpse. "You wanted death before dishonor? You got 'em both."

As we walked that night, we didn't talk much, and didn't need to. There was no place to go but home. We had no idea how long it would take to get there on foot. But we figured on it being a straight trip, even if we did have to keep an eye out for troops from both sides of a war we were done with.

We were too young and too dumb to know the true peril in any journey is what you *don't* figure on happening.

And what we never figured on was getting captured by Indians.

12

"There are not enough Indians in the world to defeat the Seventh Cavalry." —Lieutenant Colonel George Armstrong Custer, U.S. Army

---

"What's your business out here, boys?"

The question came from U.S. Army Major Liam Travers, a florid-faced Irishman commanding one of the few battalions out of Fort Riley in Kansas not sent to fight rebels earlier in the war. We ran into them on our tenth hungry, dirty, thirsty day fending for ourselves.

Most of those endless ten days had been spent hunting for edible vegetation, critters not sly enough to run or hide when we tried to shoot them, and clean water to fill our canteens. And we'd have been the first to admit we hadn't made as much progress toward home as we might've liked.

"Just passing through, Major, sir," Jake said, truthfully.

"Without horses?" Travers leaned back in the chair in his camp tent and squinted at us.

"Stolen by lily-livered Johnny Rebs who didn't care they were fightin' for a lost cause," Jake lied.

"You boys wouldn't be Confederate spies, now . . . would you?"

"No, sir." Honest, again.

"Well, if you are, I'll shoot you. And if you're not, and you're from these parts, I could use some scouts."

"Are . . . are you offerin' us a job?"

"I am, son."

"Well, Major, sir, we'll take it," Jake said before I could protest.

Travers snapped his fingers toward a soldier who looked no older than us. "Private, take these boys to the mess tent for some of that gruel masquerading as food."

As we trailed the private, we whispered at each other.

"Jake, are you loco? We don't know anything about scouting."

"We didn't know anything about soldiering, either."

"Look where that got us."

"We're in Texas, right?"

I gave a dubious nod.

"And it can't be west Texas, 'cuz we haven't walked that far."

"I reckon."

"So we're not lyin' if we tell him we're from these parts, give or take."

I warmed up to Jake's logic. "Who's to say what 'these parts' means, anyway?"

"Meanwhile, we get fed, a tent over our heads, a little pay in our pockets. So? Are we scouts?"

"I reckon we are," I said, without much enthusiasm.

After we were equipped with minimal supplies, and told our meager pay rate, Travers introduced us to the reason behind his need for scouts—a burly bearded man sprawled on a cot in a tent, snoring loudly.

"Newt Reno, meet your new protégés, Jake and Jamey Galloway. No, no, Newt, don't trouble yourself to get up."

"Uhh, Major, sir," I said, "he's sleeping."

"No, he's in a drunken stupor. Newt's drunk more than he's sober. He's also pretty full of himself. And if you're not careful, he'll regale you for hours on his adventures from the Mexican War to the gold rush, and everything in between."

"Any of it true?" I asked.

"Half, maybe. But he's a fair scout when he's not blind drunk, so you might actually learn some from him." Travers strode away, and we bounced after him like a couple of pups. "If you boys are sober and standing upright, you're already more use to me than Newt. Stay out of my way, stay out of trouble, and stay ready when I need you."

Perhaps owing to the accustomed condition of Newt Reno, nobody seemed too concerned about our actual proficiency as scouts. We soon discovered that Travers was partly right about Newt—the drunken blowhard part. But he never seemed sober, so all we learned was to stay upwind after his meals. The man could fart up a storm.

The army provided us with horses, which was no thrill to Jake. But we also had a new group of card-playing partners, with more money and other booty to lose than our dirt-poor Confederate compadres. Lucky for us, these men shared the same overconfidence in their own gaming prowess common to gamblers everywhere.

We were careful to moderate our profit-taking, so as not to spook these slightly more golden geese into avoiding us at the poker table. The more we played, the more I was convinced that we were better card players than most, and that bad gamblers hated to lose. The more they lost, the angrier they got. So, the trick was winning, but not so much that the losers wanted to kill us.

One pleasant night in early April of '65, right after my seventeenth birthday, Jake found me writing a note to add to Johnny Kirby's letter, which I still had, since we'd been nowhere near a real town in the first weeks of our current career.

"What's that for?" he asked.

"Just wanted Claire to know we gave him a Christian burial. That he died fast, not slow and agonizing. And to tell her where he was, more or less."

Jake patted me on the head. "You got a good heart, Jamey."

"I signed your name, too."

"You did?" He seemed genuinely touched.

"Sure."

"Why?"

"Because you put up with me."

We were interrupted as a courier came whooping into camp with the three-day-old news that General Lee had surrendered to General Grant at Appomattox Court House, Virginia. While our new Federal comrades celebrated through the night, Jake and me were mostly just relieved the damn thing was done.

Of course, the jubilation turned out to be short-lived. Days later, another courier brought shocking word of President Lincoln's assassination.

Though that horrific war was essentially over, the last known battle didn't take place until a month later, near the Rio Grande in south Texas, at Palmito Hill. It would take another month before Texas officially emancipated its slaves on June 19th, thereafter celebrated as Juneteenth.

On that June day, the sinking hopes of Texas plantation owners desperate to retain their slaves were conclusively crushed, drowned by the same financial tidal wave of defeat as their bankrupt brethren across the south. That included Bird Montgomery, the squire of Riverside, near what used to be Serenity Falls.

Some of Montgomery's slaves fled immediately. Others stayed and worked as if nothing had changed, since it was the only life they knew. Our young friend Salem had grown up tall and handsome, and owing to his soft-spoken politeness, Riverside's mistress, Martha Montgomery, had promoted him from field hand to house servant. In that more comfortable capacity, he'd been given better clothing, and even learned to read a little.

That's how Salem happened to be repairing loose railing on the mansion's veranda when he heard Bird Montgomery raging upstairs, arguing with his wife and God, and vowing to keep his slaves. The master of Riverside swore eternal allegiance to the Confederacy, damned Robert E. Lee for a surrendering coward and all Yankees to hellfire, then cocked his revolver and blew his brains out.

The widow summoned Salem to move the body and clean up the mess. Much to his own surprise, he didn't feel like celebrating the death of the man who'd torn his family apart. All he felt was disgust, and pity for Mrs. Montgomery, who had treated her slaves with some kindness. Montgomery's widow and sons (who'd somehow avoided fighting for sacred southern honor) packed up wagonloads of belongings, abandoned their property, and moved away—to England, some said, but nobody ever really knew for sure.

With the family departed, the more worldly slaves expected Silas Atwood's bank would take back the land. Those free blacks milled like lost sheep for a while before gathering their meager possessions, and whatever they could scavenge from the plantation. Then they also departed, to find their place in a new and uncertain world.

Salem was on his own. His father had died, and he knew of no way to locate his mother and sister who'd been sold years before. So he carefully folded the two sets of white cotton shirts, black trousers, and vests he'd worn as a house slave, stowed them in a feed sack, and started walking toward Serenity.

When he found the town, not knowing where else to go, Salem came directly to Mama's place and said he'd known me and Jake before the war. Mama took him in, gave him a place to sleep, and paid him for odd jobs around the Shamrock.

She also insisted he attend school. Juliet had taken over the teaching chores, so Mama could devote more time to business and civic concerns. His first day, Salem sat apart from the dozen or so town kids and some of Mama's younger doves, feeling very much out of place among so many white people.

"That's all for today," Juliet said at noon. "Don't forget to practice your penmanship."

Salem was so nervous, he didn't even notice his open book was upside down, until Juliet came over to him while the kids scrambled out and the whores went back to work.

"Don't look so forlorn," Juliet said. She sat next to him and turned the book upright.

Salem managed an embarrassed shrug. "See, ma'am, I can't read or write much."

"Don't worry, I'll teach you. Y'know, we have something in common." His dubious look prompted her smile. "Really. I was also a stray Cara took in, same as you."

They reached for the book at the same time, and their hands brushed. Salem's hand flinched back, as if he'd committed a sin. "Sorry, ma'am."

"Juliet. And it's okay."

It wasn't long before her special attention paid off. Salem's reading, writing, and confidence rapidly improved—and Juliet's kindness did not go unnoticed by Mama. It became clear Salem was meant for more than chores, so Mama and Juliet played matchmaker and found him a job as a printer's devil at George Rhymes' print shop and newspaper.

But it was a reluctant, better-dressed Salem Mama prodded across the street to meet George outside his shop.

"I . . . I don't know, Miz Cara . . ."

"It's better than scrubbing floors and dishes at the Shamrock."

George wiped his fingers on his ink-stained apron and shook Salem's hand. "Howdy, Salem."

"Mr. Rhymes."

"Ready to work?'

"I reckon. I don't know anything 'bout printing."

"You'll learn. Got a bed for you, too. C'mon."

With a last fretful glance back at Cara, Salem followed George inside.

With the war finished, the United States Army needed something else to do—which was bad news for the Indians. Whites have been quick to label Indians, Negroes, and Celestials as heathen savages. But after seeing what white people have done in the name of civilization, I've often wondered who the true savages are.

After a few weeks roaming the border region where Texas, Louisiana, Arkansas and Indian Territory met, mopping up forlorn remnants of rebel resistance, Major Travers received orders to turn his attention to the Indians in Texas Hill Country.

The worst was yet to come, but the subjugation of the red man was already well underway out west, even while the war with the South raged. As far back as the summer of '62, Union troops in Minnesota had crushed a Dakota Sioux uprising, hanging nearly forty Indian captives the day after Christmas. I'm not sure Jesus would've approved.

Famous scout and war hero Kit Carson had led a campaign to lay waste to the Navajo, forcing starving survivors to march 300 miles from their Arizona homelands to a New Mexico reservation in '64. Same year, troops led by another Union war hero, General John Chivington, had attacked a peaceful encampment of Arapaho and Cheyenne at Sand Creek in Colorado. Those fine soldiers slaughtered over 150 Indians—mostly women, children, and old folks.

But we didn't know all that when Jake and me were sent to spy on a local Indian band. So we rode out and watched them from a high bluff that ended in a rocky fifty-foot drop. On our third day, we were lying on our bellies, baking in the early summer sun, peering over the rim and observing the Indian camp below as they went about their business of living, same as white people would've done. Jake took a swig from his canteen and shook his head. "Damned if I know what we're going to tell Travers."

"We don't even know what we're lookin' for."

"Let's hope Travers don't figure that out."

"Well, what *do* we know?"

Before Jake could answer, the hairs on the back of my neck prickled: someone was watching *us*.

Jake shared the same suspicion. "Mmmm. We know we're in trouble?"

We looked over our shoulders. A half-dozen Indian braves had skulked up on us and stood three yards away, war paint on their faces, brandishing some lethal weaponry.

Their leader wasn't much older than us and he was a glowering savage, growling in a guttural babble of Indian and broken English. Even though we couldn't understand most of it, his contempt for us was clear. Before we could blink, his bucks grabbed us by our collars, spun us around, and yanked us up onto our knees like marionettes. They took our guns and knives. "Jake, we're doomed."

Jake's face twitched a little. "Probably—*if* we wait to get scalped."

"You got another choice in mind?"

"Do something they'll never expect."

"Like what?"

"Run for it—jump off that bluff."

I stared at him.

He shrugged. "I didn't say it was a good choice."

The leader glided over to us. Indians really can move without making a sound. He stuck the point of his knife under Jake's hat brim and flipped it off his head. A gust caught the hat and blew it over the bluff. Then he took my hat and put it on his head. When he pulled my hair up with his hand, I shut my eyes tight, expecting his razor-sharp blade to slice into my scalp any second.

What would it feel like? I'd had plenty of cuts and bruises, but nobody had ever hacked at my flesh like that. I got queasy thinking about it. How much would it hurt? Would hot sticky blood come pouring down my face, and would it blind me?

Would scalping kill me? I'd never seen anybody who'd been scalped. But I'd heard tales of men who'd survived it, and had to have their heads stitched back together like buckskin britches. I couldn't imagine what that would be like.

I can tell you this, though: when you're about to lose your scalp to savages, your whole life does not flash before your eyes. If you're lucky, you've never had the chance to discover this for yourself. But you can take my word for it.

Instead, I found myself thinking that maybe, just maybe, jumping off that bluff wouldn't have been such a bad choice after all.

13

"Timing's got a lot to do with the outcome of a rain dance."
—Thomas Dog Nose

If the expectation of imminent doom wasn't bad enough, waiting around for it was worse.

Then again, it dawned on me that *waiting* to be butchered was marginally better than *being* butchered, so that Indian could take all the time he wanted. But instead of feeling his knife, I heard a dismissive grunt, and a snicker. I opened one eye to see him giving me a sardonic little grin.

"I love doin' that to white boys," he said in flawless English. "And you two are the greenest white boys I ever saw." He let go of my hair.

My voice quavered. "Y-you're not gonna kill us?"

"Not now, anyway. C'mon, let's get you white boys out of the sun before you get heat stroke."

Seeing how we were surrounded by Indians, and uncertain of their intentions, we meekly allowed our captors to take us into some nearby woods. As we walked, the leader stepped behind us and checked our asses. "So, how scared were you? Did you shit your britches?"

Jake's indignation overcame his fear. "Do we look like we're walkin' funny?"

"We were in the war," I said, sounding all lionhearted. "We didn't shit in our britches then." He didn't have to know our war consisted of one battle we hid from.

"Did you piss yourself, at least?"

"No!"

"Not even a little?"

"Sorry."

The leader kicked a rock in frustration. "Either you're too dumb to be scared, or I'm losing my touch."

"I *thought* about pissing myself, if that helps any," I said.

"I don't need your pity. I can be plenty scary."

"Anybody can have an off day. So, if you're not killin' us—"

"I may rethink that."

"—then are you kidnappin' us?"

The Indians guffawed. "Who'd pay ransom for you two?" the leader said. As we reached a shady clearing, he gestured for us to sit down on a toppled tree trunk. "I'm Thomas Dog Nose."

At the risk of offending him, I couldn't help staring at his nose.

He squinted at me. "What're you looking at?"

"Well, I'll admit, I don't really get Indian names. But your nose does not look like a dog's nose at all."

"It's not what it *looks* like," he said, as if he'd explained this too many times before. "It's because dogs can smell things a mile away. And so can I."

"Well, bully for you," Jake said.

Thomas Dog Nose glared at my brother. "I was right. You are too dumb to be scared."

"Thomas ain't no Indian name, though," I said, changing the subject before Jake's ornery attitude led the Indians to reconsider our fate.

"I went to a church mission school for a while. One of the brothers gave it to me, after Doubting Thomas, 'cuz I was always asking questions."

"Hey, me, too!"

"Your name's also Thomas?"

"Oh. No, it's Jamey. I meant people think I ask too many questions."

"No such thing. You never know which answer might save your skin."

We introduced ourselves, blurted that we were army scouts, and admitted we didn't know much about scouting or tracking. Mostly, we'd taken the job simply to tide us over until we could figure out our next move.

"Have you decided what you're gonna do with us?" I asked.

Instead of a straight answer, Thomas started asking us about the army, white people and how we lived, the war. We told him what we could—although, honestly, there was a lot we didn't know or understand about the whys and wherefores of our own world. In return, I peppered him with a whole lot of questions about his people.

Jake even took a turn. "How come you Indians scalp white people?"

Thomas replied with an expressive shrug. "To scare 'em, I reckon. Used to be a lot more of us and a lot less of you. Used to be we didn't have to worry about losing our lands. Scalping always struck me as grisly, though. There might've been better and less bloody ways to scare you people."

"Scaring whites ain't working out so well for you," Jake said.

"You do seem to be spreading like rats. No offense."

"None taken," I said.

"Okay. So, how come white people rub out the Indians and steal our land?"

We didn't have any good answers, and the conversation kind of petered out. That's when Thomas gave us back our weapons. We were free to go. "See you around, boys," he said.

"Not if we see you first," Jake said.

Thomas cocked an eyebrow. "You won't."

Which wasn't a boast at all, as he and his braves melted into the woods. We couldn't have followed them for long even if we tried.

"See us around? What'd he mean by that?" Jake wondered.

We found out over the next week. No matter where we went to scout those Indians, Thomas and his friends managed to sneak up on us, like some kind of game. We never heard or saw them coming. But each time we met up, we and the Indians grew a smidgen friendlier and started to trust each other some.

We even learned some information Major Travers actually wanted to know, which was what tribe they were. Like many Indian groups, their band was mixed, mostly Tonkawa but with some stray Wichita and Caddo. Thomas explained the name Tonkawa meant "People of the Wolf," because they believed they were descended from a mythical wolf. So Tonkawa braves never killed wolves, and regarded them with reverence.

Like their wolf brothers, these Indians hunted rather than settling down and farming. For years, they'd hunted buffalo, a once-plentiful source of food and hides, now dwindling thanks to greedy whites killing the great beasts for sport rather than sustenance.

This Indian band wasn't generally nomadic, like the Plains tribes tended to be. Truth was, they rather liked where they were in east and central Texas. Game, edible plants, and water were plentiful, and the weather was mild. Still, the increasing encroachment of whites had taught them to be wary of staying in one place for too long.

It wasn't lost on me and Jake that we could reach a point in our scouting careers where faking it might get us killed. So we asked Thomas if he could show us some tracking and scouting skills, for real. He laughed, but agreed to give us a lesson one morning, and took us out to a stretch of trail winding through prairie and woodland. We slid off our horses, and our Indian friend said, "Tell me what you see."

We searched high and low for telltale hints, lobbing wild conjectures about what we saw and what it meant—all wrong. Thomas remained silent, simply sighing and shaking his head at our every mistake. But even a stoic Indian has his limits, and he finally muttered, "Horseshit."

Jake pouted. "Judging us harshly don't help, y'know."

"I wasn't criticizing your tracking skills—although I've seen blind Indians better at this than you two. What I'm saying is, *look* at the horseshit. *There*. On the trail."

Well, we'd seen plenty of horseshit in our time. But no matter how much we studied the manure, it wasn't revealing any secrets. So, Thomas patiently instructed us, like he was talking to dim-witted five-year-olds, which was insulting yet fitting.

I could write a whole book about all the things he taught us that day. Some of it was plain as day, once he told us. For instance, horse droppings in a pile were most likely left by wild mustangs, since they could stop when they chose and empty out without anyone urging them forward. But horses in an Indian war party, or a cavalry patrol, tended to leave their droppings strung out as their riders kept them moving.

And I knew, even if my brother didn't, how to judge the speed of a horse by the spread of its gait: one man's stride between hoof prints meant a horse was walking, two strides trotting, and three running at a fast lope. Now, even Jake knew Indian ponies didn't wear shoes. But it never dawned on either of us that unshod hoof prints framed by drag marks meant we were on the trail of Indians hauling lodge poles and the rest of their belongings in search of a new camp, not a war party.

Trampled grass got bent in the direction the animals or people were going. And that same grass could reveal whether a trail was fresh or old. "See?" Thomas said. "There's sand stuck to the underside. So, the grass had to be damp when these horses came through. When do you think that was?"

We had no idea. And we were afraid to guess.

"It's been pretty hot and dry hereabouts," Thomas hinted. He waited, but we stayed silent. "The last morning dew was two days ago. Dew burns off a few hours after sunrise. So this trail's from Indian ponies two days ago, early in the morning."

We were dumbstruck, and stared at Thomas like he was a Delphic oracle. We also failed the bear track test—what looked like an oddly single, big paw print in the sand was actually sculpted by windblown grass. Later, we found a set of hoof prints we reckoned were left by our own horses that morning. Thomas insisted they were more than three days old.

"You're just making that up," Jake said.

I peered at the imprints and tried to think of something, *anything*, I'd learned to solve this puzzle. Then I brushed the rim of the indentation with my fingertip. "Okay. Not fresh. Fresh prints have sharp edges."

"Ahh! So, what would round off those edges?"

"Umm . . . water?"

"What kind of water?"

"Umm . . . rain?"

"When did it last rain around here?"

"Three days ago?" I lit up like a prospector striking gold. "So they're more than three days old!"

"Good," Thomas said. "I was wrong. You're not complete idiots."

Not that I'd want to, but we also learned you could make soup by boiling up a concoction of prairie dogs and flour. And you could beat back a thirst by sucking on a bullet. I didn't know if I believed everything he told us, or when we might use any of this education, but I felt better for knowing it.

Thomas said he'd learned most of what he knew from his grandfather. His own father was a chief killed by a Comanche raiding party when Thomas was only five. So his grandfather became chief again and took the boy under his wing. "His name's Laughing Gull. You wanna meet him?"

Figuring this fell under our orders from Major Travers to learn as much as we could about the Indians, we said, "Sure."

On the way, Thomas taught us some simple sign language. As he explained, with so many tongues spoken among the tribes, and no way to learn them all, a common signing system had come about, enabling different tribes to communicate with each other, at least a little bit. And even knowing what little he showed us—to say "We come in peace"—could be enough to wriggle out of a situation before you ended up dead.

When we reached their camp, and were taken to see Laughing Gull, first thing we did was sign our new greeting to the grim-faced old man. We felt justifiably proud of ourselves for mastering this token of respect—until his leathery face broke into a huge grin, and he and the middle-aged bucks with him doubled over in laughter.

I looked to Thomas for reassurance. "Didn't we do it right?"

His smirk was like a weakening dam holding back his own flood of laughter. "You did."

Jake, who didn't enjoy being the butt of a joke, got a little twitchy. "Then why's everybody laughing?"

"Because I taught you to say, 'I am a horse's ass and so is my brother.' Sorry. I just couldn't help it."

Even my impulsive brother knew: when surrounded by Indians, taking a joke is your best option. Thomas promised to teach us some other sign language that might actually help us someday.

"I think you already did," I said. "Making savages fall down laughing isn't a bad way out of a pickle."

The old chief turned out to be a playful fellow with an imp-ish half-smile on his face most of the time, like he knew the best secret joke in the world and you didn't. He welcomed his grandson's new friends, and kept trying to feed us, saying we looked like skinny plucked chickens.

We were surprised to learn that Indians loved gambling with a gleeful abandon that exceeded anything I'd ever seen among whites. Thomas told us Indians had been gambling since long before the first European arrived. They'd wager on anything—card games, wrestling, foot and horse racing, archery, and more—and risk everything, including weapons, prized horses, even wives.

Laughing Gull invited us to join him in a poker game, so we sat down on a colorful blanket with him and a couple of braves. When the old man turned out to be both a terrible player and a shameless cheat, it dawned on me that maybe whites and Indians weren't so different after all.

A few braves arrayed themselves around us, brazenly peering over our shoulders, and signaling their chief as to what cards we had. Considering the company, Jake and me both knew the smart thing was to grin and bear it. Four braves with long knives topped a straight flush any day.

We visited with Thomas and his band several other times. They showed us how to play a fast-moving and riotous game called lacrosse, which was the name French traders gave it. It involved two competing teams numbering from a few men to the dozens, using sticks equipped with rawhide webbing to hurl a tightly wrapped deerskin ball through upright posts. Matches looked and sounded like warfare, and braves often ended up bruised and bloodied.

In turn, we showed them the more pastoral game of baseball, which we'd recently learned from our new army mates—and which the Indian braves found so wretchedly gentle they dismissed it as an activity for old women and children, at least until they'd added a measure of mayhem to it.

Each time we left the Indians, Laughing Gull insisted we take food, since he'd heard terrible things about army rations. Of course, we had to stop and eat it all before returning to camp—we couldn't let on we were being fed by the enemy. We were the only men in our unit gaining weight. We hoped nobody would notice.

One crisp early October morning, Jake and me were engaged in a baseball game at the army camp. Though the new sport was sweeping the country, there was still debate among players whether to follow the old Massachusetts rules, where a base runner had to be hit by the ball in order to declare him out, or the more popular New York rules where he was out if a thrown ball beat him to the base.

During the game, as Jake juggled a couple of spare balls on the sidelines while waiting for his turn at bat, a courier rode into camp with new orders for Travers. It was time to forcibly move the Tonkawa band to designated Indian Territory north of the Texas border—or wipe them out. The army didn't care which, so long as they were expunged from Texas. Having missed out on most of the war, Travers and his troops seemed to have a pent-up appetite for killing, and it didn't matter if their targets were rebels or redskins.

Next morning, Jake and me rode out for our final scouting foray before the soldiers advanced. "This ain't gonna end well for those Indians," Jake said, as our horses walked along the grassland trail. "And there's nothing we can do about it."

"We can warn 'em. If we don't, they're as good as dead."

"If we do, and Travers finds out, *we're* as good as dead."

In our single wartime skirmish, there was nothing we could've done to change the fate of our compadres who died that day. So, choosing between action (and getting ourselves killed) and inaction (to save our own skins) wasn't that hard a choice.

This was different. If we were soldiers in uniform, we'd have been obligated to obey superior officers, even if we thought they were wrong. But as civilians, we felt like we didn't owe the United States Army anything. Thomas, on the other hand, had not only *not* killed us when he had the chance—he'd befriended us. And we liked him and his Indian kith and kin.

"Jake, I'm getting tired of choices."

"Are you saying this time we don't make a choice?"

"I don't know what I'm saying."

"Because not making a choice *is* a choice."

"How is no choice a choice?"

"No choice means we do nothing," Jake said, "and the Indians die."

"Then we only got the one choice . . . which is no choice at all."

Jake frowned. "Now I really don't know what you're saying."

"I'm saying we gotta do the right thing."

"Which could get us executed."

"If we don't, we'll have to live with what happens." We rode in silence for a spell, until I had a bright idea. "Hey—how 'bout we warn Thomas. And then we just . . . disappear!"

Jake looked at me like I was an idiot. "So, you're suggesting we steal these U.S. government–property horses we're on. Don't report back to camp. Travers finds the Indians are as gone as we are. And he's *not* gonna figure we're the turncoats who left him with his britches around his ankles—and hunt us down?"

So that was it, then. We *had* to warn the Indians. Then we had to go back, pretend we'd done no such thing, and hope for the best.

When we told Thomas the news, he took it better than I expected. "Well, it had to happen sooner or later," he said, riding along with us.

"I hear some of the reservations aren't so bad," I said.

"Ehh. As soon as whites find anything valuable there, they move us someplace worse. We end up where nobody else wants to go. Y'know, I had this vision of us building some fancy gambling saloons and inviting you white boys to lose all your money to the house."

When Travers and his men rode in the next day, ready for slaughter, they found no Indians and no trail to follow—as if they'd vanished into thin air.

Though Jake and me felt like bolting, we returned to camp with those disgruntled troops. Wasn't long before we were hauled over to Travers' tent, where the red-faced major was hotter than a blacksmith's forge. We thought for certain he'd figured out what we'd done, and he'd execute us on the spot.

Instead, he damned us as incompetent blockheads, thundering a torrent of epithets, some of which I'd never heard before. "You two idiots *lost* an entire Indian tribe!"

"Indians . . . they're sneaky, sir," Jake said in a small voice. "And . . . and, I swear, they were there the last time we looked."

The major's eyes popped and I thought he'd have apoplexy for sure. But his chin drooped to his chest, his anger spent. "I'd have done better with Newt Reno. He was a boil on my buttocks. But *you* are a plague upon my house." He shook his clenched fist toward the horizon. "Turn in your horses. Get out of my camp. If I ever see you again, I'll kill you in the most painful way I can conjure. I'll flay you alive . . . I'll tar and feather you . . . I will draw and quarter you—"

His homicidal litany continued as we scuttled out, grabbed our few belongings, and skedaddled before he could change his mind. Thus ended our brief and wretched careers as United States Army scouts.

Though we were pretty sure we were headed in the general

direction of home, we were on foot again, not that Jake minded—at first. However, after three days of hiking had reminded us how big this country really was, even he moaned, "A horse . . . my kingdom for a horse."

We were exhausted. Short on water. Maybe a little disoriented. In the midst of a rest stop to continue our bickering about whether this was how we would die, I needed to answer nature's call. So I stepped behind some shoulder-high brush. When I was done, I turned around—and there stood Thomas. I nearly jumped clear out of my boots.

But I was thrilled to see him alive. And I hoped he might keep *us* alive.

"Hey!" Jake's face lit up when he saw us together.

"After all I taught you two," Thomas said, "here you are, wandering around."

"Have you been followin' us?"

Thomas guided us into a stand of trees where he'd tied his own horse, along with a surprise—a pair of saddled Indian ponies. "These should get you where you're going."

I couldn't believe it. "You . . . you're *givin'* us horses?"

"Jesus, I hate horses," Jake said, while he hugged one of them.

"You probably saved my people," Thomas said.

Jake snorted. *"Probably?"*

"So, I reckon we're all even now?" I said, not sure of Indian customs in these matters.

"Yup. Next time I see you, I'm allowed to kill you," Thomas said with a somber nod. He let my alarmed look linger for a moment, before he grinned. "Just joking, Jamey."

We rode northwest with him, to where his people had moved to safety—barely inside Indian Territory. "Right where Travers wanted you," Jake said. "And he'll claim all the credit."

"Timing's got a lot to do with the outcome of a rain dance," Thomas said. "He could've just asked us, and saved everybody a lot of trouble."

Laughing Gull greeted us as we arrived at the Indian camp. We accepted his hospitality and rested for a day. Then, even though they had little to spare, the chief had some food packed for us. As we mounted our ponies, and Thomas did the same, Laughing Gull said something to him.

"Boys? He wants you to say it . . . one more time."

"Say what?" Jake asked. But we knew.

Laughing Gull's eyebrows waggled in anticipation. We grinned sheepishly, and signed in unison: *I am a horse's ass, and so is my brother.* As the old man cackled, I figured it was a small price to pay for what these Indians had done for us. Thomas led us back to the main trail and pointed us in the right direction. Then it was time to part company.

"For white devils," Thomas said, "you two are okay."

"Same to you, for being a redskin savage," Jake said.

"See you boys around."

"Not if we see you first."

"You won't," Thomas said, with a sly half-smile. He rode his way, and we rode ours.

14

"Too much is never enough."
—Jamey Galloway

Nobody would ever call our time in the employ of not one but *two* national armies a rousing success. We'd had our fill of officially sanctioned death and destruction, and decided to avoid affiliation with anybody whose main interest seemed to be killing anybody else. Now that we had horses, and were in no rush to return to Texas, we chose to try a new adventure, roving wherever the trail might lead, with no particular destination in mind.

We did hurry out of Indian Territory, then skirted north through Arkansas, to the town of Fort Smith. From there, we sent Mama a letter, assuring her we were safe but aimed to ramble for a while. We promised to write when we could.

As I turned away from the mercantile postal clerk, Jake tugged at the saddle bag over my shoulder. "Hey. Mail Kirby's letter."

I shook loose. "I don't trust the mails yet to get it all the way to Charleston."

"It's good enough for a letter to Mama, but not to a stranger?"

"If our letter doesn't reach home, we can write again. Kirby can't. These're the *only* last words his widow and little girls're ever gonna get," I said as we left the store.

"What is it with you and that letter?"

150

"Awww, shut up and leave me alone." I felt Jake's hand on my shoulder, spun around, and shoved him.

People on the boardwalk stepped clear to avoid our scuffle. Jake collared me with both hands and banged me into the front of the building. "We're alive."

"And he's dead! Everybody said—*he* wasn't supposed to die!"

"We were *all* supposed to die. Or not. Nobody knows. God don't know."

"There has to be some sense to it."

"The only thing that makes a lick o' sense is how much Kirby loved his wife and kids. You keep that letter, they'll never know."

Jake let go of me. I knew he was right, and trying to fathom meaning from war was a ticket to the bughouse. But somehow, in my head, one man's death had come to stand for all the fallen, blue and gray. The others who died with Kirby that day— their families would never know what happened to them. Kirby's family was still waiting for word of his fate.

All I had to do was mail that letter.

But once I did, I'd never know if it reached his widow. As much as I wanted to send Kirby's letter, that's exactly how much I was afraid to let it go. And, as heavy as that choice weighed on me, I'd also been lugging a burden of guilt—for not telling him we'd mail it, for letting him die without that peace in his heart.

Still, Kirby had written his letter and sketched his drawings, without any assurance his wife and girls would ever see them. At some point, in the midst of war, wouldn't that have seemed senseless to him? Yet he had faith his letter would reach beloved hands, somehow. He'd made his peace with uncertainty, leaving him free to write and draw, leaving the rest to destiny.

I was the agent of that destiny—and the obstacle standing in its way.

Jake stepped back. "You die, I'm mailin' that letter first

chance I get."

"You won't have to." I went back inside the mercantile and up to the desk clerk. "Mister, here's one more letter to send."

Fort Smith wasn't exactly a boomtown, but it was a good place to invest most of our poker winnings in food and supplies, including a pack mule, a pair of Henry repeating rifles, and ammunition. On our way out of town, we passed a neat two-story house with a sign out front: *Fort Smith Orphans Home*. It brought Rhody to mind, and I hoped the children there received better care than she ever did.

With no timetable, and no place to be, we meandered through Kansas, Missouri, Iowa, and Nebraska. We worked at whatever jobs we could find, and played poker whenever we could. It was an uncertain existence—and surprisingly exhilarating . . . for a while, anyway.

It would be charitable to say we were not having an easy time finding our calling. I was comforted by the fact we hadn't caused any serious mayhem while trying—though that claim was tested during our stay in one small Iowa town. Or it might've been Missouri—or Kansas, for that matter. And I can't recall the name. But a building company needed workers, and hired us to carry lumber, which required no great skill.

After one uneventful and blood-free day lugging wood, we gained battlefield promotions to carpenter when two other workers failed to show up the following morning. We applied ourselves to hammering and sawing with spirited diligence, if no particular aptitude.

When the foreman came to check our work late in the day, we stood back with misplaced pride. It was immediately clear to his jaundiced eye the walls we'd framed with two-by-fours weren't truly plumb and square. "Drunken monkeys mighta done a better job," he said with a disapproving grunt.

Jake jumped forward. "Wait a sec, boss." He helpfully hammered in one more nail. A moment later, the whole thing creaked, tottered—and toppled at the foreman's feet. He was unhurt—we were summarily dismissed.

Without much regret, we moved on, working along the way at farming, logging, tending livestock, even a little mining—although a single day in a dank tunnel, with sifting sand and pebbles pelting us from above, convinced us we both suffered from severe and previously undiagnosed claustrophobia (also known as fear of death by cave-in).

In late summer of '66, we came across the seething cauldron of war veterans (of both sides), freed slaves, and Irish and German immigrants building the Union Pacific Railroad in Nebraska. We signed on for what looked like steady work laying track—but a few days of backbreaking toil at the mercy of a mean straw-boss swiftly convinced us we'd found the world's worst way to earn a dollar.

Hell on Wheels, as they came to be known, were the haphazard encampments of workers, whores, and cutthroats, which crept west along with the fitful progress of the tracks. This jumble of tents and shacks didn't strike us as a felicitous place for living, working, drinking—or even gambling, as we discovered one night in a tent saloon, playing with a quartet of railroad thugs.

The pot wasn't big, but I won it fair and square. As I reached for my small pile of profits, this walleyed Cockney leaned close, his breath reeking of rotgut whiskey. "To wha' d'you attribute the fact you never lose?"

I shrugged. "Clean living?"

An instant later, he'd whipped out a long, grimy knife and stabbed the money, pinning it to the table an inch from my fingertips.

Seeing the value of keeping all ten fingers intact, I retracted

my hands, slid my chair back nice and easy, and managed a
feeble smile. "Sometimes it is more blessed to give than to
receive. Y'all have a fine evening . . . with my money there."

So much for working on the railroad. A few mornings after
that career ended, we found ourselves riding along a shady,
tranquil stretch of trail. Seeing Jake dozing in the saddle chafed
at me like an over-starched collar.

"Hey—Jake!"

He jolted awake. "Wha—?! Whut?"

"You're sleeping—"

"Not anymore."

"—while I'm the only one worrying about our future."

Jake's eyelids fluttered shut again.

"Hey!"

He gave me a one-eyed dirty look.

Satisfied I had his attention, I said, "I've been thinking."

"That's what you woke me up to tell me . . ."

"We've been meandering for a good while now."

"So?"

"All those miserable jobs we tried?"

"Yeah?"

"Wasn't a single one we're any good at."

"Wasn't a single one I'd want to be any good at."

"So—what now?"

Jake blew out a dismayed breath. "There's nothing we're
good at?"

"One thing. Maybe."

"What?" He squinted at me, but he knew what I was thinking.

As I said, "Poker," he said, "Poker?"

In agreement, we both said: "Poker."

Compared to the many options we'd sampled, gambling
looked more and more like a tolerable means of earning

money—not to mention avoiding sweat, pain, and dismember-ment (our experience at Hell on Wheels notwithstanding, and never forgotten). So we figured we'd try playing cards for a living and see how that went for a spell.

At each town, settlement or encampment, there was always a game to join at a saloon, roadhouse, stage station, or campfire. Even though there was never what you'd call a fortune to be won, we exercised restraint as we'd done with our army mates, so as not to enrage or scare off other players by taking too much too soon.

In general, though, the heedlessness of our opponents, and the ease with which we prevailed, confirmed that greed usually trumped judgment in the minds of most players. From poor cowpunchers to rich bankers, a common impulse overran good sense: *Too much is never enough.* If we could keep our own greed in check, we might perchance turn human nature to our favor, and guide our destiny.

In late October of '68, the first day after we'd forded the Red River and set foot back on Texas soil, we crested a hill at sundown and heard the oddly musical sounds of a couple of hundred sheep in the peaceful valley below. They were tended by a family of dark-haired Basques—three men who looked like brothers, along with a pretty young woman, a small boy, and their alert dog. They'd set up camp for the night between two covered wagons, with four placid mules munching grass nearby.

Raising sheep was nothing new in Texas, going back a hundred and fifty years to the first Spanish missions. And, once upon a time, there'd been no big cattle ranchers claiming the open range for themselves. By the late sixties, though, competi-tion for the best grazing land foreshadowed the deadly range wars yet to come.

In fact, most Texas ranchers had lost much of their stock

during the war. Those who were first to round up neglected and wild cattle, burn in their brands, and build new herds were best able to meet the growing postwar demand for beef. With more settlers moving west for land and opportunity, industrialized northern cities expanding, and railroads extending their reach mile by mile and day by day, cattlemen couldn't provide beef fast enough. Some pioneering ranchers launched grueling cattle drives up the Old Shawnee Trail through Indian Territory, to new towns like Baxter Springs sprouting along the rail lines in Kansas. Others blazed new trails as the railroads and towns spread west.

As we passed the Basque camp, their sheepdog woofed softly. We waved, and they waved back. We decided to camp upwind of the sheep, so we continued across the valley, stopping at a cozy hillside clearing guarded by some big old oak trees. Once we settled in, we could see the herders' campfire, and hear their singing, and guitar and flute music.

In both camps, people and animals soon bedded down, though they and we kept our campfires burning to ward off the late autumn chill. I heard a high, lonesome flute melody carry across the open ground between us, then silence. True to form, Jake fell asleep right away, while I tossed and turned, wishing I'd done a better job clearing acorns before laying out my bedroll. But when the sound of a rifle shot boomed across the valley, Jake woke in a flash and grabbed his gun.

We both scrambled up, and discerned eight riders with torches intruding on the Basque camp. But we were too far off to see who they were. Keeping low, we scurried around the rim of our hill, approaching close enough for a better view but not so close we'd be spotted. In the moonlight and torchlight, we got a pretty good look at the leader, the only one not carrying a torch.

"Shit," Jake said.

"Is that . . . Wolf Krieg?"

Last time we'd seen him, years before, he was the young brute who'd beat up Juliet at Mama's place. This was a burly man in his twenties. But he wore the same distinctive low-crowned John Bull top hat over straw-colored hair. He wheeled his horse around the Basques, lecturing and shouting at them, though we couldn't hear exactly what he was saying. But when he momentarily looked up, we saw his face, and we knew.

"What're they up to?" I asked.

"Ain't stopping for coffee, that's for sure. Krieg's a cattleman. He wants those sheep off the range."

With their flickering torches, Krieg and his thugs looked like Satan's cavalry strutting straight out of Hell. While Krieg confronted the herder, the two younger brothers hustled the woman and boy into one of the covered wagons.

"This is not gonna end well," Jake said as we retreated to our camp. "We gotta go down there."

"Two against eight? And do what?"

"I'll think of something. Or maybe you can talk 'em to death."

Jake was determined, so we quickly saddled up our horses. By the time we looked back toward the sheepherders' camp, the argument between Wolf Krieg and the herder had heated up. One of the brothers reached for a rifle. Krieg shot him dead.

The woman screamed. The other herders dove for cover under the wagons.

"*Now* we gotta do something," Jake said. We jumped on our horses and started down the hill.

At Wolf's shouted orders, a couple of his cowboys charged the sheep, setting afire the ones that didn't scatter. Other thugs rounded the wagons, trying to run down the two surviving herders. With shots fired willy-nilly, muzzle flashes pierced the darkness. Burning sheep wailed and bolted, as if trying to flee their fate. One thug touched a torch to the covered wagon where the woman and boy were hiding, and flame scorched across the canvas canopy.

Had Jake given it much thought, he might've concluded there was so much chaos already that Krieg's men would never notice two more horsemen coming out of the darkness. But, Jake being Jake, he was improvising on the fly.

I reluctantly followed as he led us into acrid swirling smoke, and we struggled to keep our horses from spooking.

"Jamey—over here!"

Instead of blundering into the fight, we skirted behind the burning wagon. Jake slapped his reins into my hand and tumbled into the wagon. With fire crackling inches over his head, he ducked low, grabbed the boy, and slung him across my saddle. Then he wrestled the woman and himself onto his own horse. We held them tight, and dashed away.

"Jake!"

"What?"

"That was real brave!"

"I reckon."

"Jake!"

"*What?*"

"Your *hat's* on fire!"

As embers ignited his brim, he batted the smoking hat up in the air and rode out from under it. "Reckon I need a new one. Again."

We guessed the dark-eyed woman and boy to be mother and son. Scared as they were, they understood we were trying to rescue them, stopped struggling, and held on. We scrambled up the slope across the valley, and took cover under the oaks at our camp.

Only then, after we slid off our horses, did we turn to see the mob's handiwork. The mother clutched her small son so tightly I thought she might smother him. She kept him from looking at their camp, but she couldn't look away. Our war experience seemed tame compared to the feral cruelty of Krieg and his thugs that night.

Jake grabbed our rifles and a box of shells, then handed one rifle to me.

I took it but shook my head. "I can't hit anything from here."

"I don't even care if your eyes are open. When I tell you, just keep shooting."

"What for?"

"You'll see."

Jake leaned against a tree and braced his barrel on a low branch, aiming at the mayhem in the herders' camp. I did the same, for all the good it would do.

"Shoot—now!"

We both started firing. Krieg and his gang realized they were getting shot at from a distance, but we were hidden well enough that they couldn't spot us. My wild shots confused them— Jake's accurate shots scared them. As their horses bucked and wheeled, Krieg's thugs hightailed out of there. Krieg realized he was the last one left and took off after them.

Jake took careful aim and pulled the trigger—but Wolf Krieg was out of range and got away.

An eerie silence shrouded the valley, until we heard the pitiful bleating of the surviving sheep, as the barking dog tried to round up what remained of his panic-addled herd. We wanted the woman and boy to stay with us, but she insisted on returning to their camp. So we helped them up on our horses and rode down with them, into the valley of the shadow of death. Sergeant Frizzell's futile invocation of the 23rd Psalm came to mind.

Between the burning wagon and stench of charred sheep, it was like the gates of Hell had blown open that night. We expected to find all three shepherd brothers dead, until a weak voice called from under the undamaged wagon.

"Arrosa . . ."

"Paolo!" The woman jumped down from Jake's horse and rushed to the wounded man. I lowered the boy to the ground and he raced to hug his parents. The three of them fell to their knees, sobbing in grief for their dead, mixed with relief at having been spared.

Between midnight and dawn, Arrosa cleaned and stitched her husband's leg wound with sure, loving hands, as if she'd done this many times before. Jake and me gathered what belongings of theirs hadn't been destroyed, loaded up their remaining wagon, and dug one wide grave for the dead brothers. At daybreak, Arrosa somehow found what she needed to cook breakfast for all of us.

Though they didn't speak much English, and we spoke no Basque, we exchanged thanks. Paolo found a hat from one of his brothers, brushed it off, and presented it to bareheaded Jake. With a faint plume of smoke still rising from the burnt wagon hulk, they and their flock went north out of the once-peaceful valley, and we headed south, toward home.

15

"I don't recall you being this dumb before you went away."
—Juliet Rivard

Only home wasn't where we'd left it. After four years, and many miles, we reached Serenity and found . . . nothing.

It wasn't a ghost town. We'd seen those, and they looked like folks had just up and disappeared, leaving buildings behind to crumble and rot. No, it was a *gone* town, as if it had never been there. And it looked like it had been gone for a good while by the time we arrived on that mid-November day. There were a few tumbledown sheds, but not a single whole building remained. Not knowing what else to do, we rode on toward the town's original location.

We eventually reached a sign planted by the roadside—a freshly painted arrow announcing, "Serenity Falls: 2 Miles." We kicked our horses into a run and made it a race. As we got closer, the breeze carried the sweet scent of fresh-cut lumber. We could hear the echoing rat-a-tat-tat of hammers pounding nails, and the rhythmic bite of saws chewing into planks.

We rode over one more rise. Back where it had first sprouted alongside Pine Cut Run, there was a whole new Serenity Falls—bolder, brighter, and bustling. As we walked our horses down Main Street, it felt familiar yet foreign.

Many establishments, like Duncan's General Store, Charlie Stoker's hardware, Mex's livery, and the butcher shop, were back at their old locales, all bigger and fancier than before. Once a mere store, Duncan's was now an Emporium. The town felt permanent, not like a place that could ever again be banished by a rich man's whim. Speaking of rich men, Atwood's substantial brick bank still loomed over the town from its hilltop vantage point.

The town now sprawled in all directions: more farmhouses along the river side, more furrowed fields, and more neat homes north of the business district, built of board instead of logs. We rode past the Serenity Falls School & Church Meeting House, a splendid little gabled structure with tall windows.

But where was the Shamrock?

Then we saw it. Mama had claimed three connected lots, including an oversized one on a corner. She'd built the place she'd dreamed of—two stories, with a shaded second-floor balcony wrapping all around and overhanging the boardwalk beneath. Painted a cheery yellow, the building had white railings and trim, and a big roof sign at the corner proclaiming *Shamrock Hotel & Saloon.*

One of the big front windows had gracefully painted lettering—*Irish Rose Café*—and a separate door leading into a little restaurant, named for the grandmother we never knew. Out back, in addition to a barn, there was a two-room bathhouse with separate tubs for gents and ladies.

Nobody had recognized us two bearded saddle tramps, so we decided to surprise Mama. After we found our Indian ponies a cozy corner of the barn, we tried to sneak in the Shamrock's back door—but Cruz spotted us.

"Chico! Muchacho!" He strode over and wrapped his strong arms around our necks, pulled us close, and kissed us each on the cheek. Then he whispered: "Let's surprise her."

Leading us inside, he quietly opened the rearmost door in the back hallway. We saw Mama sitting at her desk, busy working on the books. "What?" she said, without looking up.

"Rosalita, are these okay with you?" Cruz asked.

"Are what okay?"

"These."

With an exasperated huff, she swiveled her chair—and saw us. We met her in a wordless embrace in the middle of the room. After a few seconds, Mama's nose twitched; we were pretty ripe after days on the trail. "Go take a bath, you two."

She released us. We took a step away.

"No, wait," Mama said, and wrapped us in her arms again. Then another sniff and recoil: "No. Bath." She shoved me and Jake out of the office and shut the door behind us.

I blinked. "We're gone three years? And that's *it*?"

Cruz herded us out to the bathhouse so fast we missed Mama watching through her yellow lace curtains. She peeked between the roses outside her window, and wiped away a grateful tear.

Our first few days back, Mama kept looking at us like she couldn't believe how we'd grown from boys into men. We'd both shaved our scruffy beards, though I kept my mustache, thinking it made me look older. I'd actually sprouted taller than Jake, but he was broader across the shoulders.

We were both pretty skinny after our travels, and Mama and Cruz seemed determined to fatten us up. Cruz's home-cooked meals were a welcome change from the army and chuck-wagon chow—and worse—we'd endured for much of our time away.

For our part, we kept gawking at all the changes around town in general and the Shamrock in particular. In addition to the bathhouse and restaurant, Mama had built an ice house, three times as many hotel rooms, and a raised stage in the saloon. By rearranging chairs, she could turn the place into a showcase for local performers, or host the many theatrical and musical troupes touring the west. She dreamed of having genuine actors present Shakespeare, right there at her Shamrock Theatre.

At our first supper together, we learned about the town's resurrection. After the war, Silas Atwood had found himself saddled with the abandoned Montgomery plantation. With land only worth what someone's willing to pay, and the southern economy in tatters, Atwood and his bank owned a whole lot of prime but nearly worthless Texas real estate—and that didn't even include the grand Riverside mansion anymore. After the Montgomery clan's departure, somebody had burned the big house to the ground one night—an unsolved mystery to this day.

So, the exiled citizens of Serenity thought Atwood might be desperate enough to consider their offer: invite the town back to its original location, reinstate the old mortgages (at a twenty-five percent discount, no less), and divide all that fertile plantation land into parcels for sale at postwar bargain rates. With few other choices, Atwood sputtered, fulminated—and agreed. By the middle of '66, the town was back where it had started, and growing.

With Montgomery taking his knowledge of Atwood's corruption to the grave, the banker knew Providence had granted him a great favor. And he toed a more righteous path (for a spell, anyway) as he rebuilt his bank's depleted assets. But Mama believed it was only a matter of time before postwar growth would tempt him back to his wicked ways.

Mama introduced us to the new merchants, including my favorite, a slight Russian Jew named Meyer Fein, proprietor of Fein's Fine Dry Goods & Tailoring. The motto painted on his window declared: "Service with a smile!" And he greeted everyone like a long-lost friend, confiding to customers in his heavy accent, "Clothes make the man, you know. Nobody takes naked folks serious." After a long, hard journey from Russia to New York, Meyer and his shy wife, Anya, had then headed west, arriving at Serenity and opening their first shop in late '65.

With the town's newly prosperous commercial district, Mama took inspiration from her childhood hero, Ben Franklin, and his Leather Apron Club in colonial Philadelphia, priming the creation of a civic association of merchants and tradesmen. The association had organized street cleaning and a volunteer fire brigade, even raised funds to purchase a Rumsey hand pumper firefighting wagon. They'd also set aside a small storefront as a town library, and Mama moved most of her books there so everyone in town could enjoy them.

Cruz, meanwhile, had recruited other Mexicans to work his land, growing crops and raising cows, goats, and chickens. Rather than paying them wages, or charging rent, he took a quarter share of their crops, eggs, and milk, leaving them the rest to use or sell for themselves. That steady supply of fresh ingredients went right into the Shamrock's ever-expanding menu.

Thanks to Cruz's culinary passion, Shamrock patrons had the best food in town. Cruz even made wine from grapes grown on his land. His Rosalita wines (after his affectionate nickname for Mama) were served proudly at the saloon and café, and sold in bottles, too.

We were happy to find our young slave friend, Salem, living in town. It hadn't taken long for him to become much more than an apprentice to George Rhymes. They'd both shared the grief of losing their families, and each filled the other's emptiness. George had even adopted Salem, and renamed his business Rhymes & Son Printing. With something to live for beyond his work, George had grown more outgoing and townsfolk elected him the first mayor of the new Serenity Falls.

With Salem's improved fortunes, I was surprised that he

seemed chilly toward us the first few times we saw him after our homecoming. Jake shrugged it off, but it bothered me until the afternoon I spotted Salem and Juliet laughing as they came out of Duncan's Emporium. She carried some purchases wrapped in brown paper, and Salem had a long, shallow wooden box under one arm.

I stood in their path. "Salem? You got a problem with me and my brother?"

"Nope."

"Well, I think you do."

Juliet glared at me. "James Galloway, you are being rude."

"That's okay," Salem said. "Jamey? You and your brother got a problem with me?"

"You've barely said two words to us since we're back."

"Salem," Juliet said, "let's go."

But I caught Juliet's arm. "Hold on."

"Jamey," Salem said, "you might want to let her be."

He didn't sound threatening. But, with Salem being bigger and stronger, I did as he suggested. Juliet hooked his arm and marched him away, like she was running the show. How is it women do that, anyway?

Then Salem stopped short, unhitched himself from Juliet, and took a stride toward me. I raised my hands in a peaceable gesture, but he didn't want to fight. Instead, he just looked disappointed—in *me*—though I had no clue why.

"You and Jake . . . you went off to the war," he said in a soft voice. "What were you fighting for?"

"Huh?"

Juliet rolled her eyes. "I don't recall you being this dumb before you went away."

"What?" The longer the conversation continued, the less I understood it.

"You went and left everybody," Juliet said, "and you can't

even say *what for?*"

Salem started to walk away, then turned back. "You fought for folks who wanted me and my kin in shackles."

"But . . . but . . . that's not . . . We didn't mean . . ." I couldn't think of what to say, or how to say it. We never supported anything the South stood for, but he was right about what we'd done. "I . . . I'm sorry, Salem. We were stupid kids. We went for the adventure."

"While slaves were being whipped. And sold. And worked to death . . . like my daddy was."

"We . . . we didn't go to win the war. And even when me and Jake had a chance to fight, we didn't. We hid." I shrugged and felt pathetic. I wanted to tell them about Jake saving that slave Tuck from the noose. But I didn't think that would outweigh the mark against us. "All we did was eat their food. Use up some rebel ammunition. In the end, we probably hurt the war effort."

"Yeah," Salem said with a sly squint. "I've seen you boys fight."

And just like that, the storm brewing between us passed like a summer cloudburst. I never knew how much he was hurt, or whether he truly forgave us, because we never discussed it again. But I'll never forgot how small I felt that day—not only because of what Salem said, but because of what we'd done.

I noticed his box. "Whatcha got there?"

"Come along and see."

We went inside the Shamrock and sat around a table near the front window. Salem pried open the lid with his pocket knife. Inside, nestled in some straw, was a brand new banjo. He took it out and laid it on the table.

Jake joined us. "You play?"

"Never one like this. I had one my daddy made."

Juliet ran her fingertip up and down the strings. "What's that wood?"

"Neck's birch. Fingerboard's ebony." Salem wasn't bragging, but he was proud of his new possession. He touched the thin ivory hide stretched across the banjo's round nickel shell.

"That there's calfskin. Cheaper ones are sheepskin."

Juliet hung on every word. "Salem says the slaves brought the banjo over from Africa. Play something."

Salem sat down, rested the round part of the instrument on his thigh, and plucked a few tentative notes. He nibbled his lower lip as he concentrated on tuning the strings and gaining a feel for the neck and frets—not that different from what I'd do when riding an unfamiliar horse. The fingers of his right hand tickled the strings and settled into a steady, bouncing rhythm as he picked out the familiar melody to "Oh! Susanna." Once he started singing in that warm gravelly voice of his, everybody joined in. Everybody but me.

Juliet, who sang all sweet and whispery, elbowed me to sing. "Juliet, I can't carry a tune in a bucket."

When the song ended, we clapped, and Salem looked at his banjo with some disbelief. "Other'n clothing and food, this is the first thing I ever bought for myself."

Then he started to pick out another tune the rest of us didn't know. During "Oh! Susanna," Salem had grinned the whole time, beaming with the pleasure he drew from all of us singing together. On this song, he closed his eyes, like he was singing to himself.

The soulful, rolling melody gave me chills. But it was a joyful song about wearing a starry crown, about calling brothers and sisters, angels and sinners, down to the river to pray and maybe learn from God how to be better people. The words were simple, and after a bit we caught on and joined in. Even me.

When the song ended, Juliet gazed at Salem, starry-eyed.

"Hon, where'd you learn that one?"

"When I was a kid, we used to sing it. After Mama and Sister got sold . . . sometimes I'd sneak down to the river. Sing it by myself. Hopin' the current'd carry it to where they were. So they'd know I missed 'em."

Late that evening, Jake found me outside, alone, leaning on the rail in front of the saloon. "What're you lookin' all moony about?"

I ignored the question.

Jake prodded. "Juliet, right?"

I kept ignoring him.

"She'd make a fine wife."

"Do I look like I'm ready to settle down? Besides, she and Salem . . ." I shrugged.

"She told me they got to be friends, on account of both being strays Mama took in. Doesn't mean anything."

"I think it does."

"Keep thinking, she's sure to end up with somebody other than you, little brother."

Back in '63, President Lincoln had officially proclaimed that a national celebration of Thanksgiving should take place on the last Thursday of November. He hoped the holiday might help reconcile North and South. Well, we know how that turned out. And it'd be another ten years before Thanksgiving caught on in the defeated southern states. But Mama decided our homecoming was a splendid excuse for embracing Mr. Lincoln's notion.

While she and Cruz hastened to prepare a feast at the saloon, Jake and me were each given half her guest list and sent out to deliver invitations to friends and neighbors. This Tuesday chore offered me the welcome opportunity to get back on my horse, Shadow, who'd stayed safe and healthy under Cruz's care while I'd been away.

My first stop was the Shaw farm, to invite our friend Becky and her family. I had not yet visited her during our first few days back. And I'll admit I was relieved that I hadn't run into her in town, either. I didn't know how welcome I'd be. Though I'd thought about her often during our travels, I never wrote because, well, I didn't know what to say.

And I still didn't.

So I had a stomach full of butterflies as I trotted Shadow out to the Shaws' farmhouse. I was not happy to find Jake already there, dismounting from his horse as I arrived. I whipped my reins around a fence rail. "What're you doing here? The Shaws're on *my* list."

"Ain't that the ideal excuse for you to come see Becky."

"And you're just being diligent."

"I'm older. I got first claim."

"Claim?" Becky squawked, as she came charging out the back door. "All you two have is *nerve!* What am I, a cow up for auction?!"

She stormed away from us. Jake shouted after her: "Mama's inviting you and your family to the Shamrock for Thanksgiving supper Thursday!"

I was so angry, I vaulted back on my horse and loped away. Jake tarried until I was out of sight, then glanced at the house where Becky had stomped inside. He tiptoed around to the kitchen window, peeked in, and saw Becky taking her own anger out on an innocent butter churn, pounding the plunger up and down like it was our heads inside that barrel.

Jake rapped on the glass. Startled at first, she recovered and tore outside, but had the presence of mind to grab a rolling pin on her way, brandishing it as she yelled at Jake.

"You two jackasses come back from your big *adventure*? During which you *never* wrote to me—"

"Becky—"

"—not even *once*? And you think I'm just waiting around for one of you to ask for my dainty hand in marriage—"

"Becky—"

"—like I got nothing better to do?"

"Becky!"

But there was no derailing her runaway wrath, barreling down the track straight at Jake. "You think you got some claim on me? After you dragged your little brother off on your war *adventure*? And then you don't come home for years?"

Jake darted in, gambling he could hobble her arms before she could swing the rolling pin. He lost that bet. She swung. He ducked and backed off to a safe distance. "Let me answer!"

"I got the only answer I needed when you marched off to play tin soldier. You got a dangerous streak I want no part of. Especially not since my mama passed. I got kids to look after."

Jake's jaw dropped. "I didn't know your mama died."

"There's a lot you don't know." Then Becky pitched that rolling pin end over end. Knocked his hat off. Barely missed his thick skull.

He scrambled back to his horse and took off.

She stomped his hat, grinding it into the gravel with her heel.

Jake never came home that evening. If you're thinking he went off to stew in the truth of what Becky had hollered at him, you don't know my brother. No, he camped out on a stool at the Camel Hump Saloon—at the far end of Main Street from the Shamrock—and stewed in cheap whiskey.

Nobody saw Jake again until the middle of the next night, the night before Thanksgiving.

That's when he slithered in through the window of Juliet's upstairs room at the back of the Shamrock. He crept over to her bed, and she smelled the whiskey on his breath even before he whispered: "Juliet . . . marry me!"

She squinted at him in the dark. "Don't say things drunk you'll regret sober."

"Aww, c'mon. It's cold." He tried to burrow into her bed. "Lemme in."

Juliet kneed him back, gently but firmly. "You go back out that window, I won't mention this to Mama."

When Jake kept trying to crawl under her covers, Juliet popped out of bed and shoved him away. He grabbed her wrist before she could scoot out of reach. At that exact moment, the door swung open—and there stood Mama, her big Colt pointed straight at Jake.

He instantly sobered up by about fifty percent and let go of Juliet. "Uhhh . . . hey, Mama. This isn't what it looks like."

"What do you think it looks like?"

Jake glanced from the window to Juliet, to the gun. No escape.

"Jacob Patrick Galloway," Mama said, "this is the gun that killed your father. Go on out the way you came in. Don't come back 'til you're ready to be the gentleman I raised you to be."

With the starch leached from his backbone, Jake started to slink out through the window.

"Jake," Mama said, "don't *ever* mistreat a lady again."

With a nod, Jake vanished, and nobody laid eyes on him all day Thursday, either. As friends and neighbors gathered for supper at the Shamrock, which was otherwise closed for the occasion, he did not appear as Mama hoped he would.

The guests numbered thirty or so, most of whom I knew. But there were some new faces, including Meyer and Anya Fein, and a shy Swede with sandy hair and twinkling bright-blue eyes, named Anders Lind. Though he was only twenty-two, and didn't speak much English yet, Anders had come to Texas determined to succeed.

Within a few months of his arrival, shortly after the town had moved back to its old location and struggled to resurrect itself,

Anders Lind had constructed a lumber mill a mile north, where the river ran fast above the falls. His mill filled a desperate need, and he prospered, supplying lumber to the growing town.

That night, Mama seated him next to Becky. Sitting directly across from them, I fumed at their stolen glances and shared whispers all through supper.

After Cruz led us in a brief prayer, we commenced eating that grand holiday feast, with an empty chair where Jake should've been.

But my brother was never one to pass up a good meal.

He arrived by the back door soon after the platters of pheasant, chicken, and turkey began circulating around the long table. Sober as a scolded preacher, he stood unnoticed in the shadows of the rear hallway, new hat in hand and head bowed, not sure he'd be welcome. Nobody knew he was there until he spoke up in a sorry croak. "Hey, Mama."

All eyes turned toward Jake, and everyone at the table stopped laughing and chatting. In the hollow silence, I marveled that he hadn't already choked on the amount of pride he'd had to swallow. But penance required more. So he shuffled forward, licked his lips, and cleared his throat. "I . . . I need to apologize to everybody. Especially Juliet. And Mama. I reckon I'm carryin' some of Daddy's demons in me. I'm real sorry."

Then he turned to go. But he paused with his back to us, hoping to be invited to the table. He couldn't see Mama silently *shushing* everybody, exacting an extra pinch of atonement from him. Jake shifted awkwardly on his feet as he weighed staying versus leaving.

When she was satisfied, Mama said, "I believe there's some food left."

Relieved and humbled, Jake found his seat, content to eat without conversation.

But I became more ruffled as the meal wore on. Between Juliet keeping company with Salem, and Becky making eyes at Anders Lind, I felt like the odd man out. By the end of supper, as Mama and Cruz accepted hugs and compliments from departing guests, I felt mighty sorry for myself. When I saw Anders leave alone, I cornered Becky and herded her into the back hallway.

"Something on your mind?" she asked with the directness I treasured at the same time as it scared the crap out of me.

"About the other day . . ."

"Jake doesn't always bring out the best in me—or you."

"I . . . I'm not sure how I feel."

"About what?"

"You."

"You may not have your brother's demons. But you got the same restlessness."

"Jake's a hard dog to keep on the porch."

"You're the pup who ran off with him."

Our voices rose.

"Now, I seem to remember you begging me not to go off to war."

"I swear, you think the sun comes up just to hear you crow!"

"Are you claiming you *didn't* have feelings for me?"

Becky looked at me like I had three heads, all of 'em empty. "If you'd've stuck around, we might've been married by now."

"You think I'm ready to get hitched?"

"Ohh, that is the *last* thing you're ready for."

"I gotta make my way in the world—"

"And you won't be doing it here."

"Maybe, in a while, when I come back—"

"Oh!" She jabbed her finger into my ribs. "Now *that's* a promise a girl can hang onto."

"That's not what I meant."

"I don't care. Others think I'm worth sticking around for."

"Who? Anders Lind?"

"He's made more of himself in two years than *you* could in two lifetimes."

"He barely talks!"

"He says enough."

"You say enough for the *both* of you."

"Next time you wander back here? I'll bet Anders and I are wedded up and having little blond babies."

"Be my guest."

Then Becky slapped me across the face and bolted out the back before I caught my breath. When I came back down the hall, Cruz draped his arm over my slumped shoulders. "Like I told you, Chico. There are many theories to arguing with a woman—"

"—and they're all wrong."

Nice as it was to be home, with soft beds and great food, and seeing how Mama and the town prospered, Becky was right about the restlessness me and Jake had in common. For what remained of that year, we spent our days working around the Shamrock, and nights playing poker. One night, though, it became clear we were running out of hometown competition.

We'd been playing what Jake and me thought was a friendly game with Nate Duncan, balding butcher Owen Jones, and grizzled hardware storekeeper Charlie Stoker. I won a modest pot—we were careful not to take too much from friends and neighbors. As Jake collected the cards for the next hand, Charlie Stoker stood up to go.

"Charlie," Jake said, "the night's still young."

"Yeahhh. But . . . my wife's expecting me."

"Expecting you to not lose so much money," Nate teased— and then *he* slid his chair back.

"Nate," I said, "you got no wife."

Charlie snickered. "Who'd want him?"

Then Owen Jones got up, too.

"Owen?!" I said. "What is wrong with all of you?"

Owen, Nate, and Charlie traded glances, like nobody wanted to speak up. After an awkward spell, Owen said, "Well, Jamey, fact is . . . you win too much. It ain't fair."

I looked hurt. "But . . . I don't cheat."

"We know," Nate said. "That's what ain't fair."

"We can't afford to play with you no more," Charlie said with a sheepish shrug.

So Owen, Nate, and Charlie shuffled off, and Jake shuffled the cards. But we both knew: there was nothing keeping us in Serenity Falls. It was time to go and see if we really could make our way in the world as professional gamblers.

Although Mama wasn't happy about our decision, she'd seen it coming, and she didn't object. She even helped us pack, and as we waited with her and Cruz in front of the Shamrock for the stage to pick us up on a chilly January morning, she said a little prayer for us: "Dear Lord, please watch over my idiot sons. Give 'em courage. And strength. Help 'em be good and peaceful. Forgive the rebellious sins of youth." She paused. "Oh, and please help 'em be smarter than they sometimes tend to be. Amen."

"Amen," we mumbled.

"When'll you be back?" Mama asked.

We both shrugged. Mama sighed and cast a glance heavenward: "Dear Lord, you have your work cut out for you . . ."

16

*"Money talks, mes amis. Mostly,
it says . . . au revoir."*
—Gideon Duvall

You know what? Losing fifty-thousand dollars can spoil your whole damn day.

We spent the next couple of years moving from small towns to bigger towns, to cities. In general, we won more at poker tables than we lost, quit before we were broke, and moved on before wearing out our welcome.

During that time, I came to regard poker not as gambling, but as a science governed by the laws of probability, based on the predictable presence of fifty-two cards in a deck (barring the occasional sneaky extra ace). The game required patience and strategy, and the concrete nature of the cards combined with human eccentricities to keep the venture intriguing. Years of practice, and the tracking lessons of our Indian friend Thomas Dog Nose, had honed my ability to discern details most would miss—the darting of eyes, a nervous swallow, a subtle slump of a shoulder—any of which might reveal the strength of an opponent's cards, or his character.

By the time Jake and me reached the gambling mecca of New Orleans at Mardi Gras time in February of '71, we felt ready to compete with the best players for the biggest stakes. Decked out in new finery matched to the setting and company, we did well in that genteel city's parlors, casinos, and saloons. Our winnings enabled us to enjoy the gracious life there, including a hotel suite; warm afternoons whiled away at baseball games; and evening musical shows at the St. Nicholas concert saloon, with its opulent décor and pretty serving girls.

Come autumn of '72, as we were thinking we might go home for Christmas, a letter from Mama arrived, reporting plenty of good news from Serenity Falls. To compete with corrupt Silas Atwood, she'd opened an honest bank (complete with a massive E.R. Morse Fire & Burglar-Proof Safe—"built in Boston, best on the market"). George Rhymes had added telegraph services to his print shop. Meyer Fein now had a partner, a Chinaman named Chen Ma, doing alterations and laundry.

But there was bad news for me: Becky had up and married industrious Anders Lind, whose lumber mill was thriving, as were their two blond, blue-eyed babies. If that wasn't enough to sour my mood, Salem had been courting Juliet, which took some grit. Although marriage between Negroes and whites was legal in Texas, the idea was not exactly popular.

I knew I should be happy for my friends, but I was jealous, and disappointed. The two girls I'd liked most had moved on, as if I'd never existed.

"Why shouldn't they?" Jake said, rubbing some proverbial salt in my wound.

Not only had I lost my appetite for a visit home, but I needed a new challenge. So Jake and me decided to leave New Orleans, and set our sights on the splendid Mississippi riverboats we'd heard so much about.

To our dismay, we soon learned the heyday of riverboat gambling was already passing into history. Gaming on the smaller packet steamers was dying out, as more gamblers headed west to boomtowns where cowpunchers and miners had wages to burn. Some gamblers had stayed on the river, where they now had less competition. But there were fewer fancy paddle wheelers, and the increasingly rare high-stakes games were not open to every Tom, Dick, and Harry who happened to book passage. First we'd have to make a name for ourselves on the river, which we tried for a spell—just long enough for us to miss the comforts of New Orleans.

We were back there by Mardi Gras in early '73, and soon invited to a private game at the posh St. Charles Hotel. With its palatial white columns and sandstone façade, the St. Charles looked like a Greek temple. Inside, no luxury was spared, including the paneled parlor where we sat down with five players considerably older than us, and all acquainted by fellowship in the same wealthy circles. But we didn't know them, and our one-night admission to the city's upper echelon made me wary.

Our genial host was Emile Doucette, a banker in a charcoal pinstriped suit. But the man to beat was Gideon Duvall, a dark-haired, bearded presence with a jutting chin. He looked thirty-five, elegance incarnate in black broadcloth and fine silk. A man of supreme confidence, Duvall had a soft French lilt in his voice, and the convivial glint in his eye said life itself was one grand game. But he showed no mercy to his tablemates as the stakes rose.

Throughout the evening, Duvall was attended by a round-shouldered little fella he called Mike, a frayed dandy with wispy gray hair. He appeared to be Duvall's manservant, fetching drinks and cigars for his master without being asked, as if he could read the big man's mind.

As the final hand played out, with Gideon dealing, Doucette wondered, "Will our two young peacocks get plucked?"

"Or peck us to death?" said a man named Falcon, tall and thin in a crimson velvet frock coat.

Jake shook his head and threw down his cards. "Well, this peacock's done-for."

Gideon gave the rest of us a mild glance. *"Messieurs?"* Everyone but me folded. Gideon smiled and laid out his cards. Four queens.

Doucette whistled. "Tough to beat a quartet of ladies."

"Wanna bet?" Jake said.

I modestly set down my hand: the three, four, five, six . . . and *seven* of diamonds.

The rich men gasped and laughed. Gideon's queens may have been prettier, but my workmanlike straight flush prevailed.

"C'est la guerre, mes amis," Gideon said with a philosophical shrug. As I raked in my winnings, he stood, flashed a crocodilian smile, and shook my hand with a bone-crushing grip. "Next time? Different outcome, son." He headed for the exit, but his companion, Mike, gave me a long look before trailing in his master's wake.

I flexed my tender fingers—until Doucette filled them with ten crisp thousand-dollar bills. "Comes to poker," he said, "Gideon Duvall's the Big 'Gator. You bested him your first time."

As Jake came over, I saw he held a handwritten note. "What's that?"

"Invitation," Jake said.

"From who?"

"Gideon Duvall."

"To what?"

"Rematch. On the *Queen of New Orleans*. Sailing from Memphis to St. Louis, in a week."

Doucette whistled again. "That's a rich game. A word of advice? Don't press your luck."

"Luck's not why I won," I said, not meaning to brag.

"That confidence could serve you well," Doucette said, "or cost you every penny."

Doucette's warning didn't keep us from taking the train to Memphis, where we boarded one of the Mississippi's last great floating palaces. Widely known as Her Majesty, the *Queen of New Orleans* tooted her steam whistle, churned muddy green water into white foam with her mighty paddle wheel, and cruised north toward St. Louis.

The first couple of days and nights were set aside for relaxation, including fine dining, brandy and bourbon, cigars, music, and dancing—and a little unofficial friendly gambling. When we brushed shoulders with Gideon Duvall and his companion, Mike, on the upper promenade deck, Gideon gave us a nod and a smile. "Let the games begin," he said.

Once they did, two days of elimination rounds in the *Queen*'s fancy parlor weeded out the pretenders, while smart play and serendipity allowed both me and Jake to reach the big game. We'd be among the seven most proficient (or luckiest) finalists—including Gideon Duvall, of course. Still, rarefied company and rising stakes notwithstanding, I slept well. Maybe that was foolish. And you know what they say about fools and money.

When play resumed the next day, Jake bowed out early, carelessly close to broke. One by one, the others folded. Once again, it came down to me and Duvall.

As spectators gathered, we went back and forth for a spell, each cautious, unable to inflict ruinous damage on the other. Then, a mite past midnight, with fifty-thousand dollars in the balance, I believed I held the winning hand. So, I bet everything, then laid out my cards: the nine, ten, jack, queen, and king of clubs. Straight flush, again. Our audience gasped—just as I noted Gideon's lack of concern.

He had all diamonds. The ten, jack, queen, king . . . and ace. His royal flush beat my straight. The crowd whooped, and Mike collected Gideon's chips.

I stared, unblinking. *How could I have been wrong?* As Gideon accepted accolades, Jake tried to pull me out of my seat. But I was dead weight.

Howard Weinstein

Gideon flashed that pearly smile. "Money talks, *mes amis.* Mostly, it says . . . *au revoir.*"

Mike handed him six twenty-dollar gold coins. "To the valiant vanquished," the conquistador said, as he flipped one coin apiece to the conquered.

Jake caught his. Mine conked me square on the head. It took some effort, but Jake steered me outside into the chilly darkness and kept me company as I paced the upper promenade, round and round. Replaying the final hand in my brain, over and over.

By the time I regained the power of speech, I was more mournful than angry. "Fifty. Thousand. Dollars. Fifty grand. Fifty grand!"

"Lotta money," Jake said.

"Gone. Like black magic."

"I saw."

"Duvall could *not* have had those cards."

"But he did."

"How?" Before Jake could answer, I silenced him with a finger. "Don't tell me, 'cuz you don't know."

"Yeahhh, I do. He cheated."

I stopped. "H-h-how did I not see it?"

"You got greedy. He played you like a fiddle. And you rosined up the bow."

"You knew?"

"I thought for sure *you* knew."

"And you *didn't tell me*?!"

"Jamey, I'm your big brother—"

"Who's supposed to look out for me!"

"You're a great poker player. But you need to pay attention if you're gonna beat cardsharps like Duvall."

"Awww . . ." The boat's steam whistle moaned in sympathy. "You could've told me." I plunked my elbows on the rail and buried my face in my hands, imagining what it would've felt like to run my fingers through fifty . . . thousand . . . dollars.

"Look," Jake said, not unkindly, "I play reckless 'cuz you almost always win. If you're gonna start being reckless, I gotta rethink this whole system."

That did it. I charged at Jake and tackled him right there on the promenade. Our scuffle proved pitiful and brief, all grappling and grunting with no actual punches—lasting only until four rawboned crewmen pried us apart by our pants scruffs. They hauled us before the amused captain, a grizzled Irish seadog puffing on a meerschaum pipe carved like a mermaid figurehead on a ship's prow.

"Can't have ya bustin' up Her Majesty now, boyos," he said. "Can ya swim?"

"Yes, sir," I said.

"My brother started it," Jake said, as if that explained everything.

The captain cackled. "Brudders, eh? Well, brudders, y'can jump, or we c'n toss ya."

"You sure we can't bribe you?" Jake asked.

The captain cocked an eyebrow. "With what?" He was right about that, since Duvall hadn't left us with much. "You'll find yer gear at the St. Looie dockmaster. If ya make it that far. Now, overside ya go."

We straddled the rail, and clung there like reluctant monkeys on their first vine.

"You first," I said.

"Coward," Jake said. In the dark of night, somewhere south of St. Louis, he swung over and plunged feet-first.

I followed two seconds later. As I hit the frigid water, I jammed my hat down to keep it on my head. Jake's hat floated free and I watched it disappear, carried downstream by the current. "Why do you even wear a hat?"

"Hey—wanna bet who reaches shore first?"
Arms and legs flailing, the race was on.

17

"Human folly tends to be a lot more entertaining when it don't actually involve you."
—Mississippi Mike Morgan

We collapsed on the sandy riverbank, two exhausted heaps with chattering teeth and blue lips.

"I won," Jake said between gasps.

"Who cares." I stumbled to my feet. "I saw it first."

"Saw what?"

"That." I pointed toward a ramshackle fishing shack half hidden in nearby woods.

I wondered if the *Queen*'s captain did us a favor, or if fortune had favored the foolish. Even in moonlight, it looked abandoned, with gaps in the walls, a door hanging off corroded hinges, roof half caved in. We found a rusty stove inside. Jake splintered some roof boards for firewood. I broke open a footlocker, rooted around, and discovered a box of dry matches and some musty blankets.

We managed to fire up the stove, stripped down, wrapped those blankets around us, and toasted ourselves and our soaked clothing. We dozed, woke at dawn, then dressed and hiked along a riverbank trail that eventually led us into St. Louis. Seeing the *Queen* tied up at the wharf reminded me of my money in Gideon Duvall's pocket—and of how much I wanted to pummel my brother for not warning me. And while that might've been momentarily satisfying, it wouldn't serve much purpose.

We claimed our belongings at the dockmaster's shed, then faced facts: we had forty-five dollars between us—not enough to get us anywhere worth going, or into a decent poker game to revive our fortunes. But it's hard to think on an empty stomach, so we fortified ourselves with biscuits, stew, and coffee at a waterfront tavern.

As we ate, Jake noticed me nibbling my lower lip. "I know that look."

"What look?"

"Your ruminatin' look. Tell me your 'brilliant' plan?"

"So you can mock me?"

"Awww, poor little you."

"Mock all you want." I wiped my mouth and got up.

"Where you going?"

"Wait here. I'll be back."

"When?"

"When I'm done."

I grabbed my carpetbag, darted out the door, and disappeared around the corner. Jake shrugged and helped himself to my leftovers.

A few blocks from the river, I found what I was looking for—a modest little church that looked empty as I went inside. I spotted some Bibles on a shelf. Just as I grabbed one and tucked it into my coat, the preacher came out of the shadows. He was dressed in black, not all that different from me, though plainer.

"Things must be bad if you're stealing a Bible, son."

An hour later, I met up with Jake outside the tavern. He sized me up, noticing I'd flattened the brim and punched out the crown of my black hat, which already looked pretty beat up from our dip in the Mississippi. I'd also taken off my silk brocade vest and ruffled shirt, and wore my black coat over my gray-flannel undershirt.

He grabbed the book tucked under my arm. "You stole us a Bible?"

"Borrowed." I took the Bible back and struck a humble pose. "What do I look like?"

"A preacher. So?"

"So, I'm gonna preach a sermon."

"What? When?"

"Tonight."

"Where?"

I showed him where—the Maison Rouge Saloon & Dance Hall three blocks away, a classy joint with a red-and-gold-painted entry and ornate carved doors.

"Jamey, how's this gonna make us any money?"

"When I'm done, you'll pass the hat."

I led him inside. There was a moderate midday crowd of gambling patrons and working girls. The proprietor, a jovial chatterbox in a plaid suit, greeted us. "Brother James!"

Jake's eyebrows arched. "Brother James . . . ?"

I ignored him. "Howdy, Mr. Wilson."

"Y'all set for the show tonight?"

"Mr. Wilson—please. It's a *sermon.*"

Wilson chortled. "More like throwing Christians to lions. Or . . . like seein' pigs fly!"

I started feeling sheepish and shifty, so I hastily introduced Jake. "This here is Brother Jacob."

Wilson pumped Jake's hand. "Ahh! From the orphanage!"

To my relief, Jake played along. "Yeahhh, from the orphanage."

Neither of us had ever seen a man as tickled as Wilson. "*Some* punkins," he said, "preachin' to gamblers. I doubt you'll save many souls. Although the Lord does work in mysterious ways. See you boys tonight. Yessiree. Preaching—to gamblers!" He laughed as he walked away and went back work. "That's *some* punkins!"

Jake gave me a dubious squint as we went back outside. "That's *some* punkins, Jamey. Except for one big fly in the ointment. Why would confirmed reprobates gambling the night away give any money to a preacher?"

He made an unfortunately good point. And I had no good reply. So I stalled. "Well . . . see, that very phrase comes right out of the Bible."

"What phrase?"

"A fly in the ointment." I flipped some Bible pages. "See? Right here, in Ecclesiastes: 'Dead flies cause the ointment of the apothecary to send forth a stinking savour.' "

"How does that answer my question?"

"You got any better ideas?"

"Don't get touchy, Brother James. Just don't offend anybody to where we get beat up. Or worse."

"What kind of idiot do you take me for?"

"An idiot pretending to be a preacher, so we can fleece hard-case gamblers out of their hard-won money. That kind of idiot."

"It . . . it sounded better in my head."

"It always does."

I couldn't admit it to Jake, but I had no clue what I was going to say. And he was right—I had to be careful. Sermons were rarely entertaining—but this one had to be. Even if we didn't collect a cent, leaving *them* laughing would make it more likely *we'd* leave upright.

We found ourselves a quiet corner of the Riverview Hotel lobby a few blocks north.

Neither fancy nor seedy, it was the kind of transient place where nobody would care if we bided there until showtime.

After I bummed paper and a pencil from the desk clerk, we camped out in a couple of overstuffed wing chairs. I opened the Bible, and started thinking hard.

By the time I was done scribbling and crossing out, two hours later, I felt like my head was a jumble of biblical porridge—an image that reminded me how hungry I was. So we spent more of our dwindling funds on supper, and then walked to the Maison Rouge.

Wilson grinned as he took us backstage to wait behind crimson curtains. "Got yourself quite a crowd."

Then he ducked out to introduce me. "Ladieees and gents! La Maison Rouge proudly preeeesents a novelty act for your entertainment and soul-savin' pleasure—Preacher Brother James!"

I'd pictured myself commencing with a grand entrance, but my feet disagreed and stood still. Jake grabbed my hat and gave me a shove. I popped out through the curtain, clutching my borrowed Bible like a shield. Wilson was right about the crowd. I felt like a condemned man at my own necktie party.

Despite Wilson's enthusiasm, the gambling continued unabated. I was greeted with general indifference—but no immediate threats of violence, so I cleared my hoarse throat. "Th-thanks for letting me visit with y'all this evening, brothers and sisters."

And that's when my mind went blank. My saving grace: nobody was listening much anyway. Then a few desperate ideas percolated from the bottom of my brain, like flotsam stirred up by a dust devil. It didn't really matter where I started, so I blurted: "Y'all know my favorite commandment?"

"The eleventh?" someone heckled. "Thou shalt shut up?"

I tried to chuckle. "I'm afraid that one got edited out, brother. No, sir . . . it's th-th-th-the tenth. Sure, it has a lot of them 'Thou shalt nots' in it. Thou shalt not covet thy neighbor's house, or thy neighbor's wife . . . or manservant, or maidservant . . . or his ox or his ass . . . or anything else. But it *doesn't* say thou shalt not win thy neighbor's money in a fair poker game." I heard a few laughs—somebody was listening.

"I-I-I've been where you are, folks. Checking the cards. Makin' sure the other fella doesn't see ya sweat. Truth is, most of what I've learned about prayer *came* from playing poker." That earned a bigger laugh, and some nods of recognition. I fumbled with the Bible before I found my page. "Why . . . why, right here in Ecclesiastes . . . the good book says, 'I saw under the sun that the race is not to the swift, nor the battle to the strong—' "

"But that *is* the way to bet," Jake called out, spurring more laughs.

" '—neither yet bread to the wise, nor riches to men of understanding, nor favor to men of skill . . . but time and *chance* happeneth to them all.' "

Jake chirped an "Amen!"—and a surprising number of gamblers echoed his affirmation.

"Amen!"

"Preach it, Brother!"

That gave my confidence a lift. "Y'know, I don't think the Bible even condemns gambling—'chance happeneth to them all.' But it does frown on cheating: 'Thou shalt not steal.' Which reminds me of this poker player. He throws down a royal flush, and he goes to gather up the pot. But the dealer, he draws on him and shouts, 'You're cheatin', mister!' And the player, well, he shouts right back, 'I am not!' And then the dealer, he says, 'You *are*! I know for a fact I did *not* deal you that ace!' "

To which the room roared with laughter.

So I headed down the home stretch: "If you think about it, there was even gambling right there in the Garden of Eden. Didn't Adam double down on that apple? 'Course, he lost. So, I reckon the moral there is—beware of dealers who're snakes. And speaking of animals, I was at a horse race back home in Texas, and seeing all the betting—and losing—it struck me that horses must be smarter than us. Have you ever seen a horse go broke bettin' on people?"

More laughter, and genuine applause.

"I've known many a man who counted heavily on luck. But if you're relying on that little rabbit's foot in your pocket? Don't forget how that worked out for the rabbit. So, I think you can be both a Christian and a gambler. And if you play straight and fair, you never know when some guardian angel might just slip you that ace you're praying for. Thank you kindly for your time, folks. Brother Jacob over there'll be passing the hat. We'd be much obliged if you'd toss in a dollar or two for . . . for the orphanage in Fort Smith."

With a humble wave, Jake scooted between the tables, holding my hat out—and collecting a surprising bounty. He saw Gideon and Mike at one high-rollers' table. Gideon gave a nod of approval—but kept his money to himself.

I met Jake at the entrance, where he was stuffing the collection offerings into his pockets. Wilson greeted us with a grin and a back-slap. "Brother James! That was better than a lot of our actual entertainment. You wouldn't happen to sing . . . or juggle?"

"Sorry."

Wilson shook my hand. "I was right, though, 'bout the Lord workin' in mysterious ways."

"Heh! You don't know the half it," I called back as Jake and me dashed out the door.

I returned the borrowed Bible to the empty church, with a note of thanks and a five-dollar donation. (And I did eventually mail a bigger contribution to that orphans' home back in Fort Smith. Seemed like the right thing.)

Like rodents seeking a safe burrow, we scurried back to our quiet lobby corner at the Riverview Hotel, and Jake tallied our proceeds. "Hnnh. You managed to charm two-hundred and fifty-seven dollars out of a saloon full of gamblers."

"At least all of Mama's Bible lessons didn't go to waste."

A voice startled us from behind: "I wish I'd have thought of that dodge."

Jake pulled his gun. I clutched at the money. But it was no robber—it was Gideon Duvall's stubby sidekick, Mike.

"What do you want?" I said.

"Gideon'd like to see you lads at his house."

"Why?"

"He enjoyed your sermon."

"Not enough to contribute," Jake said.

"Human folly tends to be a lot more entertaining when it don't actually involve you."

"I don't suppose he was tickled enough to gimme back my fifty-grand," I said.

"No. But I did sway him to part with five hundred."

Jake's eyes narrowed. "What's the catch?"

"No catch. You're free to go your merry way."

Jake towered over Mike and tried to look threatening. "How do you know we won't beat him senseless and take back *all* our money?"

"Wouldn't blame you if you did."

The possibility of retrieving even five hundred outweighed wounded pride, so we went.

Mike took us by horse-drawn streetcar—"the proper use for horses," according to Jake—which let us see a little more of St. Louis beyond the waterfront district. As our coach clacked along on steel rails embedded in the cobblestone boulevard, Mike mentioned that St. Louis was the fourth biggest city in the country, after New York, Philadelphia, and Brooklyn.

We jumped off in a wealthy neighborhood and followed Mike past a corner bakery, onto a block of impressive four-story brick and stone townhomes. The Duvall house was the first one. Mike led us up broad granite steps and inside a spacious foyer with mahogany wainscoting, fine drapes, artwork, furniture, and rugs all around. A wide curved staircase led to unseen upper floors.

Mike escorted us into the front parlor and doffed his well-worn gray hat in salute to an elegant, elderly lady. She sat on a sofa, sipping coffee, with a little black French poodle dog reclined on a tufted cushion next to her. "*Bonjour,* Madame Duvall," Mike said.

"*Bonsoir, Monsieur* Morgan," she said with a sly smile, and an exotic French accent. "And these young men?"

"Jake and Jamey Galloway. Lads, this here's Madame Duvall, Gideon's mother."

We mumbled greetings and bowed stiffly.

"Do not worry, I do not bite," she said, with a nod toward her dog. "And Charlemagne bites only my son."

As if on cue, Gideon entered and Charlemagne jumped into a fit of ferocious barking and snarling. The dog never left his perch, though, as if he couldn't be bothered. Gideon gave him a wide berth and sat in a leather chair across the room. "I hate that dog, *Maman.*"

"That is why I keep him."

Mike bent down and the pooch jumped right into his arms.

"Charlemagne is an excellent judge of character," Madame Duvall said. The little dog hopped down, circled us, sniffed at our feet, then sat up on his haunches with a grin on his little face, and waved his tiny paws at us. Then he hopped back up next to Madame Duvall. "Charlemagne approves."

"*Mes amis,* Mike has prevailed upon me to grant you five hundred dollars of my winnings, so you can leave the city in some comfort."

"What if we don't want to leave?" Jake said. "What if we'd rather beat the snot out of you, and take back the entire fifty-grand? You did cheat."

"Mon dieu," Madame Duvall said. "More angry men who want to beat you? Does this never end?"

"Maman, this is not your affair," Gideon said. Then he turned to me and Jake. "The experience of losing to a man who can cheat God right out of his Heavenly throne will eventually enrich you far more than a few thousand dollars."

"It was a lot more than a few," I said. Fists clenched, I took a menacing step toward him—and stopped when I heard the click of a small gun being cocked. We turned to see Gideon's mother pointing a smile and a filigreed pocket pistol at us.

18

"Never cheated an honest man.
But scoundrels're fair game."
—Mississippi Mike Morgan

"*Maman!* I can do this without your help." Gideon sighed. "One of these days, she'll permit angry men to thrash me. Just not today."

Not that we liked apologizing at gunpoint, but it seemed the prudent choice. So that's what we did—to Madame Duvall, not her snake of a son.

Without lowering the gun, she gave us a gracious smile. "*Au revoir. Revenez nous voir de nouveau.*"

"She says goodbye, and come see us again," Gideon translated. "But she's only being polite, *mes amis.*"

Mike guided us out the front door and down the steps. Under the flickering light of a gas streetlamp, he handed us five one-hundred-dollar bills. "Now, something's better'n nothing, but I got a proposition for you."

Jake tilted his head. "Is it gonna cost us any of that five hundred?"

"Nope."

"Then what's your offer?"

"Coaching you and Jamey in the fine art of cheating."

I shook my head. "I don't wanna cheat."

"What could you possibly teach us?" Jake asked.

"First rule: whatever the game, expect your opponents to cheat."

"What's the second rule?" I said.

"Outsmart 'em." Mike gestured to a cellar apartment beneath the Duvall house. "Come inside, and I'll tell you more."

Admittedly, I was curious. "You live here?"

"Rent-free. I take care of Gideon, he takes care of me."

We shrugged and followed him downstairs. Inside, he lit three lamps, and the amber glow illuminated a cramped flat with a low ceiling, furnished with shabby cast-offs—a rickety table and four spindly chairs, a couple of tattered wing chairs, sagging shelves loaded with books.

I was drawn to four ornately framed items hanging on one wall, and looking very much out of place. The smallest frame held a diploma for a Michael Morgan from the University of Maryland School of Law in Baltimore. The three larger frames displayed oil paintings. Two were famous portraits: George Washington and Thomas Jefferson, signed by renowned artist Gilbert Stuart. The third was a true oddity—which I recognized from books as the Mona Lisa.

While I wondered how these valuable artworks came to be in a drab cellar apartment, Mike stoked the cast-iron stove in the narrow kitchen, and heated up some leftover coffee.

"So you're, what," Jake said, "Duvall's servant?"

"Now, maybe. Used to be I were fairly well known as Mississippi Mike Morgan."

That hooked our attention, but I was sure the claim was bogus. "Mississippi Mike Morgan was a legend."

"And you heard he disappeared years ago." Mike sat at the table and casually shuffled a deck of cards.

I looked at his threadbare frock coat and the moth holes

nibbled in his hat. "They say Mississippi Mike dressed like a king."

"And he was real tall," Jake said.

"Legend builds a man up, lads—and time cuts him down to size." As Mike spoke, his hands worked wonders with those cards. "Thirty years back, I were among the first gamblin' kings on the big river."

I noticed he had big hands and long, slender fingers. "You—he—never cheated."

"True fact. But I knew every cheat in the book. So, I were never cheated by no man, neither."

"If you're him," Jake said, "what happened?"

"The nerves. Lost a game I shoulda won. After that, it never flowed natural again."

"Why didn't you just quit?" Jake asked.

"All is vanity. Played 'til I had nothin' left."

Then his card-handling picked up speed. As we watched in awe, Mike flipped, shuffled, mixed, spun, and dealt those cards in ways I didn't think any man could. After one shuffle, he dealt the ace and queen of hearts and set the deck aside. Then he scooped up the two cards with one hand, and when he tossed them down again, they'd miraculously turned into the ace and queen of *spades*.

He dealt out four aces, and put them back on top. Then he cut the cards, which placed those four aces in the heart of the deck—and then somehow dealt *all four aces* from the top again. Next, he dealt out five pairs, at a pace deliberate enough for us to follow. Or so we thought, until he revealed he'd dealt himself an unseen third card.

He dealt himself the aces of spades and clubs from the top, then placed them back in the deck together. He shuffled and cut twice, shuffled again, then dealt out four pairs—and when he turned up his own pair, they were the *very same two aces* he'd started with. He dealt the aces of hearts and diamonds, then put them back into the deck faceup. No matter how he shuffled, mixed, or cut after that, when he dealt as if distributing hands to five players, those two red aces always turned up together. Whatever his tricks and techniques, it was all equally effortless and unseen.

"That wasn't cards," I said when he'd finished, "that was magic."

"Difference is, a magician *wants* you to know he's performing a trick," Mike said, with a mysterious half-smile. "A cardsharp don't."

Jake could handle a deck better than most, but he was completely amazed. "Nerves—?"

"The cards and me, we're best friends . . . until I'm dealt into a game."

"Then what?" Jake asked.

"The shakes. The sweats. See, lads, half of gamblin' is ninety percent mental."

I tried to grasp the tragedy of Mike's life, and wondered if the same fate awaited me. "How'd you hook up with Gideon?"

"A man needs to eat. When I got the nerves, I thought for sure I'd end my days floating facedown in the river. When I met 'im in '56, I were doing card tricks for pocket change. He were young. Somethin' about the way he walked. And played."

"What?" I asked.

"Potential. Like you. So I set out to build 'im into the next great poker man."

"Why?" Jake asked.

"Pass along what I knew. Maybe just to see if I could." Mike sighed. "But I picked the wrong man."

"Because he cheats?" I said.

Mike nodded. "He could win fair and square, in his sleep. But Gideon's a 'gator."

"And 'gators," Jake said, "don't much care how they catch their prey."

"Once you knew how he was, why stick around?" I asked.

"He pays me okay. And I do believe I'm the closest he's got to a friend."

"Well, I don't want to win by cheating."

"Jamey, you are my chance to atone for Gideon . . . by creating a great honest poker man. Like I were. I can teach you, so you won't never lose to a sharper like Gideon again."

Jake and Mike watched me frowning and pacing.

"He's . . . ruminatin'," Jake said.

"Why do you think you lost to Gideon, anyway?" Mike asked me.

I stared at him like he was loco. "Because he cheated."

"Nope. You lost because you didn't *catch* him cheating."

"Oh, that makes me feel *so* much better."

"Mistakes ain't nothin' to be ashamed of. Everybody makes 'em. But if you can't swallow your pride and learn what lessons they got to teach, you'll repeat 'em over and over."

Well, that would make me an idiot. So I sat at the table and tugged my hat low over my eyes. "All right, then. Teach me."

Mike opened two fresh decks, sliding one over to me and one to Jake. Then the man once known on the big river as Mississippi Mike Morgan set about tutoring me, with barely a respite for sleep, food, or pissing.

With saintly patience, he explained various tricks employed by expert card mechanics—stacking, switching, marking . . . false shuffling, cutting, and dealing . . . bottom dealing, second dealing. Hopping, copping, culling, crimping . . . peeking and mucking. Swapping in a "cold deck" with prearranged cards, so the dealer could control the entire game. Then he showed us how to execute each one, saying, "If you can't do it, you can't spot it."

We practiced, again and again, until we were able to perform them all with some meager competence. Then Mike challenged us to try and catch him in the act. At first, even when he told us which move to watch for, we still missed it. We begged him to slow it down for us, but he just laughed. Little by little, we did improve, and soon my detection skills exceeded Jake's.

But Mike wagged a finger at me. "Don't turn boastful, Jamey. You wasn't born with your brother's cunning. So he will always be a better cheater than you."

"Ha," Jake said.

Mike's finger aimed at Jake. "*You* are devious. But Jamey's powers of concentration will always beat yours. So, he'll have the better chance of catching a cardsharp in the crime."

Mike declared an intermission to stretch our cramped legs, taking us into his tiny back-room "museum" where he displayed tools of deception he'd collected over the years. Some were as simple as a vest with two elastic strips stitched inside, one for tucking away a reserve ace or two, another for holding a tiny pencil for marking cards. Others were complex mechanical holdout contraptions for hiding cards up a sleeve, some ridiculously clumsy, others diabolically undetectable.

Mike told us how gamblers easily slip marked and rigged decks into games by planning ahead and bribing bartenders and flirty barmaids eager for an extra buck. He explained cheating was not only knowing how, but *when* to deploy a tactic. "A true sharper knows the rhythm and rhyme of the game. Play a *good* cheater, you'll have this uneasy feeling you're being had. Play a *great* cheater? You'll think you're winning . . . until you ain't."

Jake rubbed the back of his neck. "So a cheater might not be working alone?"

"A cardsharp might have a whole crew hiding in plain sight. You got to read the room."

We settled back to working with the cards. After a while,

despite all the coffee consumed, Jake fell by the wayside and snored with his head on the table. A little after sunup, Mike and me took our coffee cups outside, sat on Gideon's stoop, and enjoyed the cool morning air.

"Sweet Jesus," I said, munching a fresh muffin from the corner bakery. "I had no idea there were that many ways to cheat."

"Now you know," Mike said.

"You sure you never cheated?"

"Never cheated an *honest* man. But scoundrels're fair game."

"Was I a scoundrel?"

"Nope. That's why I chose to teach you."

"The scoundrels—tell me about 'em."

Mike looked wistful. "Ahhh. Well . . . they was gamblers, bankers, mine owners. Coast to coast, north to south. Many a man too mighty for the law to touch."

"Why them?"

"They wronged folk what didn't deserve it, or couldn't fight back. I hold nothing against wealth, mind you."

"Us, neither."

"It's corruption I don't cotton to. So we'd even the scales."

"You and Gideon?"

"Yep."

"How?"

"Flimflam schemes."

Ahh. *Now* I understood the framed art on Mike's wall. "Those paintings inside—*you* did 'em?!"

"I got an eye," he said with a modest tilt of his head. "It's all about selling the illusion."

"That law school diploma sure fooled me."

"Oh, that one's real."

I gaped at him. "Y-you're a lawyer?!"

"I were. For about a week. All it took me to figure the law

ain't about justice. It's about winning and losing."

"Tell me about the schemes."

Mike smiled. "I'll admit, there was a fun to it." As he regaled me with accounts of their exploits, the intricacy of a well-crafted confidence game fascinated me—like clockworks, where gears and pulleys and levers had to mesh with precision. The names alone conjured audacious gambits of great risk and retribution—the salted diamond mine, the Spanish Prisoner, the fortune teller, the rare-fiddle game, the Chinese curse, the undiscovered da Vinci, the Royal Spanish land grant.

As Mike finished, Jake came outside to join us and grabbed the last muffin. "So," Mike said, "what's next for you lads? Poker?"

I winced like a man with a hangover. "Ugghh. My brain's all jumbled."

"Well, un-jumble it," Jake said.

"Don't rush him, Jake. But don't you waste God's gift, Jamey. Seems you've reached one of them forks in the road. I suggest you take it."

With that bit of cryptic advice, Mike's tutelage ended. We left him and walked the streets for a while. When I made it clear I was not yet ready to try poker again, we decided to go back home for a visit. Considering the distance, neither horseback nor stagecoach had much appeal. Then we discovered that the railroad had only recently extended into northern Texas. We could catch a train from St. Louis that very night. It would take us as far as Dallas, where we'd buy ourselves some horses for the last stretch of the journey to Serenity Falls. Jake grudgingly agreed a few days in a saddle wouldn't kill him.

We went to the train depot and bought our tickets. Before we boarded, I was drawn to the locomotive, at rest on the rails. The Indians called it the Iron Horse, but I knew horses—and there was nothing equine about this beast. It was more like a mythical armored dragon, made real in iron and steel, puffing smoke in repose, breathing fire in ground-hugging flight powered by forged pistons, rods, and driver wheels, rather than leathery wings.

The train left the city behind and crossed the heartland and hills. I watched out the window, until the clickety-clack of wheels and track rocked me into a deep sleep. I had a dream, about St. George and the dragon, a story I'd read as a child. When it looked like St. George was losing his battle against the dragon, he retreated to pray for God's help. And he decided to melt down his armor, even though it might've been the only thing that could keep him alive.

But this knightly hero didn't use the molten metal to make another lance or sword. No, he forged a strongbox, and he poured out all his fears and doubts, and lack of faith, right into that box. And he locked them inside, bound with chains. Then, without his armor to protect him, he went back to the battlefield, slew that dragon, and saved the kingdom.

When I woke the next morning, I felt exhausted. Whatever the meaning of my dream, I doubted I could ever do what St. George did—trade fear for faith.

As for what Mike Morgan had taught me, I didn't know if I'd ever make any sense of it. Even if I did, if I was as inept at skulduggery as Mike had noted, then what good would all that beguiling knowledge do me, anyway?

Shakespeare wrote, "Life is a tale told by an idiot, full of sound and fury, signifying nothing."

I was pretty certain I was the idiot he had in mind.

19

**"By the pricking of my thumbs,
something wicked this way comes."
—William Shakespeare, *Macbeth***

From our many miles traversing this grand and varied land, I learned there were countless captivating and surprising sights to see. But the most unexpected was a Scotsman dangling upside down from a tree on a pleasant March morning.

Once off the train in Dallas, Jake and me bought three cheap horses, a pair of saddles, and supplies for the ride home, five days at an easy pace. We also traded in our trusty old percussion Remingtons for Colt Army six-shooters, which had been modernized to shoot metallic cartridges.

Along that last leg to Serenity Falls, with Jake dozing in his saddle, something caught my eye alongside the road up ahead. "What the hell is that?"

Jake opened his eyes and squinted. "Whut?"

"Up there."

We got closer and made out a man hanging by his feet from a tree limb, like a Christmas goose in a butcher's window. He waved a gun around like a madman, so we knew he was alive. We didn't know right off he was Scottish, since his shouting sounded like gibberish. He seemed to be warning us to stay back, yet begging for rescue, which was a little confusing.

He was a wiry little fellow with a wild reddish beard, not much older than us, wearing only a dirty gray-flannel union suit. The way he raved and flailed his gun, it was likely his aim wouldn't be real accurate, and we stopped at a presumably safe distance. Jake called out, "Point that gun away, and we'll get you down."

After the man tucked the gun to his chest, Jake cut the rope tied around the tree trunk and lowered him down. I guided him to a soft landing—and snatched the gun from his hands. The man flopped flat on his back, so relieved to be on terra firma he didn't care much about the gun.

"Och. Keep it. The boggin' bastards only gi' me one bullet, anyway."

I helped him sit up against the tree and he swigged from Jake's canteen.

"Who strung you up?" Jake asked.

"Scouts I hired. Turned out to be boggin' thieves."

"What're you doing out here, anyway?" I said.

"Railroad engineer . . . surveyin' fer New York investors . . . thinkin' o' buildin' rail lines in Texas. God knows why." He stuck his hand out. "Angus McDonnell."

We all shook hands. "Jake Galloway. My little brother Jamey."

He had a knife wound in his right shoulder, which Jake examined and cleaned up as best he could. Then I helped Angus to his feet. "Think you can ride?"

He could stand okay, but he had trouble putting one foot in front of the other without reeling so badly I had to catch him to keep him from toppling.

"Whoo," he said. "M'head's still a wee bit burlin'. But I reckon I c'n hang on, so long as the beastie does the walkin'."

We boosted Angus up on our packhorse and took him with us. The more he talked, the more we understood his heavy brogue, to where we could be pretty sure of half of what he said. As he got used to being upright again, he proved to be a chatty, good-natured companion. Had I trekked to a foreign land, and ended up hanging from a tree, I might not have been kindly disposed toward the residents of that country as a whole. But his enthusiasm for America, and the work he'd come here to do, seemed undiminished.

"I came here a year ago," he told us. "Worked on railroads in England an' Scotland a'fore that. Heh, they're sooch wee places. I reckoned America's big enough to keep me workin' fer ever." He spread his arms wide, shouting with joy: "This country's boggin' huge!"

Viewing familiar territory through a newcomer's eyes helped me see it fresh. A day from home, as we rode downhill through a narrow slot canyon, Angus looked it all up and down, from the channeled sand under our feet and boulders along the trail, to the tops of the rocky walls above us. I had never before noticed how many different colors striped across the rock face.

"Geology! Everywhere!" The joyful echo of his voice made us laugh. "This canyon, did y'know an ancient stream cut through all o' this rock? Took millions o' years! But water always wins, if you're nae in a hurry." He looked behind us, as if measuring the grade of the canyon. "Does it rain much here?"

"Nope," Jake said. "Why?"

"I wouldnae want t'be caught ridin' through if it did."

"Funny," I said, "they call this Horsethief Canyon. Old-timers say it was named after some rustlers hid out here. Figured they could post guards at both ends, and no lawmen could sneak up on 'em."

"Aye . . . but it rained. Buckets."

I nodded. "Flash-flooded the canyon. Drowned every last rustler. Horses, too. People say when it storms around here, it's not thunder—it's all those horses running for their lives."

Later, as he talked about his railroad work, I asked, "How

come there aren't more railroads in Texas, anyway?"

"Most places, the Washin'ton blokes dole out acres o' free public land to the railroad companies. The more track they lay, the more land they get."

"And do what with it?"

"Build on it. Or sell it. Either way, they get rich as King Midas."

"How's Texas different?"

"Texas kept control o' public land. And they're a wee bit stingy about givin' it up. Sooner or later, though, you'll have rails goin' every which way."

Had that already been the case, we never would've met Angus hanging from a tree.

As soon as we reached Serenity Falls, we saw evidence of the town's continued growth since our last visit home. New rows of saplings lining the streets would eventually provide welcome shade. Amid expansion at the outskirts and filling of central vacant lots, everything was pretty much where we'd left it. We took Angus directly to Doc Stump's office, to have his shoulder wound checked out.

Doc looked up from reading a medical journal at his desk when he heard us walk in. "Can I help you?" He recognized us, and a grin spread across his face. "Ha-hah! I'll be damned."

We introduced him to Angus, and Doc set to work. The little Scotsman continued to babble nonstop about the wonders of America, how he'd been set upon and robbed, how Jake and me had saved his life. When he finally paused for a breath, Doc said the wound didn't appear infected, but he'd clean it out and stitch it up, just to be safe.

"That okay with you, Mr. McDonnell?"

"Och, call me Angus. Yer stitches won't be m'first, or m'last."

Doc wanted him to stay in town for a week, to confirm it was healing properly. We said he was welcome to be our guest. Jake ran out and fetched some of our old clothing for Angus to wear. As his patient dressed, Doc took us aside. "Is he all right in the head?"

"Far as we know," Jake said.

"He never shuts up."

"Well, he was hanging by his feet for a spell," I said. "That could shake your brain loose a little."

Doc noticed Angus sitting on the edge of the examining table, his shoulders trembling with quiet sobs. "Are you *sure* he's all right?"

I put my hand on the Scotsman's shoulder. "Angus?"

He waved me off, embarrassed by his tears. "Och . . . I dinnae ken what woulda happened to me if you hadnae come along. I dinnae ken how I c'n ever repay yer kindness."

"We'll think of something," Jake said with a grin that faded when we felt the floorboards start to shake under our feet. "What the hell is that?"

Angus brightened with geological excitement. "Earthquake?"

I shook my head. "We don't have earthquakes here."

"What we have is cattle," Doc said. "Krieg's cattle."

Jake and I went outside, with Angus right behind us. From Doc's boardwalk, we saw a dust cloud rolling in over the hills to the southwest. The wind carried the sound of a big herd of bawling beeves—heading straight into Serenity Falls.

Up and down Main Street, townsfolk grabbed kids, belongings, and small animals, rushing them inside homes, barns, and shops—as if they'd done it before.

"How long has this been going on?" I asked.

"Started about a year ago," Doc said. "With more settlers coming west, and the beef boom, ranchers've all been expanding their herds. Looking for any advantage, like a faster and easier way to market. Lately, Krieg's beasts're coming through town every week."

"Through *town*? Why?"

Doc waved his hand around. "He wants all this land—where the town and farms happen to be. Rangeland . . . access to water. Like he's aiming to take over the whole damn state."

"But he's already the biggest. Isn't he?"

"Yeah, and now he has the power to intimidate farmers and smaller ranchers into abandoning their claims and homesteads."

"I remember when you saved that mangled leg of his," I said.

Doc frowned. "I should've shot him when I had the chance."

As we watched, Bar KR hands thundered three hundred head right on through the heart of town. We remembered when Krieg had come through with a small but orderly herd, early in the war, and just that one time. This was cattle chaos, with animals careening up on boardwalks, trampling goods on display, a few even running into buildings.

"Last month," Doc said, "one even ran inside your Mama's place. Cruz guaranteed it didn't come out again—and we had fine steak dinners for a week."

It took a considerable while before they'd all forded Pine Cut Run where the river ran smooth and gentle. Angus stood next to me, eyes wide. "Laddie! Y'didnae tell me y' came from sooch an excitin' town."

"I didn't know we did."

As the last of the cattle passed by, Doc stepped into the street. "I'm fed up with this."

"Where you goin'?" Jake said.

"To kick the council into calling a town meeting. For tonight."

We took Angus over to the Shamrock, where Mama and Cruz greeted him like family. After all three of us had enjoyed hot baths, they sat us down to a fine meal in the Irish Rose Café, and caught us up on all the news of the past few years.

As to be expected, there'd been births and deaths. Printer

and mayor George Rhymes had been taken by a fever, rest his soul. The only comfort came from knowing he was reunited in the hereafter with the wife and boys he'd buried while coming west. Meyer Fein, of the thriving Fein's Fine Dry Goods & Tailoring, was elected to succeed him as mayor.

George had left his business to Salem, including the newspaper, print shop, and telegraph service. Salem and Juliet were married now, and had a baby on the way. Not everyone in town approved of a white girl being with a Negro, and some boycotted Rhymes & Son Printing. But there was a community of folks who'd known Salem and Juliet for a long time, rallied 'round the couple, and made them feel safe and welcome.

Mama could see how the news about Juliet marrying *anyone* pained me, but she sternly reminded me I'd had my chance at Juliet, and Becky, too. "I'd have been happy seeing you marry either girl."

"Well, I didn't."

"No. You kept gallivanting around with your brother. So you have no cause to be anything but happy for your friends."

She was right. But that didn't mean I had to like it.

Angus begged me to show him around, and I welcomed any excuse to take my old faithful pony, Shadow, out for a ride.

"This Krieg bloke, he fancies himself a gallus laird, does he?" Angus asked as we rode alongside Pine Cut Run.

"A what?"

"A big-headed lord o' the manor."

"That's him, all right."

"And he's right about yer wee river."

"How do you mean?"

"It's what we call a steep-gradient stream. Upstream, y've got rapids leadin' t' yer falls." From where we stood, we could hear the rushing water boiling over and around rocks. "He cannae cross there. Downstream, mair rapids, wi' water runnin' fast an' shallow over rocks, and mair falls. But through here, it levels out."

"Isn't it deeper and wider here?"

"Aye. But it flows slower."

"There've gotta be other crossings."

"Aye, but miles away, and nae as good as this. Here's also a bonnie spot fer buildin' a railroad bridge."

At the Shamrock that evening, a quarter of our four hundred residents gathered for a hastily called town meeting. Mama, Sheriff Huggins, Doc Stump, and Meyer Fein sat at a table on the stage. Silas Atwood was notable by his absence.

Doc spoke for the town hotheads. "It's plain as day. We have to stop the Kriegs from running their cattle through town again."

"How?" Cruz said. "With your little pocket pistol?"

"Guns and guts built this town. I thought we had enough of both."

An argument rumbled for a while until Mama banged the gavel to quiet the room, and Cruz said, "Krieg is a bully. Tell him he can use the crossing. But only if he buys a permit and pays a per-head toll. That way, we have control—and make some money, too."

Some folks liked the idea, others thought it was loco. How would it be enforced?

"We raise an army," Mex the blacksmith said. "We be ready. Guns and rifles. There's more of us than them."

"But they are willing to pillage and kill," Meyer said, "and we are not."

"Why not?" Mex said.

"Because it's uncivilized," butcher Owen Jones said, still wearing his bloody trade apron.

Becky spoke up, balancing her third blond baby on her hip. "Y'know what's uncivilized? Cattle stampedin' down Main

Street. I need a safe place to raise my kids. I never know when that herd's gonna come chargin' through."

"Becky's right," hardware storekeeper Charlie Stoker said. "Wilhelm Krieg used to be my friend. Now he's threatening our lives and property. If we're not willing to defend ourselves, with shooting if need be, then we don't deserve to call ourselves Texans."

"Charlie, you propose a war," Meyer said.

"Mister Mayor, that's up to Krieg."

"Sometimes," Doc said, "blood must flow to serve a higher good."

"Listen—*please*," Meyer said. "I come from a land where the powerful take what they want from the weak. Then the weak rise up to smite the powerful. And the *tsuris*—troubles—go on and on. America has to be different. If we stoop to the level of the Kriegs, are we any better?"

Jake and me had been away so much, I didn't know how welcome my opinion might be. But I remembered what Wolf Krieg did to those sheepherders. "You can't go gun to gun with the Kriegs."

Jake held up his pistol. "Wanna bet? Force is the only thing they understand."

"Yeah, they understand how to use it," I said. "There's gotta be a better way."

"And what way is that?" Becky said.

"I . . . I don't know."

The debating and arguing erupted again. Mama banged the gavel, and Meyer Fein spoke as the crowd settled down. "We have Yiddish saying: The worst peace is better than the best war." He sighed. "We can argue all night. But nobody seems to have better idea than Cruz. I move we vote on it."

"Second that motion," Jawbone said.

Meyer sighed again. "*Oy, gevalt.* All in favor . . ."

A few hands popped up right away. Other folks wary of committing themselves looked around. More hands rose, slowly. When called to oppose, fewer though equally sluggish hands went up. In the end, there was a narrow and unenthusiastic majority in favor.

But once the vote was done, the mayor showed his practical side, calling for all the property-owning townsfolk to chip in two dollars, to raise funds for hiring armed help. That proposal also passed, though without any greater zeal.

"And where are these armed men supposed to come from?" Mama said.

Cruz mentioned the Slade cattle outfit had recently been forced to shut down. He'd overheard some of those unemployed Lazy-S hands at the saloon blaming the Kriegs for their misfortune. Hardware man Charlie Stoker said he knew some of them; he'd talk to them about serving as hired guns.

The sheriff volunteered to give Wilhelm Krieg the news he'd have to pay to run his cattle across our stretch of Pine Cut Run. "I ain't sure how wise it is for a hummingbird to spit in a rattlesnake's eye, but I'll ride out there tomorrow."

As the meeting broke up, Angus was as excited by seeing democracy in action as he'd been about our local geology. "Y'know, you Americans, the way y'govern is rare as rockin' horse shite in the rest o' the world. Even yer crabbit folk, with their grumblin' and seagull skretchin'—it still came down to a vote, instead of a fray."

He was right. But a fray with the Kriegs loomed, and I couldn't see any way around it.

20

"Wilhelm Krieg has succumbed to the affliction of many a self-made man: he worships his creator."
—Dr. Calvin Stump

I bolted awake in a cold sweat. In my nightmare, I'd been back in that Valley of Death on the night Wolf Krieg and his thugs had attacked the Basque shepherds. Then my brain had whipsawed me onto Main Street, in the middle of a town ablaze. *Our* town.

Safe in my dark room at the Shamrock, I checked my watch on the nightstand. Half past three, but I knew I'd never fall asleep again. So, I dressed and padded downstairs to the kitchen. That's where I found Mama, also wide awake.

We sat at the table, commiserating over some of Cruz's apple pie. We agreed that something had to be done about the Kriegs, and confronting them head-on was likely to be a terrible mistake. Mama shared my fears that we were sending our sheriff on a dangerous fool's errand. We tried to think of other options, but came up empty.

That morning, we were among a dozen concerned townsfolk gathered on Main Street as Jawbone Huggins climbed up on his big draft horse.

Mama squinted at him. "This one time, *please* take your gun."

"They'll be less likely to feel obliged to shoot if the only thing I'm armed with is bad news." He turned his horse and cantered out of town.

Jake and me sat at a rear table in the café. Mama fetched us some coffee, and Cruz joined us with plates of eggs and bacon. "Lookit, I can't just sit around," Jake said. "I'm going to help Charlie Stoker recruit us some guns."

I looked annoyed. "Can't you wait?"

"For what?"

"We've already seen what the Kriegs're willing to do to anybody who stands in their way."

"That's why we gotta defend ourselves."

"Jake, do you *want* Wolf Krieg to torch this town?"

"How's doing nothing gonna stop him?"

"I didn't say do nothing."

"If you got some brilliant plan, now's the time, little brother."

"Well . . . it's not so much a plan. It's more like . . . an idea."

"Is it a *good* idea?"

"Hush," Mama said, "and let your brother talk."

With a deep breath, I tried to formulate anything that sounded halfway intelligent. I thought back to how I'd licked Jake in the brawl that had won me the dubious right to go off to war with my idiot brother. "What if there was a way to take Krieg's strength and turn it into a weakness?"

"Like baiting a bull to charge the red cape," Cruz said, catching my drift.

Mama gnawed on a strip of bacon. "So what's Krieg's red cape?"

"I don't know," I said. "I don't know enough about him. Did people always hate him this much?"

"No," Mama said, "folks were too busy hating Bird Montgomery and Silas Atwood. But, then, I didn't really know Wilhelm Krieg."

"Other folks did," Cruz said.

"Then we oughta talk to 'em," I said. "Maybe find out something we can use."

Jake pushed back from the table. "You go waste your time if you want."

Jake left, and I headed out to talk to old-timers who'd known Krieg the longest.

Mex at the livery told me he'd heard talk from Krieg's longtime foreman Bulldog Quill that ranchers were already worrying about a future with less access to open range for grazing, and more competition for land and resources, including water.

Butcher Owen Jones confirmed the booming demand for beef as the population out west grew. Controlling as much undivided rangeland as possible—and access to Pine Cut Run, for both water and cattle crossing—would give Krieg an advantage over other ranchers. He'd already been muscling small farmers out of the way, farther outside town.

Jake was at Stoker's hardware store when I got there. Charlie Stoker had been among the first settlers here, starting his business back in '49, and seemed to know Krieg best of all. Krieg had arrived in '50, and the two men soon became close friends. Charlie knew Krieg had been born in Germany in 1820. After his parents died in a fire, he'd come to America, arriving in Philadelphia when he was twenty. There, he'd saved his pennies to pay for English lessons from a young tutor named Felicity, who was also a music teacher.

They'd married and had two sons, named after their favorite composers, Mozart and Bach. Wolfgang, called Wolf, was born in '43. Johann, nicknamed Jo, came along in '46. Then they'd settled in Texas to raise cattle.

As soon as he could afford it, Wilhelm bought his wife a piano, and Felicity started teaching her older son to play when he was little. Charlie recalled Wolf as an affable child who'd eagerly perform for his parents' friends and neighbors whenever they visited the Kriegs' growing home. That sure didn't sound like the Wolf Krieg we knew.

Then Wilhelm Krieg had suffered grievous losses. His son Jo drowned when he was just six. His beloved Felicity died giving birth to their daughter, Victoria, in '55. After that, Wilhelm could not bring himself to look at their piano, even thought about chopping it up for firewood. Young Wolf never touched the piano again. Without his mother and music, he turned sullen.

The shrouded piano had been consigned to gather dust in a back room of the Krieg mansion—until four-year-old Victoria had discovered it. As if given the gift by her dead mother, the little girl taught herself to play, with astonishing brilliance. Though it caused him more sorrow than joy, Krieg listened to the music that flowed through her, like some mysterious and bittersweet legacy from the mother she'd never known.

Charlie remembered being entranced by Victoria's talent; others were spooked, and whispered of the strange girl possessed by spirits. But Victoria soon had no audience other than her father, as he cut ties with old friends like Charlie and concentrated on building his cattle empire. Unsure about raising a young daughter, Krieg had sent Victoria to boarding school in Philadelphia for several years.

"She'd be about eighteen now," Charlie said. "Some folks claim they seen her roaming the Krieg range alone. Riding naked on a bareback white stallion, her hair flowin' in the wind."

That grabbed Jake's attention. "Really?"

"Don't put much stock in saloon gossip." But Charlie confirmed that Krieg's withdrawal had become nearly complete after his leg got crippled. Charlie plainly missed the admirable friend he once knew, the poor immigrant who'd tamed wild lands, took risks few would, and built a fortune from nothing. "Must be ten years since I seen him. He sends Bulldog into town for ranch business. I reckon nobody knows how grief might change a man."

Doc Stump delivered a less charitable summation: "Wilhelm Krieg has succumbed to the affliction of many a self-made man: he worships his creator."

When I was done talking to people, I knew more about Krieg—but didn't know how that might help us. I knew he'd simply claimed expanses of open range illegally, and had also bought twenty thousand acres of public land at bargain prices. He'd reached a peak of such predatory arrogance that he no longer saw Serenity Falls as home to farmers, merchants, craftsmen, and families.

To him, their properties were simply jewels missing from his crown. In a way, like most folks, Krieg was only trying to forge order from chaos. But to gain his own security, he was all too willing to take it from others.

I was headed home when Jawbone came riding down Main Street. Seemed like half the town gathered to find out the news as he swung out of his saddle in front of the Shamrock. He stepped up to the boardwalk and waved his hands to quiet the clamor.

"What happened?" Mama said.

"I told Krieg what the town voted."

"What did he say?" Meyer Fein asked.

"Well . . . he laughed." The sheriff sighed. "Said nobody says no to Wilhelm Krieg. Said if the town wants a war . . . then, by God, he'll give us one."

Mama looked at Jawbone and shook her head. "At least they didn't shoot you, ya big idiot. So . . . what now?"

Meyer's shoulders slumped. "A fight we do not want."

I took Mama aside. "Get the mayor, the sheriff, Cruz, Jake,

and Angus together in your office."

"Is this about your idea?"

"Yeah. Maybe. I don't know. Just get 'em. I'll be right back."

I ran down the street to the printing shop. I did have an idea—but knew I'd need a lot of help to pull it off. Salem looked up from his workbench when I walked in.

"Hey, Jamey."

"I need to send a wire."

"Where to?"

"St. Louis."

21

"You say 'conspiracy' like that's a bad thing."
—Jamey Galloway

I faced everybody Mama had gathered in her office. It was time to deal. I took a deep breath and began: "Don't think of Krieg as an enemy."

"Well, he sure ain't our friend," Jake said, as he juggled a pair of shot glasses.

"Think of him as a mark."

Jake caught both glasses and stared at me. "Your brilliant idea—"

"I never said brilliant—"

"—is a *confidence scheme*? This ain't no game, Jamey. The Kriegs wanna wreck this town."

"You're right, no game. And we're running out of time. But we need a choice that avoids a lotta killing. And this has to stay just between us."

"Just this little group?" Mama said. She looked dubious. Hell, they all did.

I nodded. "The more people know, the more likely somebody spills the beans."

"You do realize you're talking about a conspiracy," Sheriff Huggins said.

"You say 'conspiracy' like that's a *bad* thing." I glanced

around the room. "Does anybody—other than Jake—really think a shooting war with the Kriegs is a good idea?"

Nobody said a word—except Jake. "Jamey doesn't know the first thing about doin' this."

"But we know somebody who does," I said.

"And he's heading here, on the next train from St. Louis," Salem said, as he and Juliet came in, with a freshly received telegram.

Jake gaped. "Mike Morgan—?!"

I was done knuckling under to my brother. "He's done this sort of thing. Lots of times."

"Years ago. Now he's a broken-down bum."

"If he can help, we have a real chance to save this town."

"And if he can't?"

"Then we're no worse off for asking."

"Not to interrupt," Jawbone said, "but who the hell is Mike Morgan?"

I told them all about Mississippi Mike, his adventures and the schooling he gave me in St. Louis. When I was done, the group reached the general consensus (much to Jake's displeasure) that we might not have much to gain, but we had little to lose. And in the absence of any better choices, my uncertain ghost of a plan might be the town's last best hope.

Juliet Rhymes customarily began her day by kissing Salem goodbye at the front door of Rhymes & Son Printing at seven, then walking down Main Street to the Shamrock for a morning cup of Cruz's robust coffee with Mama, before preparing for her school day. She loved the cool quiet and singing birds, before the onset of the daily hustle and bustle of a growing town.

But the morning after Krieg's declaration of impending war, and our decision to summon Mike Morgan, Juliet opened the print shop door, stepped out on the boardwalk—and heard the distant percussion of a single hammer, pounding four nails. A second hammer joined in a duet. A third created a chorus, like a team of big woodpeckers scattered around town.

Juliet concentrated, trying to isolate the closest source of the noise. She walked a block, turned a corner, and found young bank teller Hobie Shroder dressed in a brown business suit, posting a large broadsheet announcement on the wooden wall outside Stoker's Hardware.

"Hobie!"

Hobie, the youngest bald man in town, jumped back so abruptly his derby fell off. That's when Juliet got a good look at the poster's big bold print:

The Serenity Falls Bank & Land Company announces all town mortgages, without exception, shall be paid in full, thirty days from today . . .

There was more, but she didn't need to read it. She backed the mousy teller up against the wall, hissing his name again with a harshness that scared him. "*Hobieeeeee*. Atwood's foreclosing on the whole town?! How could you put these up?"

He tried to slink sideways, but she grabbed him by the scruff of his pants and yanked up, hard. Hobie yelped. "I—*aye!*—can't afford to lose my job."

"Even if the rest of us lose everything?" Juliet released him in disgust. Then she ripped down the broadside and took it with her as she marched over to the Shamrock. She passed folks already looking at the same posters on other walls, with reactions ranging from fear to fury.

Over at the bank, Silas Atwood's grand temple to Mammon, sweat beaded on Atwood's forehead as he paced his office like a caged varmint, wearing a visible track across his Oriental rug.

"Goddamit. I shoulda never let you talk me into this."

Wilhelm Krieg, his partner in mayhem, sat in a leather wing-back chair, like the emperor on his throne. "You see, we live with our choices, Silas. You chose to piss away this bank's assets on ill-considered speculation and a mansion in Austin."

"One man's speculation's another man's fortune. It's not my fault I got bad luck."

Krieg exhaled a drifting ring of smoke from his cigar. "I am changing your luck."

Atwood slumped into his big leather desk chair. "How's letting you pay off the peasants' mortgages at ten cents on the dollar changing *my* luck?"

"My money refills your vault. So you do not end up in prison."

"Or tar and feathers."

"Here is how it will be. I need your bank functioning. From now on, *no* investments without my approval."

They were interrupted by a ruckus from the bank lobby. "Nooo," Hobie wailed, "Mr. Atwood's in a meeting!" As the office door flew open, poor Hobie's valiant effort to block intruders failed—and Mama, Meyer Fein, and the sheriff barged in.

Atwood shrank back in his chair as Mama slapped the broadside onto the desk. "You can't do this Bird Montgomery boondoggle all over again!"

"It's legal," Atwood said.

"Stealing our property and selling it to *him*?"

"Mr. Krieg's a bank client, like anybody else."

"He's destroying this town!"

"You got no proof."

"Him sitting here? That's all the proof we need."

"I am innocent of such accusations," Krieg said. "But I did promise you years ago there would be consequences for offense against my family's honor."

Mama's temper flared like a flame doused with kerosene. "You would hold a grudge for that long?"

"I am a patient man." Krieg rose from his seat, wielding his fancy cane like a club.

Jawbone stepped between them, and his size alone was enough to force both combatants back a step. "Now, Mr. Atwood," the sheriff said, "it's not too late for you to reconsider this whole thing."

"Do your job, Sheriff," Atwood said in a shaky voice, sounding more like a plea than an order.

"If people get riled, I can't guarantee anybody's safety."

Atwood dug in. "This action is lawful. You enforce it—or I'll find a federal marshal who will. Now, everybody—out."

Mama took a menacing stride toward the banker, like she aimed to strangle him. Meyer and Jawbone intercepted her, hooked her arms in theirs, lifted her off her feet, and hauled her out the door as she yelled back at Atwood and Krieg, "You are both gonna regret this!"

"May all their teeth fall out—except the ones that hurt," Meyer muttered as he and the sheriff carried Mama outside. They set her down on her feet to see if she'd try to charge back into the bank. When she didn't, they all retreated to the Shamrock, where Cruz, me, and my brother waited in the office. There we all were, stewing, trying to figure out what to do next. Cruz brought us some food and coffee, though nobody had much appetite, nor much to say.

I looked around at a roomful of glum faces. "Jake, you remember Mike Morgan's first lesson?"

"Just tell me, so I can die a happy man."

I ignored his sarcasm. "Whatever the game, expect your opponent to cheat."

"And how does that help us?"

"Well, it doesn't. Not yet, anyway."

"Silas Atwood is a serial idiot," Mama said. "He sinks himself back up to his neck in bad deals, and the only way he can save his ass from catastrophe is to become a rich man's puppet—all over again!"

"I reckoned he'd be more careful," Jawbone said, "once your bank started giving him some competition."

Though Mama's bank was thriving, it had only been operating for a few years. Given a choice, many townsfolk had shown a clear preference by coming to her for deposits and loans, but Atwood still held most of the long-standing mortgages.

"Silas never admits his mistakes, much less learns from 'em," Mama said. "With all the charlatans coming west, he doesn't have the brains to keep from becoming beholden to somebody like Krieg."

"And he don't have the backbone or *cojones* to stand up to him," Cruz said.

Atwood's anatomical shortcomings aside, gloom had settled over us like a chilling fog. Even Mama's fury had dwindled down to melancholy. "Maybe Josiah Ford really did curse this town with his dying breath, all those years ago," she said.

Jake stalked out. There had to be a way out of this kettle of fish, though I had no idea what. Things would come to a boil, one way or another. I was counting on Mike Morgan, and his arrival couldn't come too soon, what with Jake and others still keen on a fateful—and likely fatal—fight.

When I went looking for my brother, to try to bring him around to my way of thinking, I found him at the workbench in the barn behind the Shamrock—cleaning and loading his guns. "What're you doing?"

"What does it look like?"

"Jake—pull in your horns!"

"No. And when I'm done with my guns, I'm going to load *yours,* if you're too dumb to do it yourself."

"What do you think Krieg and his men are doing right now?"

"Same thing."

"You want a war?"

"I didn't start this. But I'll be damned if I'm gonna let them finish it without a fight."

22

"Greed bewitches. Always has, always will."
—Mississippi Mike Morgan

The week it took Mike Morgan to journey by rail and stage from St. Louis to Serenity Falls felt like eternity in Purgatory to me, giving me too much time to think of all the ways we could fail to stop Krieg and Atwood.

Though no evictions would take place until the thirty days had elapsed, morale in town was lower than a snake's belly in a dry ditch. Some folks, figuring there wasn't much point in lingering, decided to give up and beat the exodus. But unlike the Biblical Exodus, when the Israelites fled Egyptian bondage for the Promised Land, the townsmen of Serenity Falls thought they'd already settled in their land of milk and honey. Now they were about to be forced into the wilderness, with no Moses to save them.

To the dismay of brother Jake and Charlie Stoker, efforts to raise an armed force to lock horns with the Kriegs proved futile. With those looming foreclosures, there was little enthusiasm among our townsmen for a war. Despite Jakes's dogged desire to fight, few shared that sentiment.

As for me, well, no one in our little band of conspirators saw Mike as quite the savior I'd made him out to be. Truth was, even I had doubts. But seeing Mike's stage roll into town did raise my hopes, if only a little.

Mama, Jake, and Cruz stood behind me in the shade of the Shamrock's boardwalk. I stepped forward as the coach door opened and Mike got out. But my grin turned grim when I saw who climbed out after him—Gideon Duvall.

"What the hell're you doing here?" I spun toward Mike. "What the hell is *he* doing here?!"

Gideon flashed his pearly smile, slid between me and Jake, and draped his arms over our shoulders. "You boys're as happy to see me as Atlanta was to see Sherman."

I glared at Mike, who tried to placate me. "He volunteered."

"Then he can volunteer to get right back on that stage," Jake said, "and go I don't give a damn where."

"He wants to help," Mike said.

"*C'est vrai,* boys," Gideon said.

Jake fixed a gimlet eye on Gideon. "Why? There's no money in it. For either of you."

Mike grabbed their luggage handed down by the stagecoach driver. "Ain't about money. It's about saving this here town. We know that."

"It's about love, and beauty," Gideon said. "I love taking down bullies. And an artful swindle . . . ahh, *c'est magnifique.*"

Jake yanked me aside. "No Gideon."

I wasn't any happier than my brother to see Gideon, but here he was. "He knows how to do this."

"There ain't much to learn from the second kick of a mule," Jake said. "Or did the first kick make you forget that fifty-grand he stole from you?"

I answered with a silent glare.

"You know Gideon's full of shit."

"That's what I'm counting on."

"So how can we trust him?"

"We don't have to trust him, just keep an eye on him."

"*Mes amis,* you know me to be a master at this sort of deceit," Gideon said. "I can make a considerable contribution to your quest for reparation. Your choice."

"Worth the risk," I said to Jake.

"What if you're wrong?"

"Then you can shoot him."

"Deal," Jake said, pronto. Gideon's eyebrows arched in alarm.

We all went into Mama's office, where Jawbone, Meyer, Salem, Juliet, and Angus joined us. After we briefed Mike and Gideon on the whole dirty situation, Mike let out a low, slow whistle. "You folks are way out on a skinny limb."

"And Gideon's just the man to saw it off," Jake said.

"Just here to help," Gideon said, undeterred by Jake's hostility.

Mike peered closely at my face and Jake's. "Would the Kriegs recognize either of you lads?"

"Not if they tripped over us," I said.

"Good. Jamey, you recall what I taught you?"

"Know your mark. Offer him something he can't resist."

"And?"

"Figure out what he's willing to give up to get it."

"By knowing them things—?"

"You can turn the mark's strength into weakness."

"And what do the Kriegs want?"

"Wealth, power, and land."

"What do you want?"

"Enough cash to pay off all the town's mortgages."

"Look," Jake said, "we got less than three weeks 'til this whole town's evicted."

Gideon's eyes twinkled. "Then we better get started."

"Doing what?"

"Why, selling Mr. Krieg a railroad," Gideon said.

Jake cocked his head like a confused pup. "We don't own a railroad."

"When we're done," I said, "neither will he. But we could end up with enough of his money to save this town."

"Or we could end up in jail," Jake said.

"Your way, we could end up dead," I said.

Juliet's eyes narrowed. "Why would somebody like Krieg fall for a swindle?"

Mike tapped a finger to the side of his head. "The human mind is a predictable thing. There's an ol' Scottish saying—"

"Aye," Angus said with a slight smile: *Muckle wad aye hae mair.*"

Mike translated: "Those who have much always want more."

"Folk like y'r dour Mr. Krieg," Angus said, "they're nae as sleekit as they fancy themselves. So we c'n convince'm there's a fortune in his future."

"Greed bewitches," Mike said. "Turns smart men stupid. Lures 'em to their doom. Always has, always will."

In the absence of any better course of action, our gang of budding artful dodgers followed the path set by our mentors. With Gideon's guidance, Meyer outfitted Jake, Angus, Mike, and me with appropriate business attire and city derbies, and Mike and Gideon coached us at playing our roles.

While the rest of Serenity Falls slept, lamplight glowed inside the Rhymes & Son print shop on the north side of town. To the metallic music of mallets tapping alloy type sorts into their chases and the hum of well-oiled levers and gears, Salem and Juliet worked their hand press through the night, creating the counterfeit documents our scheme required.

Mike and Gideon's supervision and knowledge provided assurance of authenticity. And Mike had thoughtfully brought along his own printer's stereotype plates, metal casts already cut with the engravings Salem needed for meticulous reproductions of the filigreed border, numerals, and delicately etched train illustrations prominent on genuine stock certificates. Mike even pitched in as an able printer's devil, and they were done by dawn.

With the ink barely dry, Mike and Gideon did a final inspection. "That's mighty fine work," Mike said.

Gideon put an arm around Salem's shoulder. "You could have a real future at this game, son."

Salem arched one skeptical eyebrow.

With all as ready as possible, our plan to ensnare the Kriegs got rolling later that morning when Salem wrote out a bogus telegram and handed it to young Zachary Gannon, his beanpole, bucktoothed apprentice. Zach hopped on his horse and raced to deliver it to Wilhelm Krieg at his ranch. The message announced:

Chicago: Dayton Dilmore advance agent for Hollister & Dodge Development Co. arriving in Serenity Falls soon. Will call to discuss major land deal.

23

**"It is better to be feared than loved,
if you cannot be both."
—Niccolo Machiavelli**

With Jake holding the reins, the one-horse covered buggy bumped down the rutted road. Seeing Mike Morgan looking like he was about to throw up, Jake pulled to a stop.

On the plus side, Mike no longer resembled a threadbare pauper. He'd been transformed by Meyer Fein's fine pinstriped wool suit—and his own imagination and knowledge—into Erasmus Richter, fictional assistant to the very real U.S. Senator from Texas, James Winright Flanagan. Erasmus Richter was in from Austin, on his way to stoke the fire that would power the state's drive to catch up with railroad development elsewhere in the west.

But on the buggy ride to Krieg's ranch—with Jake now dressed in the natty outfit, derby, and guise of Dayton Dilmore, land agent for Hollister & Dodge—Mike's nerves started jangling, like he was about to sit down to a big poker game on the Mississippi.

"I am feeling mighty queasy here, Jake," Mike said, as he leaned over the side. "I hate to ruin these nice duds." The noise from his gut sounded like a retching dog.

"Do you want to get down?"

"Naww, I can puke from here."

Jake wasn't at all sympathetic. "You said you could do this."

"I been wrong before."

"Then I'm turning back."

Mike let out a rattling belch. "Naww. Drive on. Maybe it'll come back to me. Like swimmin'. They say once you know how, you never forget."

"You a good swimmer?"

"Nope. Sink like a stone."

Jake shook the reins and imagined himself strangling me at his earliest opportunity. But they pressed on, and he could only hope his partner would pull himself together in time. Without Mike Morgan taking charge, Jake doubted how he—a gunslinging gambler—could ever portray a business man. *We're doomed,* he thought.

As they turned off the road onto Krieg's property, Jake glanced at Mike—and did a double take, astonished to see a miraculous restoration. Mike's face shone with jaunty confidence. Even the way he sat, he actually looked taller. For the first time, Jake allowed himself a tiny twinge of optimism.

He stopped the buggy in front of Krieg's fine *casa grandé*, which wouldn't have looked out of place on the richest of antebellum plantations. Jake hopped down and waved to Krieg, who sat watching from a rocking chair on the broad columned veranda, his trusty Winchester Yellowboy across his lap.

"Hello, there," brother Jake called, with a broad salesman's smile—and a wary eye on that rifle. "Wilhelm Krieg?"

The Winchester swung his way.

Jake halted. "Dayton Dilmore, sir! Advance land agent for Hollister and Dodge Development Company—I sent a telegram?"

Krieg said nothing. The Winchester didn't waver.

Neither did Jake's smile. "Sir, may I come up there for a chat?"

"I do not chat. State your business."

"Fair enough. I like a man who's direct." Jake took a step toward the house.

"From there," Krieg said, as Wolf came outside to join him.

"Well, all righty," Jake said. Still smiling. "We hear you're about to take ownership of a great deal of valuable land near here."

"How come you know so much?" Wolf asked.

"It's my job to know." Then Jake baited the hook: "So, how'd you like to turn that land into a fortune that'll dwarf what you can earn from cattle?"

Wolf took a bite. "Hnnh. How?"

"Whatever scheme," Krieg said with a dismissive snort, "I have no interest."

Mike climbed down from the buggy. "Herr Krieg, my name's Erasmus Richter. Senior aide to Senator Flanagan. He sent me to see you, personally."

"Poppa," Wolf said, "it don't hurt to hear 'em out."

Krieg glowered, but he did lower his rifle.

"That's Poppa's best invitation, gents," Wolf said. "C'mon in."

Krieg leaned heavily on the ivory handle of his fancy carved cane and rose to his feet. His old leg injury turned the simple act of standing into a painful task.

Jake skipped back to the buggy to retrieve a tube-shaped leather carrying case. Then he and Mike followed the Kriegs inside, where classical piano music flowed from a back room and filled the vaulted entry hall. They all went into Krieg's paneled study and Wolf closed the door.

A massive mahogany desk with strong curved legs and clawed lion-paw feet dominated the spacious room. Rows of leather-bound classics filled floor-to-ceiling bookcases. (Mama would've killed, or at least inflicted serious injury, to lay claim to Krieg's matched Shakespeare collection.) Heavy burgundy curtains allowed only a little bit of daylight to filter through the tall windows. A gun rack on the wall displayed a score of pre- and postwar pistols and rifles. A portrait of a beautiful young woman with lush chestnut hair hung on the wall opposite the desk. Jake wondered: Krieg's wife, or daughter?

Wolf stood all hunched, arms crossed, as if he hadn't yet earned a comfortable place in his father's inner sanctum. Krieg set his rifle in the wall rack, then eased himself into the suede cowhide chair behind his desk. "Now, then, tell me about this potential fortune."

"Sir, I don't blame you for asking," Jake said. "But I'm bound by my fiduciary responsibility to our major investors. All I can say is, it involves a lucrative land use that my company specializes in. It'll give you monopolistic power over other ranchers and businesses for a hundred miles around. And it'll generate more profits than you've ever dreamed of."

"You may underestimate my capacity for dreaming," the elder Krieg said, while maintaining his detached reserve.

His son, however, had no such hesitation. "You can make this happen?"

"I'm not authorized to discuss details until this local land is in your hands. But then, I promise, you'll find it was worth the wait."

"Herr Krieg," Mike said, "we have something in common."

"What is that?"

"We both hail from Germany."

"I wondered by your name, but you have no trace in your speech."

"I were a mere babe when my family sailed across and settled in Baltimore. So I never grew up with the language, or memories

235

of the old country you must have." Without waiting for an invitation, Mike settled into the tufted-velvet chair across the desk from Krieg, and slid it closer.

"Then I shall call you Herr Richter, if you please," Krieg said.

"I'd consider it an honor."

At first, this conversational detour flummoxed Jake. But he soon realized that Mike's every word, touch, and smile blended like the ingredients of a gourmet recipe in the hands of a master chef. He was cooking up a spell over the Kriegs, without their ever noticing they were being hoodooed. Jake couldn't believe Mike was the same man who'd been fighting a losing battle with his nerves not thirty minutes earlier.

Mike's warm gaze never wavered from his host's eyes. Jake marveled how he used simple, subtle gestures to transform an audience with a monarch into a visit between friends, making himself that much harder to dislodge. "If you were a different kind of man, Herr Krieg, I'd say you should be flattered by the attentions of a United States senator. But flattery is rubbish to men like you."

"It is."

"And the senator knows men like you are the future of Texas."

"I am," Krieg said, unencumbered by false modesty.

"Flattery appeals to vanity. And you are not a vain man, but a practical one. So I present you a practical vision—unending wealth and influence for the Krieg family, for generations to come."

Krieg set his arms on the desktop and leaned forward. "Tell me more."

"The senator's concerned Texas will be left behind, due to lack of railroad development."

"How does this concern me?"

Mike leaned an elbow on the desk and rested his chin on his

hand. His voice lowered to a confidential purr. "Hollister and Dodge're seeking Texans owning the right land—like the land you're about to lay your hands on."

To Jake's amusement, Krieg and Wolf mirrored Mike's movement and leaned even closer themselves: *Maybe Jamey was right about Mike after all.*

"I will not sell so much as an acre," Krieg said.

"Oh, they don't want you to sell."

Jake gripped Mike's shoulder and gave a fast, nervous shake of his head. "Mr. Richter! We're not supposed to say anything yet."

"Son, you can't expect a man to buy a pig in a poke."

Jake scowled. "Well, if you think so . . ."

"I do." Mike turned back to the Kriegs. "Hollister and Dodge want a partner—in a new railroad." Then he snapped his fingers toward Jake. On cue, Jake opened the leather tube, fished out a rolled map, and handed it to Mike. Mike set it down, but didn't open it. Wolf Krieg looked like he'd explode if somebody didn't spread that map out in a hurry. "First, what we say here on the sly must not leave this room. I assure you, it is to your advantage. Others hear tell of this, it all falls apart."

Krieg nodded gravely.

"Good," Mike said. Then, like a fan dancer lowering her feathers, he ever-so-slowly unfurled the map across the desktop, revealing a detailed surveyor's chart of local topography—and the path of a proposed railroad.

Wolf peered at it with fascination. "So, why aren't there more railroads in Texas, anyway?"

"Could be ill feelings from the war," Mike said. "Many who sided with the Confederacy regard the railroads and banks as sulfurous agents of the North. Do you, Herr Krieg?"

"It was not my cause."

"Good. That's what we heard about you."

"We?"

"I been negotiating in secret with the company. They aim to take the lead in building rail lines in Texas. One of those lines could pass through right where you are about to come into possession of all this land."

Wolf put a hand on his father's arm. "Poppa, we can't rely on cattle forever."

"Cattle I know. Railroads, I do not."

"But they do."

"Match made in heaven," Mike said. "Growth for Texas— money and power for you."

Wolf's finger traced along the map. "Back east, they've had railroads everywhere for years. Poppa, it's the future—the west is booming!"

"For whoever hauls goods to market first," Jake said. He could see that this whole railroad notion had tipped Wilhelm Krieg's orderly and sovereign world on its side. As for Wolf, he was hooked like a hungry trout.

Krieg remained unconvinced. "Why my land?" As if he already owned it.

Mike leaned back, resting his clasped hands on his belly, as if distancing himself from the offer. "Doesn't have to be. Land is something Texas has plenty of. But you're about to own the easiest crossing over Pine Cut Run, which is a troublesome river, with those falls and rapids."

"Poppa," Wolf said, "if we don't build this railroad, somebody else will. And we'll have to pay to use it."

"If you own it," Jake said, "everybody pays you."

Mike stood, as if to leave. "Look, we just come to measure your interest."

"We're interested!" the son said, a little too eagerly.

But the father would not be stampeded. He stood and limped slowly to the door. "Herr Richter, Mr. Dilmore—I will think on this proposal. But I prefer not to waste your time. You may return for my decision."

"I've come a long way, sir," Jake said. "My instructions are to wait as long as it takes."

"Very well. Then I will give my reply in two hours."

"Thank you, sir."

Mike checked his gold watch. "While Dilmore stays, I'll go back to town. Wire the senator, tell him we met. There's a young company fella due in any time—Levi Hollister, son of the co-founder. Soon as he arrives, I'll bring him here. In case you decide to go ahead."

Krieg opened the study door and called out: "Victoria—come here."

The piano music stopped. Moments later, Krieg's daughter appeared in the doorway. She looked eighteen, as Charlie Stoker had guessed, and much like the portrait in the study. She appeared the very embodiment of Victorian elegance in a floral skirt and prim ivory blouse, lace-trimmed collar buttoned to the top of her graceful neck, chestnut hair neatly gathered and pinned. "Yes, Poppa?"

"I need you to occupy Mr. Dilmore, while I consider his business proposal."

Victoria eyed Jake with a sassy twinkle. "Yes, Poppa." She glided from the study toward the front door. "Mr. Dilmore, I hope you don't mind the company of a cloistered ranch girl."

Jake followed her out onto the veranda. "Heh! I've seen ranch gals," he said with a crooked grin, implying she was anything but.

She showed him around the outside of the mansion, explaining when various additions had been built over the years. Of course, Jake looked more at her than the house. With her refined appearance and manner, she seemed older, and out of place on a cattle ranch.

"As you can see," she said, "this house has many accrued layers, like my father."

"He's an interesting man, all right."

Victoria laughed. "He's a bastard—though my brother is the family champion by far."

"Does your father know you talk like a drover?"

She shrugged. "I grew up around ranch hands, and children do copy their elders. So he shouldn't be surprised. Are you?"

"Little bit."

"Good," she said with a sly half-smile. Then she unpinned her hair and shook it loose over her shoulders.

Her tour of the grounds brought them to a large, neatly trimmed garden enclosed in wrought-iron fencing behind the house. "This was Felicity's idea. She wanted something civilized, to remind her of the city where she grew up. After she died, it was neglected for years. But I had it restored."

"You involved with the family cattle business at all?"

Victoria's eyebrows arched. "A girl? My father would never allow it."

"So . . . what keeps you busy?"

"Hmm. I'm still deciding on that. Oh! I do seek opportunities to confound my father."

"I'll bet he adores you."

"Sometimes."

"He's got your portrait in his study."

"Oh, that's Felicity, not me—from when they were first married. I'm told I look very much like her."

"I'll say."

"Sometimes, I think the resemblance comforts him, like she's still here. Other times . . ." Her voice trailed off.

"Why do you call your mama by her name?"

"She died giving birth to me. So I never knew her. I don't

really think of Felicity Krieg as my mother. She's . . . an ancestor."

"Must've been hard, growing up without her."

"It's all I knew."

"You had your daddy."

"He was . . . unprepared to raise a baby girl. My upbringing was left mostly to nannies, tutors, and spinster aunts. Oh, and boarding school in Philadelphia."

"My mama was born in Philadelphia."

"Really. Have you ever been there?"

"No, ma'am. Never been back east."

At the back of the gardens, they reached the family burial ground. Victoria paused at the graves of Felicity and Jo. "When I was little, I'd come out here and talk to them. I'd wonder what they were like . . . how my life might've been different." She sighed. "Sometimes I think my father would have been happier if the infant died in childbirth instead of the mother."

"My daddy died when I was little. I sometimes wonder the same thing, how my life might've been."

"People think my father's heart turned to stone after Felicity died. I think it's the same heart, but he did build a fortress around it. German men aren't allowed to be sentimental."

"Not only German men."

"His grief fueled his ambition, like wood for a fire. Sometimes I think his plans are all he has left. And, as you may have heard, nobody says no to a Krieg." As they left the gardens, she asked, "Do you know Machiavelli?"

"Not personally."

She laughed. "Italian Renaissance philosopher I read in school. Said it's best for a leader to be both loved and feared. But if you have to pick one—"

"Pick fear," Jake said.

She looked at him with an admiring—and alluring—tilt of

her chin. "You know Machiavelli better than you think. Come—meet my best friend," she said as their walk ended at a grand stable housing a dozen fine riding horses.

Jake did his best to hide his unease around that many hooves. Victoria led the way to a stall where a white stallion reared up at his first glimpse of Jake, who nearly jumped out of his shoes. Victoria's musical laughter settled the horse down.

"Not fond of horses, Mr. Dilmore?"

"They're not fond of me."

"Well, you're not a ranch hand. Westerners do seem to romanticize their bond with horses."

"I've known people like that."

Jake took a cautious step back as Victoria opened the stall and went in to greet her horse. "Truth is, for most folks horses are beasts of burden. Or a way to get from here to there." She kissed the horse on his nose, and unbuttoned her high collar to let him nuzzle her neck.

"You two have a . . . close relationship."

"I wasn't joking. Lucifer really is my best friend."

"Lucifer?" Jake imagined an entire catalogue of infernal deeds that might have earned the horse that name. "He's white. Why not . . . Angel?"

Victoria slipped out of the stall and back to Jake. "Aren't we all fallen angels, one way or another? Good and evil, struggling inside?" She gazed into his eyes.

"I reckon." He felt her warm breath on his cheek.

"Don't you think that's much more interesting than just being good . . . all the time . . . without considering . . . alternatives?"

She gave him a slow, soft kiss. Knowing where he was and who her father was, he balked at kissing her back. Mostly.

"I'd like to take you for a ride," she whispered into his ear—and then turned to haul her fancy tooled saddle off the rack in front of the stall. Jake could hardly say no. So she readied Lucifer and their mellowest old mount for her guest.

"You may be disappointed," she said with a coy glance as she led both horses outside.

"About what?"

"I won't be taking my clothes off."

Jake blushed.

Victoria laughed. "You can't believe everything you hear from gossips."

She hiked her riding skirt and sat astride her horse, not sidesaddle like most women. It didn't really surprise Jake that she seemed unconcerned with conventions of modesty. He climbed up on his horse the usual way, and Victoria led at a walk.

"I never really believed you did that," Jake said.

"What?"

"Riding naked."

"Oh, I never said I didn't. I simply said you can't believe everything you hear." With a saucy laugh, she prodded her horse to a trot. Once they were away from the house, she kicked Lucifer into a full gallop, racing across their rangeland with a fearless abandon Jake found both intoxicating *and* unnerving, as he scrambled to keep up without falling off and breaking his neck.

After a few miles' ride over rolling hills, they stopped at a shady glade. While the horses grazed and drank at a spring-fed pool, Victoria took Jake by the hand. They walked around the edge of the pond, carefully picking tart, purple dewberries off spiky stems. Victoria took down a blanket she had tucked behind her saddle and spread it on the grass.

"This is nice," she said, as they sat and shared the berries. "I don't socialize much."

"With men, you mean?"

"My father expects I'll be an old maid."

"What about all those ranch hands you learned to talk like?"

"Oh, fraternizing with the help is not encouraged."

"I suspect you've broken that rule a time or two."

"A time or two."

"Must be tough, smart girl like you, not seeing much of the world beyond this ranch, big as it is."

She squinted toward the horizon. "Don't feel sorry for me. All the while I was in Philadelphia, I felt . . . caged, by brick and cobblestone. The only things that kept me from going mad? Music lessons, and dreaming of coming back here . . . to all this space and wildness."

"Civilization's coming. Even here. All this, it's gonna change."

"All the more reason to enjoy it while it's here. Look at those horses. Animals live in the moment. Why shouldn't we?"

Then Victoria Krieg shed every stitch of her clothing and dove into the pond. My boggled brother weighed the propriety of looking away. But she didn't want him to, and he knew it.

"Dayton! Come in with me."

"Your father seeing me all wet when I go back?" He shook his head. "Let's just say I'm wary of his close relationship with his Winchester."

She swam for a while, pausing to splash at Jake. Then she marched dripping wet up the bank, and kissed him. "Remember . . . nobody says no to a Krieg."

"Well, when you put it that way . . ."

Jake surrendered. They settled down onto the blanket, and had themselves a pretty good time.

24

"It ain't leading a man into temptation if he's already memorized the map."
—Mississippi Mike Morgan

Since Jake and Mike's early departure that morning, the rest of us conspirators had attempted to go about our daily activities, while keeping an edgy eye out for their return. When the buggy rounded the bend and rolled onto Main Street, first thing we noticed was Mike driving alone. By the time he'd parked in the barn and unhitched the horse, the mayor, the sheriff, Salem, and Juliet had all beelined over to join Mama, Cruz, Angus, Gideon, and me at the Shamrock.

We pounced on Mike as he walked in the back door.

"Where's Jake?" Mama said.

Mike tried not to smile. "Left him in good hands, I believe."

"Well," Meyer said, "what happened?"

"The mark has been roped. You ready to close the deal, Levi Hollister?"

All eyes turned to me. "In theory."

"In theory," Mike said, "there ain't no difference between theory and practice. But in practice, there is." While I blinked and tried to figure that one out, he asked again: "Are you ready?"

"You bet," I said with a feeble smile that convinced no one.

Once I was all primped and proper, thanks to Meyer, Mike

and me climbed aboard Mama's four-seat surrey and headed back out to the Krieg ranch. On the way, I begged Mike to help me rehearse again. But he refused.

"You're ready, Jamey."

I am not, I thought.

"Trust me."

I do.

"Trust yourself."

I don't!

Considering how little I'd known about the railroad business a few weeks earlier, and how much information Angus had stuffed into my head in the past few days, the odds were no better than fifty-fifty I'd remember what to say and when to say it. By the time we drove up to the Krieg mansion, I had no choice but to plunge in.

We came up the front steps just as Jake and Victoria returned from their excursion. She greeted us, and tossed Jake a flirty smile—which instantly turned him skittish. As she ushered us into the house, she flustered him even more with a playful pat on his rump.

Mike took that moment to pluck a weedy bit of wildflower out of Jake's hair. Jake blushed and gave us a dopey shrug.

I've been in many a house, large and small, mansions and hovels. Every home smells like something, or a mixture of many things. Old wood, new lumber. Cooking, good and bad, sweet or pungent. Tobacco smoke, fireplace ash. Lamp oil and candle wax. Trash and manure. Cattle and wet dog. Perfume and soap. Sweat, beer, and dust. But as we followed Victoria through the expansive entry hall, the Krieg mansion smelled like . . . nothing. As if nobody lived there. The damnedest thing.

Victoria ushered us into the study. She went to open the burgundy drapes wider, but Krieg shook his head, as if barring the intrusion of too much sunlight. So she left the drapes as they were, excused herself, and shut the door behind her. There we were, facing Wilhelm Krieg at his desk, with second-fiddle Wolf standing behind him. Mike introduced me, we pulled up some extra chairs, and I spread the map Mike had left with the Kriegs as our only tangible inducement, in the absence of actual rails and rolling stock.

I pointed at a long, crosshatched line. "Right here'll be the first railroad to connect this part of Texas with Dallas and points north."

Wolf looked like a hungry hound approaching a roastin' pig. "Then Austin to the south?"

"That's the plan."

Wolf squinted at the map, as if seeking mystical secrets hidden in the neatly printed lines, letters, and symbols. Then he pressed his thumb on the spot where Serenity Falls was located, and symbolically rubbed it out. "The old town—gone."

"Yes, sir," Jake said. "The new town—I think Kriegsburg'll be a good name. Built right about here." He pointed to a spot an inch away.

Even Wilhelm Krieg's accustomed scowl brightened a touch.

"I'm told by Mr. Dilmore and Mr. Richter that you Kriegs are pioneers," I said, my words flowing without hesitation (to my great relief). "So's Hollister and Dodge. As this great state grows, we'll be the ones moving people, and everything they make and buy."

"You envision big things, Mr. Hollister," Krieg said.

"Why dream small?"

"When's all this gonna happen?" Wolf said, commandeering the conversation.

"As soon as those mortgage foreclosures are done," I said, "Hollister and Dodge is ready to start."

"But it takes years to build a railroad."

"True," Mike said, "but construction profits roll in early."

"Construction profits?"

I nodded. "You bet. We'll set up a separate construction company. We'll use money from government subsidies and bonds. Hire ourselves to build the danged thing. Inflate cost estimates. Pay workers less than the estimates—and pocket the difference." I spread my hands like a magician at the finale of a dazzling trick. "Profits!"

Wolf grinned. "I read where Thomas Durant did that same thing with his Crédit Mobilier company. That's how he got rich building the Union Pacific."

"Except they got greedy," I said, "and they got caught. We keep a low profile, and stay out of trouble. Once the railroad's operating, you'll not only be able to move your own cattle to market safer, faster, and cheaper—you'll charge other ranchers for transporting theirs, too."

"Think about it, Poppa," Wolf said. "No more cattle drives!"

"There's also the lumber industry," Mike said. "It's been stunted by the difficulty of moving logs and boards great distances. But those East Texas piney woods are just begging for rail transportation."

Wolf could see a golden future unfolding. "Hnnh . . . I didn't even think of lumber."

"That's not all," I said. "Bigger railroads'll offer a fortune to buy you out."

"Why would we ever sell?" Wolf said, irked at the prospect of having his acquisitive aspirations wrenched from his grip.

"You don't have to," I said, "unless you want to. If the Krieg family retains its ownership stake, you can ride the rails all the way into the twentieth century, collecting royalties and fees bigger than you can imagine."

"Oh, I can imagine a lot," Wolf said.

"More and more people'll come to Texas, and they'll use our rails to travel and ship goods in and out."

"Poppa," Wolf said, "it's like having a license to print money!"

"And you'll gain even more land," Mike said, "to use as you please."

Wilhelm Krieg frowned. "But Texas has halted land grants."

"That's the *public* policy, sure. Right there in the new state constitution. But the senator knows people who can pry loose that land for you. You can keep it, develop it, or sell it. You'll have more than a ranch. You'll have a kingdom."

"We can't lose," Wolf said. "God's not making any more land. Poppa, we gotta do this."

Krieg was plainly enticed, but determined not to be dragged along by his son. "As pleasing as this appears, there is a price?"

"Well, yes, sir, there is," I said. "To be a partner, Hollister and Dodge requires you to be among the five biggest stockholders, buying a minimum of two thousand shares. But your involvement will be a clarion call for others to invest. Selling shares serves two purposes—to reward partners like you, and to raise capital needed to build the railroad."

"So what's our deal?" Wolf asked.

"Rest assured," Mike said, "I arm-twisted the board into some excellent terms. Mr. Hollister?"

"For you, twenty-five dollars a share," I said. "Public price'll be a hundred. And every share you buy, Hollister and Dodge'll give you two more."

"*Ten* more," Wolf said.

"*Ten!?* The board'll hang me!" I took a solemn breath, as if contemplating my own demise. "I . . . I'm authorized to go as high as . . . as three."

Krieg sat back and let his son haggle. "Nine," Wolf said.

"Four."

"Eight."

"Five," I said, with a wince.

Before Wolf could speak, his father thumped his fist on the

desk. "Done."

"*Poppa*—"

"Done." Krieg's verdict was final, and Wolf knew it.

I bowed my head. "This could cost me my job."

Wolf scoffed. "Your father's the company founder."

"Co-founder," I said. I looked at Krieg. "And besides, don't fathers hold their sons to a higher standard?"

"We try," Krieg said, with a dubious glance at Wolf.

I slipped a packet of documents out of my leather case and spread them on Krieg's desk. I reached for the pen in his inkwell, crossed out some numbers, and wrote in adjustments. "So, your buy-in is fifty-thousand dollars—two thousand shares, at twenty-five dollars a share. That's a seventy-five percent discount off the public price. With free shares, you'll own twelve thousand to start."

Wolf liked the sound of that. "Poppa, that's over a million dollars' worth of stock!"

"As other investors come in," Mike said, "stock prices'll go up, you can make a killing selling those shares."

For the first time, I saw it in Wilhelm Krieg's eyes: he could picture himself as the gold-plated owner of railroads barreling up and down the great state of Texas. "And when we issue more stock to raise capital," I said, "you'll be first in line to buy additional shares, at insider prices. You'll be part of a never-ending cycle of wealth."

Krieg nodded almost imperceptibly. "Yes."

"This all rests on one touchy question . . . forgive me for asking, sir," I said. "You *can* come up with the investment money, right?"

Before Krieg could answer, Wolf thumbed a gesture toward the door. "All of you, wait outside."

Mike, Jake, and me left the study. But Wolf didn't shut the door all the way. It remained open a crack—enough for us to overhear him saying they didn't have fifty-grand in liquid assets. "But this kind of chance, Poppa—it's worth taking out a loan."

"No loan," Krieg said. "My dear friend Atwood will provide."

They summoned us back in, and Krieg assured us he'd have no trouble raising the required amount, in cash.

I blew out a relieved breath. "For a second there, I was afraid I'd have to start hunting for a new partner."

"No need," Krieg said.

"I really shouldn't tell you this yet," I said in a furtive murmur. "But . . . aww, what the hell. Twelve thousand shares'll give you two thousand more than our current primary investor."

Wolf puffed up with predatory pride. "That's the way it should be. Nobody bigger than us. And nobody says no to a Krieg." His dead-pale eyes gave me the same chill as that first time Jake and me met him, when we were kids and he'd flicked a lit match at Jake's face.

"I want to know, who is this other investor," Krieg said.

"Well, sir, I'm afraid that's confidential—at least until our transaction is complete and you're an official partner. But I can tell you, this other fella will not be pleased. He thought he was gonna be king of this venture. Well, that's his problem, right? Do we have a deal, then, Mr. Krieg?"

"First, I need evidence this railroad can be built where you say."

I looked hurt. "Well, sir, you have the assurance of the Hollister and Dodge board that we can." I sighed in exhaustion, as if he was beating me down. "I'd heard you were a fair man, though not a foolish one. So I came prepared. Our chief engineer's waiting in town. I'll bring him here tomorrow."

"Even better," Wolf said, "meet us at that river crossing. He'll answer our questions. We'll hand down our decision."

"Fair enough," I said. "Mr. Richter and Mr. Dilmore'll fetch you tomorrow morning."

"Contingent upon that," Krieg said, "I will gather the funds."

"I reckon you'll want to confer with your attorney before we finalize this whole thing," Mike said.

"I have no use for lawyers."

Mike chuckled. "Like Shakespeare said, first thing, let's kill all them lawyers."

"I would let them live—elsewhere."

"I know the senator wouldn't want you to have no doubts about the deal."

"Herr Richter, do I appear to you a man troubled by any shadow of doubt?"

"No, sir. Until tomorrow morning, then—say, around ten?"

With handshakes all around, I retrieved and rolled the map, and we three left the house and boarded the surrey. Jake gave the reins a shake and the horses headed for town. "There's something squirrelly about that Wolf Krieg," he said.

"Maybe," I said, "but he did do half the selling for us. I almost feel bad about leadin' 'em into temptation."

"It ain't leadin' a man into temptation," Mike said, "if he's already memorized the map. And remember this about Wilhelm Krieg: the most dangerous critter in the world is a man convinced beyond doubt of his own virtue."

Krieg left the ranch for town soon after us, driving alone in his expensive leather-topped buggy. His first stop was Salem's print shop, where he wired Hollister & Dodge in Chicago. As we'd anticipated, he wanted to confirm his deal with the home office. He waited and watched while Salem pecked at his telegraph key—but, out of Krieg's sight behind the counter, the link to the wires stretching pole to pole across the country had been disconnected.

"I will be at the bank, meeting with Atwood," Krieg said. "If a reply arrives while I am in town, bring it to me at once." He dropped an extra dollar on the counter, limped out, and drove to the Serenity Falls Bank & Land Company atop the town's highest hill.

When Atwood heard Krieg's demand for fifty thousand in cash—immediately, as a no-interest loan, to be repaid at his leisure—the banker slowly lowered his ever-present cigar and gawked at Krieg sitting on the other side of the desk. Atwood's mouth moved, but it took a while before he dredged up a few dry words: "I—can't—do that."

"You can," Krieg said, "and you shall."

Atwood slumped forward. His forehead clunked against the desk. "If I don't, you know enough of my secrets to ruin me."

"I would take no pleasure."

"Ain't that a comfort."

"This will work out well for you, Silas."

Atwood tilted one doleful eye toward Krieg. "How?"

"Because it will work out well for me. I shall be too mighty to fail." Krieg stood and poured two glasses of bourbon from the bottle on Atwood's desk, as he told the banker about the railroad deal.

The more Atwood heard, the more he felt light-headed. Maybe Krieg's demand didn't spell calamity, after all. The Krieg ranch was the bank's single largest customer; the more money Krieg piled up, the more he would deposit. And Atwood had no real choice—he couldn't afford to alienate Krieg to the point where the rancher (and newly minted railroad mogul) might take his business to a more substantial bank in Austin or Dallas. He was obliged to provide whatever Krieg demanded.

They heard a knock at the door. Hobie Shroder entered with Salem, who handed a telegram to Krieg. Krieg read it to himself and smiled, which he wouldn't have, had he known the message from Hollister & Dodge confirming authorization for the deal was bogus.

With a deep sigh, Silas Atwood escorted Krieg out of his office. Without explanation, he dismissed his tellers and clerks, and closed the bank thirty minutes earlier than usual. Then he led Krieg down a hallway to a back room with an armored door, secured with the three sturdiest deadbolts known to man.

Atwood fished his key ring from his vest pocket, opened each lock with a different key, and opened the vault to reveal a matched pair of monumental safes. Without bothering to hide the combination from Krieg, he twisted the dial on the right-hand safe three times and swung open the stout steel door. He emptied the cash contents onto a table, counted out bills worth fifty thousand, stuffed the money into a leather satchel, and handed it to Krieg.

"Silas, this will be the best investment of your life."

His mouth too parched to speak, Atwood simply watched in silence as Krieg departed with an alarming portion of his bank's cash.

25

Where vice is, vengeance follows.
—Scottish proverb

Next morning, with a cool spring breeze and warming sunshine, Jake and Mike took the big surrey out to fetch the Krieg men at their ranch. Angus and me drove directly to the Pine Cut Run crossing to await their arrival. On the way, I had to verify that our Scottish friend was ready to play his part.

Indeed, he was eager to pitch in. "Laddie, y'saved m'life. It's the least I c'n do. We Scots have a sayin': Where vice is, vengeance follows. The Kriegs're vice. And we are vengeance."

The surrey soon arrived and parked close to the water. While everyone else climbed out, Krieg remained in his seat. After I introduced Angus, he delivered a sprightly lecture on Pine Cut Run and the surrounding land, with the sheen of authoritative expertise needed to establish in Wilhelm Krieg's mind that this deal was the real thing. And he stressed that the same geology which made for an ideal cattle crossing also affirmed it as "a bonnie spot" for a railroad bridge.

The Kriegs were sufficiently impressed to invite us back to the ranch to conclude the agreement. Angus and me followed the surrey in our smaller buggy.

"You sounded very convincing," I said.

"It's easy when y're tellin' the truth. Anybody buildin' a railroad here, that's exactly where you'd put it."

"I was never sure this plan would work."

"Y're about t'find out."

"We couldn't have made it this far without you, y'know."

Angus winked. "I reckon it was Providence led you t'find me danglin' from that tree."

Arriving at the ranch, we all followed Krieg into his study. Seeing the pain in every halting step he took, I felt a trace of Christian charity toward him. Then again, counting the misery he'd inflicted on others, he deserved to feel some misery of his own. Savoring another soul's distress did trigger a twinge of Christian guilt—which I promptly squashed like a bug.

Once the documents were signed, Mike ceremoniously gathered the papers together in a folder and slid them across the desk to Krieg. In exchange, Krieg lifted a satchel off the floor and passed it to Mike—who handed it to me. I finally got to feel the substantial heft of fifty-thousand dollars.

"Congratulations, gentlemen," I said to the Kriegs. "You are now partners in a bold new venture."

Next came handshakes and celebratory brandy, poured by Wolf into six glasses on the desk. As we each took one, Krieg wondered if we'd be importing an army of Chinamen to build the railroad. "I read that is what the Central Pacific did. And I have been curious: why Chinamen?"

Mike hoisted his drink. "They built the Great Wall of China, didn't they? They must know something. To the railroad—long may she roll."

"To the railroad!" we said in unison, to the chiming of fine crystal goblets clinking together.

Wolf then raised his drink even higher. "To the end of Serenity Falls . . . sooner rather than later."

With the deal done, I couldn't wait to sweep all that money out of Krieg's reach. As the rancher escorted us out, Mike paused on the veranda. "Herr Krieg, there's another little private matter the senator asked me to discuss with you, if that'd be all right."

"Of course."

We left the smaller buggy at the ranch for "Mr. Richter" to use later. Then the fictional Dayton Dilmore, Levi Hollister, and the very real Angus McDonnell climbed aboard the surrey and drove away. When we reached the road, I ducked under the front seat and pulled a blanket off a bona fide arsenal of firearms we'd stocked there should the need arise to protect our treasure from outlaws.

I took the reins, while Jake and Angus kept rifles ready and eyes peeled in the gathering dusk. The last time I'd had a chance at holding fifty grand, it ended up in Gideon Duvall's pockets. This time, the money was ours—right there in my brother's lap—and that fact caused me sufficient trepidation that I had our horse team pacing back to town twice as fast as normal.

Meanwhile, Wilhelm Krieg and Mike repaired to the front parlor for more brandy, and fine cigars.

"Herr Krieg," Mike said, "there's one more small transaction the senator asked me to take care of. In exchange for ongoing constituent services to you—such as arranging for special land grants—how would you feel about some consideration for the senator's reelection campaign?"

"Is there an amount the senator has in mind?"

"There is. Five thousand."

Krieg allowed himself a hint of a smile. "Compared to fifty thousand, that seems a pittance."

"Not for nurturing such a mutually beneficial relationship like a babe at the bosom."

Krieg excused himself, went back to his office, and returned with an envelope containing a stack of cash. He handed it to Mike.

"On behalf of the senator, I thank you kindly for your support, sir," Mike said as he tucked the money into the pocket inside his frock coat. "I can assure you we'll see your interests are looked after."

"Are you not going to count it, Herr Richter?"

"That'd be an insult to a trustworthy man. We'd not do that to a neighbor."

"Neighbor?"

"The senator and his friends'll soon quietly buy up some of the land adjacent to the projected route."

"Ahh, the value of which should rise considerably once the railroad is built."

"Yes, indeed."

"I prosper, and so does the senator."

"One hand washes the other, Herr Krieg," Mike said, with a pantomimed gesture. "Why, back in '63, Senator Samuel Pomeroy of Kansas introduced the land grant bill that made the transcontinental railroad possible. It were such a big help to the Atchison-Topeka that the shareholders elected Pomeroy president of their operation. Washed hands all around!"

They shared a laugh, and Krieg insisted his new friend stay for dinner, which Mike gladly did.

Back in town, we parked behind the Shamrock and, under guard by Jake and Angus, I hustled the money directly into Mama's office. Once she slid the satchel inside her E.R. Morse safe and shut the heavy door with a satisfying *thunk* of security, I allowed myself to settle into her desk chair with a sigh of relief.

"My boys," Mama said, regarding me and Jake with wonderment. "I'll be honest, I didn't think this would work." She gave us each a doting pat on the cheek, and then she and Cruz went back to tending the saloon and café. Angus went with them to celebrate with song and drink, leaving me and Jake alone in the office.

My brother cocked an amused eyebrow. "It must be killing you that you can't tell Becky all about your brilliant plan."

"*Our* brilliant plan," I said, happy to share the credit. But I knew I couldn't share the tale, not with anybody who didn't already know.

His social business with Krieg concluded, Mike Morgan drove back to town alone. It was nearly midnight by the time he came upstairs to the room he shared with Gideon at the Shamrock. Gideon, still fully dressed except for his frock coat and hat, looked up from a corner chair where he sat reading a copy of the *Serenity Falls Mercury* newspaper.

"How'd it go?"

"Smooth," Mike said.

"He 'donated' the extra five thousand?"

"He did." Mike double-tapped the bulge inside his coat pocket. "I intend to sleep with this until I can stash it in Cara's vault first thing in the morning."

"Feels good, running the ol' game again."

"It does. Been a while since we got to sleep the sleep of the just, in the name of friends."

Gideon's eyes narrowed. "Are they really friends?"

"Close enough." Mike shed his coat, carefully folded it, and placed it next to the pillow on his bed. He'd pulled off his shoes and had his trousers down around his ankles when a commotion exploded outside on Main Street—pounding hooves, shouting voices . . . and shooting. Lots of shooting.

Gideon darted to the window and peered outside. *"Mon Dieu!"*

Mike saw the hellish flicker of flames dancing through the glass and across his companion's face. He pulled his trousers back up and rushed to Gideon's side. They looked out in horror at a mob of masked horsemen tearing through town, carrying torches, veering here and there to light buildings ablaze. One nightrider hurled his torch like a spear, shattering the window of Duncan's Emporium across the street, setting the store on fire.

Mike smelled smoke curling into the room under their door. "Holy Jesus! The hotel must be on fire, too!" He wrestled his shoes back on. "Gideon! The money!"

Gideon scooped up Mike's coat and hat, then grabbed his friend by the arm and pulled him out. With choking smoke already filling the Shamrock's main room, they scurried down the branched staircase. The saloon had still been open, with a moderate crowd on hand. Mama, Cruz, and security man Dutch de Groot hurried patrons out both front and back doors.

Jake and me raced around to all the rooms, clearing out hotel guests, working girls, and their clients. Not all were as completely dressed as they might have preferred. With little time to gather up clothing, we grabbed blankets and sheets so they'd have something to cover up with once they got outside.

Mama dashed through the smoke to her office. Clutching her bank records and ledgers in her arms, she scrambled out the back and herded all her girls together and away from the burning building.

As soon as residents realized the town was under attack, some charged out with guns and rifles, chasing and shooting at the invaders. Jake and Doc Stump were among the defenders. Between the smoke, flames, and chaos, not to mention moving targets, nobody could be sure how many marauders there were, or if any of them got shot. But the gunfire forced them to flee even faster than they'd come thundering in.

Without wasting time to hitch up the horse team, volunteers hauled the town's Rumsey fire engine to the center of Main Street, ran the long siphon hose down to the river, and manned the pumper handles. Once pressure built up inside the tank, the fire wagon's nozzle shot water a hundred feet. The firemen concentrated the pumper's stream on the block including the Shamrock, doggedly determined to save what they could.

With gunfire ending, I joined the bucket brigades already stretched down to Pine Cut Run. It seemed like the whole town pitched in—men, women, and children, some barely dressed, all terrified yet resolute. As we passed full buckets one way and empty ones the other, I thought back to that hellish night years ago when the Basque sheepherders were attacked, and about my own recent nightmare that turned out to be a premonition.

Jake joined me on the line. "The lead rider . . . did you see his hat?"

I nodded. We both knew: the burning of Serenity Falls was Wolf Krieg's handiwork.

26

"Cry 'Havoc,' and let slip the dogs of war!"
—William Shakespeare,
Julius Caesar

Remnants of dark smoke curled high into the eastern sky at sunrise.

Too distant for Bulldog Quill to smell it, he could see it from the Krieg ranch miles away as he walked from the bunkhouse to the *casa grandé* for his daily dawn meeting with the boss. He'd already heard from ranch hands who'd been out drinking the previous night that Serenity Falls had half-burned to the ground.

Bulldog was fairly certain who was behind it: did the old man know? When he saw a seething, stone-faced Wilhelm Krieg standing on the veranda, he had his answer.

"My son is at the stable," Krieg said. "Bring him here, now."

"He don't take orders from me, Boss."

"Then bring him at gunpoint. Or knock him senseless and drag him."

Bulldog about-faced, found Wolf, and relayed the summons. Wolf not only didn't resist—he strode toward the house so fast the foreman had to hustle to keep up. They found Krieg still on the veranda, gripping the rail so tightly Bulldog half expected the wood to splinter in his bare hands.

"Did you burn that town last night?" Krieg said.

Wolf cocked his head. "What if I did?"

"You may have touched off a war between us and those townsmen."

"So what?"

"Your attack will harden their opposition. Hollister and Dodge will not want delays and open conflict. They want us to have that land. Our deal *depends* on it."

"You can tell Hollister and Dodge the way to win any war is by destroying your enemy's will to resist. Who's gonna stay and fight for a town of ashes?"

The residents of Serenity Falls wondered the same thing, as daylight allowed a full accounting of the wreckage. The town's valiant firefighting efforts proved to have been not entirely in vain. Though Mama's saloon had been reduced to smoldering ruins, the café and many of the hotel rooms upstairs survived. But half the businesses and homes were rubble, and some townsfolk were already packing up whatever they still had—for some, only the clothing on their backs—and preparing to leave forever.

While Doc Stump treated some burns, few were serious, and there were no human deaths. Sadly, three horses died, trapped in the livery stable before Mex and his hands could rush them out. I feared my old pony, Shadow, was among the casualties, until I found him running loose near the river. When he heard me whistling for him, he trotted over and I hugged him around his sooty neck.

Back at the Shamrock, Jake, Cruz, Dutch, and me helped Mama dig through her charred office. Turned out her E.R. Morse safe really was fireproof. Scorched on the outside, the blistered steel box had done its job and protected all the records, valuables, and money stored inside—including the fresh fifty grand from Krieg. It also cheered Mama to learn the fire had miraculously halted short of the town library, sparing her beloved collection of books.

Neighbors helped Cruz and Dutch hoist the safe onto a sturdy wagon for temporary relocation to Salem's undamaged print shop on the north side. Mama spread the word that customers' deposits were secure, and her bank would reopen for business soon. She wished she could also tell people how we were trying to save the town from the Kriegs. But she couldn't, of course.

Speaking of banks, Silas Atwood's brick building remained unscathed on its hilltop.

Our grim band of conspirators gathered at Salem's shop. That's when we realized Jake was nowhere to be found, even though we all swore we'd *just* seen him somewhere or other. He was gone, and I had a pretty good idea where. I ran over to the corral outside of what was left of the livery. Mex told me Jake had grabbed a horse and taken off about fifteen minutes earlier.

"Dammit. Did he have his gun?"

"*Sí.* Rifle, too."

I whistled to Shadow at the far end of the corral, where his head was eyeball-deep in a trough of oats. He gave me a sideways glance that declared how much he didn't want to move. I whistled again. He stamped his foot in protest before he sauntered over to me. Even though he was nineteen, I knew he still had some speed left in him.

I saddled him up and rode out, slowing down long enough to shout to Mama: "Jake took off by his idiot self."

"Where?"

"The Krieg ranch."

"Go! Stop him before he gets himself killed!"

In a cloud of dust and cinders, me and Shadow lit out after my jackass brother. As the better and faster rider, I knew the miles to the Krieg ranch gave me a chance to catch up to him. Whether I'd really be able to *stop* him was another matter.

About halfway there, Jake heard hooves pounding behind him. He turned to see me pulling alongside. "Jamey?! What the hell are you doing?"

"What the hell are *you* doing?"

"You know what."

"Then I'm doing it with you."

"You don't have to."

"Blood's thicker than water. But let's take a shortcut!"

I let Shadow assume the lead, knowing Jake's horse would follow—right down a narrow trail through a thick pine forest. I knew the way, and kept my head tucked as we weaved through a maze of low-hanging branches.

Taken by surprise, Jake struggled to control his horse, and directed a sputtering stream of curses my way as pine branches whipped him in the face. He did his best to duck and protect his eyes. Though we emerged from those woods after a few minutes, it must've seemed like hours to Jake. Before he opened his eyes and realized we were out in the open, I'd snatched the reins out of his hands, and brought both horses to a stop.

I felt a little bad seeing him wipe trickles of blood from scrapes and welts on his face, but barely stifled a laugh when he spit out bits of pine bark and needles. His hat was missing, knocked off somewhere during our wild ride. I reached up to brush more pine needles out of his tangled hair.

He swatted my hand away. "What're you, trying to get me killed?"

"I'm trying to stop you from getting *yourself* killed. Jesus, Jake—for once in your life, look before you leap."

"For once, you leap without looking so damn much. You know who torched our town!"

"And how are you, the lone lunatic, gonna fix that by riding up there—"

"There's two of us."

"Okay, two lunatics. 'Cuz I'm such a good shot—and I don't even have my gun."

"Goddammit. Then let's go back to town and raise some rabble. Those people got nothing left to lose."

"Roust as many armed men as we can find?"

"Yeah, ride right out to the Krieg ranch—"

"Cry 'Havoc,' and let slip the dogs of war?"

"Yeah."

"Either the Kriegs die? Or we do?"

"If they die, this town stays to rebuild. If we die, we're no worse off."

I stared at him. "Dead is a *whole* lot worse off!"

"Better a live coward than a dead hero?"

"That philosophy is why we're alive to stand here arguing about it."

"I'm tired of rolling belly-up for bullies. It's time to take a stand."

"Suicide ain't a stand. It's just dumb."

"Then I suppose you got a big idea?"

"Come back to town, and I'll tell you."

Jake shook his head. But, at that moment, he was in no condition to lead a two-man frontal assault on the Krieg ranch. So he followed me, slowly and carefully, back through the pines. We spotted his hat—stuck in a tree, skewered by a sharp branch. I reached up, tugged it free, and handed it to him. He fingered the holes punched clean through the crown.

"Looks like you'll be needing another new hat."

"Better than needing a new head," Jake said, with a philosophical shrug.

27

"Gettin' mad gets in the way of gettin' even."
—Mississippi Mike Morgan

Jawbone Huggins inspected Jake's scraped-up face. "You look like you got a fast shave from a blind barber."

"Never try to save an ungrateful cat stuck up an unforgiving tree," Jake said—with a testy glance at me.

With our gang reconvened at Salem's place, we set about trying to figure our next move. Jake and me recounted how we knew of Wolf Krieg's affinity for fire. We were sure he was behind this, even if we couldn't prove it.

As to why he would torch Serenity Falls, when all this land would soon belong to the Kriegs anyway, I could only think of one reason: "He just couldn't wait for it to fall into his lap. He had to destroy this town his own way."

"We've already got Krieg's money," Juliet said. "Why not pay off the mortgages and be done with it?"

"Because we'll never be done with it," Mama said.

Jawbone agreed. "If Krieg can't take this land by foreclosure, he'll try and take it by force. It's only a matter of when."

"We finish this," Jake growled, "once and for all."

"Gettin' mad gets in the way of gettin' even," Mike said to Jake.

"Then what can we do?" Juliet asked.

"We raise the stakes in the game," I said, without hesitation.

"You still think this is some game?" Jake said. "Lookit what they did to this place."

"And you want to hit 'em back."

"I want to *kill* 'em!"

"Why play to their strength, instead of ours?"

"We got no strength."

"We got Krieg's fifty thousand, which he got from Atwood."

"So why would Krieg pay out even more?"

"Because we already have 'em roped. We have 'em thinking this railroad deal is the goose that'll lay 'em an awful lot of golden eggs."

"But in the fable," Juliet said, "they get so greedy, they end up killing the goose."

"Exactly!" I said. "If we can tempt Wilhelm Krieg into being too greedy for his own good, he'll kill that goose without even knowing it."

The sheriff was dubious. "You're bettin' this town's fate on one man's greed?"

"Most bets have a fool and a thief," I said. "The trick is to make sure the other fella's the fool."

"This here's a classic situation," Mike said. "But if you don't know where you're going, it's a good bet you'll end up someplace else."

"I know where," I said, "and I know why."

Mike looked me in the eye. "Good. The why comes first."

"Like the Bible says, 'a false balance is abomination to the Lord. But a just weight is His delight.' It's time this town got that just weight."

"As long you're not trying to be a hero," Mike said.

"Oh, heroism's overrated—and a short-lived occupation, as Sam Houston learned."

"All righty, then. How you gonna get where you're going?"

"Krieg and Atwood're dancing this two-step together—so we kill two birds with one deal. We need to take enough money to pay off all these mortgages—so Atwood can't threaten the town with extinction every time some rich bastard clinches his *co-jones*. And we need enough money left over to help everybody rebuild."

Mama liked what she was hearing. "That'll tell Krieg we're not going anywhere. If he means to take this land, he'll have to try it without a banker in his vest pocket."

"So you aim to call Krieg's bluff?" Mike said.

"I do. We play the ace up our sleeve."

Jake shook his head in disbelief. "What ace?"

"The other big stockholder. Bring him here to try and buy out Krieg's shares. There can't be two kings. And Krieg only knows one way to answer a challenge."

Mike rubbed his chin, and started to fret. "Though, the more you complicate a plan, the more likely it unravels."

Spurred by Mike's hint of doubt, Jake pounced. "What if Krieg's not as greedy as you think?"

"Yeah," Salem said, "why're you so sure he'll want to buy out the other fella?"

Despite his qualms, Mike spoke up. "To inveigle a man like Krieg into wanting something? You only have to tell him he can't have it."

"Why wouldn't he just play it safe," Juliet said, "and sell his shares to the other stockholder?"

"If you were Krieg," I said, "knowing what he *thinks* he knows, would you?"

Juliet thought about it. "I guess not."

"His whole life," I said, "Krieg's gambled—big. Jake, what've we learned from pert near every poker player we ever faced?"

"They think they're better gamblers than they really are," my brother said, grudgingly.

It was time for me to close this deal with my dubious co-conspirators. "Krieg's convinced he's investing in a sure thing. He'll have Wolf pushing him to buy out this other investor—to be the emperor of Texas. And, as we're all sick and tired of hearing, nobody says no to Krieg."

"A plan can get you in," Salem said, "but that don't mean it'll get you out. Maybe Juliet's right about settling for the money we already have."

Juliet agreed. "That's a good-sized stake for rebuilding the town somewhere else."

"Is that enough?" I said. "After eviction? And having our town burned down around us? How many people lost everything they would've taken with 'em?"

But Jake resisted. "The Kriegs gotta pay for what they've done. And not just money. They should pay with their lives. They sowed the wind, let 'em reap the whirlwind."

"I call your Bible verse, and raise you," I said. " 'Avenge not yourselves, but rather give place unto wrath.' "

Juliet chimed in. " 'Vengeance is mine; I will repay, saith the Lord.' "

"Sometimes the Lord's busy elsewhere," Jake said.

I gave my brother a steely squint. "Okay. Say a miracle happens. Say we actually kill Krieg, without getting ourselves killed. How does us hanging for murder help this town?"

"No jury'll ever convict us."

"Knowin' the facts," Sheriff Huggins said, "I'd have a hard time even arrestin' you. But some circuit judge might decide different. And I might not be able to talk him out of it."

I turned to Mike. "You've done bigger games than this. Krieg thinks he's holding the winning hand. But that's not enough for him. He has to destroy his opposition. We'll be giving him the chance to do that."

"It's still a gamble," Mike said.

"Isn't everything?" I turned to Jake. "We can take down Krieg—*and* break the bank."

"What if this doesn't work?" Salem said.

"Then we've still got Krieg's fifty grand. We'll be no worse off than we are now."

Mama quoted Shakespeare. " 'Though this be madness, yet there is method in it.' "

"Jake," I said, "are you willing to keep your gun holstered, for now?"

"For now. But we need somebody to play the other investor—somebody good."

"One man," Mike said. "Gideon."

Jake waved his hands. "Oh, no! Him advising us was one thing. But trusting him to be out front? *Uh-uhh.*" Then he glanced around the room. "Where is he, anyway?"

That's when we realized . . . nobody had seen Gideon Duvall all morning.

Mike's face went pale. He clutched at his coat, shut his eyes, and winced. His hand dug into his inside pocket, and came out empty. "Gone."

"What's gone?" Mama said.

"Money. Five thousand Krieg handed over last night, to add to the pot. But I don't know when . . ." Mike groaned as he remembered Gideon had carried his coat during their hasty escape from the burning hotel. After the chaos, he'd never thought to take inventory. "Gideon took it. He must've got a horse and slipped out of town."

Jake ran over to the livery, then returned with confirmation that a man matching Gideon's description bought a horse and saddle early in the morning. So Gideon had absconded, but where to?

Mike knew. "He's like a salmon swimming upstream. It's a sure bet he's headed back home to St. Louis."

Jake stood and turned toward the door: "I'm gonna find him. And I'm gonna kill him."

I grabbed Jake's arm. "You can't kill him!"

"Why the hell not?"

"Because we need him to play the other investor. Nobody else here can."

"Can't Mike bring another one of his confidence *amigos* here?"

Mike shook his head. "It'd take weeks. We don't have time."

"And we don't have Gideon either."

"But he's within reach," Mike said. "It's him, or nobody."

I looked at the group. "It takes one predator to eat another. Gideon's the one who can angle Krieg into buying a wagonload of worthless stock."

"But he needs minding," Mike said, still smarting over the money Gideon had swiped. "Or he'll turn around and make you his next meal."

That was a lesson I wouldn't forget. Figuring Gideon was on his way back to Dallas to catch the train to St. Louis, Mike and I prepared to chase him down.

"Why can't I go?" Jake said, standing in my way.

"Because you'll shoot him as soon as you lay eyes on him."

"You're probably right."

"Besides, we need you here to help Salem and Juliet print up a whole lot more stock certificates and railroad documents. Those have to be ready when we bring Gideon back."

"*If* you bring him back."

"Oh, I'll bring him back."

Gideon had a six-hour head start. With luck, we might catch up to him on the way. Less lucky, I hoped we'd get there in time to take the same train leaving Texas. But we'd chase him all the way back to his fine townhouse in St. Louis, if we had to.

I wasn't afraid of Gideon Duvall at all.
I was a little afraid of his mother.

28

"Whistling past the graveyard don't necessarily keep you out of the grave."
—Mississippi Mike Morgan

Gideon reached Dallas before we reached him.

We raced into town, left our horses at a local livery, and rushed to the depot just as the eastbound train was leaving. With no time to spare, we took a literal leap of faith and hopped aboard as the train chugged away from the platform, whistle blowing and drive wheels gaining speed.

It didn't take long to spot Gideon in the first-class club car, with its oak paneling, polished brass fixtures, and emerald velvet upholstery. The train had barely cleared the station, and he was already engaged in a poker game with unwitting victims. He didn't notice us, until he felt the cold steel barrel of my Colt against his neck.

A lesser man might've been startled. Gideon smiled. "What took you so long, son?" He set his cards down, stood, and nodded to his poker mates. "Sorry, gents. I'm needed elsewhere. I may be back. Or, I may not," he said, with a melodramatic glance at my gun.

Mike led the way outside to the open platform at the end of the car. With my pistol still poking into his ribs, Gideon turned to me. "I thought your brother was the gunman."

"Consider it insurance against your premature exit."

He gestured at the landscape flying past us. "Where would I go?"

"Depends how desperate you are."

"*Qu'est-ce que c'est, mes amis?*"

"For starters, the five thousand you stole from your own friend during the fire."

"You took advantage of me," Mike said, looking hurt.

"I swear, I don't know what happened to that money. I was in as much danger as you, Mike."

"Not enough to keep you from slippin' five grand out of his coat pocket," I said.

Gideon spread his hands in a gesture of innocence. "I have no such money. And you have no proof."

"You stealing from Mike? That's not even the point."

"What is?"

"The game is still on."

"We need you to play the other big stockholder," Mike said, "so we can lure Krieg into going broke buying out his competition."

Gideon slipped a cigar out of his coat pocket, struck a match, and lit it. "The game, as you call it, proved beneath me," he said, blowing a smoky billow into my face. "And that fire? Not worth risking my neck for your cause."

My thumb tickled the hammer on my gun. "I am real tempted to overcome my aversion to shooting people."

"Don't lower your standards on my account."

"The easy thing would be to kill you and toss your carcass overboard for the coyotes and buzzards."

Gideon's eyes crinkled in amusement. "Not your style, *mon ami.*"

"Styles change, *mon ami.*"

"I doubt you could kill in cold blood."

I flashed my brightest smile. "If I can't, my brother can. You dodge me, Jake has temper enough to hunt you down. And he's a very good shot."

"Listen to the lad," Mike said. "After the town burned, it were all they could do to keep Jake from a murderous spree out to the Krieg ranch. And you're a lot less fearsome than them. You really want to spend the rest of your days looking over your shoulder for Jake Galloway?"

"I'm not given to violence," Gideon said to me. "But I am given to gambling. And, in the absence of any burning reason to choose otherwise, I'll gamble that I can elude your brother. So we're at an impasse here."

"Then let's gamble, for real. You and me. Winner take all."

"For what stakes?"

"You win? Keep the cash you swear you didn't take. I win? You give back the money—*and* go back to Serenity Falls to finish the job."

"I'm not compelled. To hear you tell it, I already have that five grand. And you don't have someone to be your mysterious investor. So I'd be risking a tidy sum and taking part in your scheme, at no advantage to me."

Mike whispered in my ear.

"Nope," I said, with an emphatic shake of my head. "If I lose, we'll have nothing."

My alarm kindled Gideon's curiosity. "Hnnh. If you're not interested, maybe I am."

"Consider it," Mike said, prodding me.

"*No.* No way."

Gideon reached for the handle of the coach door. "You need me, and I have no use for you. So I'll be on my way."

Damn him for guessing right that I wouldn't shoot him. So I grabbed his shoulder. But Mike blurted, "Jamey'll also put up the fifty grand from Krieg."

Gideon's eyebrows arched. "Ahh. Now, *that's* compelling."

I glared at Mike, but he just shrugged. "You gotta make it worth his while."

"Not so fast," I said, more to Gideon than Mike. "We need that money to rebuild the town. Without it, there *is* no town. So, if I'm risking all that, playing for my home—hell, for the homes of everybody in Serenity Falls? Then it's only fair you play for *your* home. The deed to your house in St. Louis."

Gideon gnawed on his cigar.

"You can claim you're not concerned about Jake Galloway killin' you," Mike said to his erstwhile partner. "But whistling past the graveyard don't necessarily keep you out of the grave."

As Gideon mulled his options, I taunted him. "Lookit, Gideon the Great. Afraid of losing."

"Not at all." He extended his hand to me.

I shook it before either of us could reconsider. "Terms are agreed, then."

"I'll write it up, me as witness," Mike said. "Then I'll deal, and you'll play."

We went back inside the club car and found an empty table. Word somehow spread through the coach that something big was up. By the time Mike finished scribbling our hasty agreement, other travelers had gathered around us to watch. Gideon signed first, then Mike, who slid the paper and pencil over to me. They both saw me hesitate.

"Second thoughts?" Gideon said.

I signed, with an extra flourish at the end. I folded the paper and handed it to Mike—who then leaned close to Gideon and said, "Now I'll tell you what you need to know about Jamey's game."

My eyes almost popped out of my head. "What?!"

Mike looked pained, but not enough to stop. "He's been my meal ticket for twenty years. Did you think I'm fool enough to throw that away, boy?"

"*Et tu, Brute?*"

"I already taught you about Gideon's game. Only fair I do the same for him."

"A plague on both your houses."

As that stooped little man murmured in Gideon's ear, I couldn't hear everything. But I heard enough.

First, Mike reminded him he was the best player around, a poker genius. Then he revealed what I knew to be my fatal weakness, something I struggled to control. "The lad's good. You won't never be able to tell when he has a great hand. He just don't show it. But when he's got a bad hand? He tries so hard to cover it up, his face goes blank as a boulder. He won't blink at all, for near a good twenty seconds."

There was more after that, but not much. Gideon offered me one last chance to back out. But Mike wagged a finger at me. "You do that, you'll end up losing your nerve, just like me. You won't never win a big game again."

My confidence faltered. I was certain I was about to be suckered by two snakes in the grass—and they could see it in my eyes.

More in regret than anger, Mike picked at my doubts. "I reckon I were wrong about you, boy."

Gideon comforted Mike with a shoulder squeeze. "You tried to turn a sow's ear into a silk purse."

"And now I see I wasted my time. Son, you're a coward. And a mama's boy."

"Hey," Gideon said in mock protest, "nothing wrong with being a mama's boy. Just ask my *maman.*"

"It's plain you ain't up to the job of playing with the Big 'Gator here," Mike said.

Gideon said, "Your fear's smarter than you are, son."

My ears burned with shame. I felt cornered. And alone. In a

rail coach full of people, I was alone. I didn't have Mama watching out for me, or Cruz advising me, or brother Jake arguing with me. No Juliet or Becky to try and impress. Maybe I should've thought longer and harder about what I was fixing to do. But I subdued my furious humiliation, and kept my voice flat and frigid. "Even big 'gators get caught napping. Let's deal."

We started out with fifty-thousand dollars' worth of chips each. Mike cracked open a fresh deck of cards, allowed both of us to inspect them to our satisfaction, then dealt opening hands. Now that I knew Mike was a traitorous son of a bitch, I'd have to keep a sharp eye on his hands as well as Gideon's.

It's been said by men far wiser than me that nobody remembers the first hand of a poker game, only the last. That's generally true, even for the players. So I'll tell it to you, short and sweet, exactly as it happened:

Gideon starts out winning. I fold one bad hand after another. I warn him I'll kill him if I catch him cheating, and the same goes for treacherous Mike. Gideon smiles, unruffled.

Then the tide turns. I take several hands in a row. Gideon starts to sweat a little. But he also sees my tells in action. I don't have many, but if you know what to look for—and he does, thanks to Mike Morgan's betrayal—they're plain to see. Gideon must feel some extra confidence, knowing Mike's appraisal of me is proving accurate.

More passengers gather to watch, lured by the high-stakes intensity of the match. Next hand, I spot Gideon cheating, with a holdout card. He tries to dismiss the faux pas with a chuckle and a charming smile.

With a less charming smile, I draw my gun. "Next hand'll be played with you stripped to your union suit."

Gideon protests, but he has no choice. So off come the fancy duds—not incidentally revealing assorted means of cheating he's been holding in reserve. As he sits there, resplendent in red flannel, he tries to salvage some dignity by demanding fresh cards.

So Mike sees the porter and comes back with three new, sealed decks. I pick one, which Gideon consents to using. Play resumes. The pot ebbs and grows, gradually mounting past ten thousand. But the make-or-break stakes are held out by two crafty rivals.

During a brief respite to stretch our legs, Gideon compliments me. "Son, I didn't expect such spirited competition. But, in the end, you will lose."

Back to the table. Mike deals.

I don't want this game to last all the way to St. Louis. Time's running out for the folks back home. Determined to speed things along, I up the ante with our biggest opening yet—five grand.

Gideon gives me a friendly warning: "Haste makes waste." Then he considers . . . calls . . . and raises five grand.

I think for a bit, ask for three cards, then call. Gideon takes two cards, calls again.

It feels like the end is near. I take one new card. I check my hand.

That's when Gideon sees it—damned if Mike wasn't right. My face goes blank, eyes unblinking, for pert near twenty seconds. Gideon is sure he's witnessed my fatal tell, revealing a weak hand, despite my best efforts to hide it.

"Let's finish this, old man." I call, and raise—with everything I've got.

Convinced I'm bluffing, the Big 'Gator smells blood in the water. Whether my play is audacious or reckless, Gideon is sure he's won. With ceremonious deliberation, he pushes all his neatly stacked chips ahead.

I check my cards again. With a deep, drawn-out breath, I set them on the table. Facedown, like I'm folding.

Gideon smiles.

He reveals his hand. Three aces and a pair of deuces. A stylish full house. He reaches for the pot.

That's when I let out the slightest drawn-out grunt: "Uhh-hmm . . ."

Gideon pauses. Despite his years of practice, faint doubt flickers in his narrowed, steady eyes. He recovers, and stares at me, deadpan. But I only engage that reptilian gaze for a moment. I'm already looking down at my cards, as if I don't know what's there.

But I do. I turn them up. One by one.

I show a trio of sevens. The gathered crowd is hushed, wondering if I have four of a kind. When the next card is a six, there's a collective groan: *The kid's lost,* they're thinking.

I leave my fifth card facedown, for what seems like an eternity.

Then I bend up a corner, and slowly flip the card over. The crowd gasps in surprise—it's the fourth seven.

"Well," Gideon says with a wry half-smile, "I'll be buggered."

He instantly realized that I'd deployed my own fatal frailty to reverse-bluff him into believing I had a losing hand. He watched as I gathered up the chips, wincing only when I reached for the note promising his house deed. "How long until *Maman* and I have to move out?"

"You can stay, as long as you pay rent."

"I'd rather start over. We'll vacate by the end of the month."

"Your choice."

"I see your devious hand in all this," Gideon said to Mike. "You two ran a scheme on me."

"Nope," Mike said, "I did. Jamey didn't know nothing. The only way to sell you on the switch, to get him genuinely riled at me, and set you to watchin' for his tell, was if he really thought I snaked him."

I shrugged. "He's right. I'm not that good an actor." I turned to question Mike. "But how'd you know I'd find a way?"

"I knowed you had a good teacher. You done the rest."

"Well-played, *mes amis*," Gideon said, as he dressed.

"Aren't you angry?" I asked.

Gideon replied with a devil-may-care gesture. "I've won and lost many a fortune. I'll win again. And I'll be more careful next time I face you across a poker table."

"Last thing I need is a house in St. Louis. You want to win it back?"

"How?"

"Just make sure the game against Krieg works."

"Ahh. Incentive. But why trust me after all this?"

"Oh, I don't. I trust you're suited to the task, you have too much pride to do it poorly—and you'd like your house back, so you don't have to explain to *Maman* how you lost it."

"Well, I do like your plan. It can work. In the right hands."

"Yours."

"Of course."

"My brother *will* kill you if you double-cross us again."

"You have my word as a gentleman."

"Is that worth anything?"

"I rarely give it. When I do, it is sound. There is one requirement."

"What?"

"I always choose my own moniker."

"Got one in mind?"

"Gabriel Goldsworthy."

We stepped off the train in Denison, last stop in Texas, at the Red River. From there, we sent two telegrams—the first to Salem and the gang in Serenity Falls, saying we were on our way back for the final round. The second went to Krieg, from Gabriel Goldsworthy, revealing his identity as the other large investor in the Hollister & Dodge railroad enterprise. He'd be in Serenity Falls in a few days, and would pay a call to discuss their mutual interest in railroad stock.

Then we caught the next train back to Dallas.

29

"Take care when capitalizin' on another man's calamity."
—Mississippi Mike Morgan

Richly dressed Gabriel Goldsworthy and Levi Hollister (Gideon and me) drove the four-seat surrey out to Krieg's ranch. Mike followed in the smaller buggy. When we arrived, Victoria escorted us to the study, where old man Krieg and Wolf waited. Krieg and Gideon immediately squared off like two chesty gamecocks.

Gideon struck first, announcing he'd been quietly buying up railroad stock from smaller investors. "I am now the single largest shareholder. I intend to buy you out."

Wolf started to swear, but his father cut him off. "I will sell nothing. And I will be second to no man."

"You may know the range and its ways, but the stock market is my range. If you don't sell to me, I'll crush you. You have 'til noon tomorrow."

"Another sunrise will not change my mind. Set foot on my land again at your peril."

"Or, what—you'll shoot me?"

"I will. And I will enjoy it."

Before the men could come to blows, I grabbed Gideon's arm and hustled him out the door, leaving Mike behind.

"Might've overplayed your hand there, 'Mr. Goldsworthy,' " I said as we came down the mansion's front steps.

"You must sell the illusion." Gideon flashed his pearly teeth. "Besides, where's the fun in playing it safe?"

Inside, Mike conferred with Krieg. "This Goldsworthy is a carpetbagger. The senator wants a Texan partner for Hollister and Dodge."

"He will not have the ballocks to come back," Krieg said. "If he does—"

"You should buy *him* out," Mike said.

"We think alike, Herr Richter."

Next day, with the sun high, Krieg sat on his veranda, his Winchester across his lap. Wolf stood behind him. Krieg checked his pocket watch. By ten minutes past noon, satisfied his challenger had backed down, he got up to go inside.

Wolf held the door open, but stopped and squinted into the distance. "Well, I'll be damned."

Krieg turned to see a covered buggy rattling up the lane, carrying a lone occupant: Goldsworthy. Krieg waited until it was thirty paces away, aimed his rifle, fired—and prepared to shoot again.

The bullet pinged the body of the buggy—*much* too close for Gideon's comfort. He flinched, yanked the horse to a halt, bailed out, and scrambled for cover behind his vehicle. From relative safety, he waved his hat: "Don't shoot, Krieg!"

"I told you I would," Krieg yelled back.

"Things have changed—in your favor. Let me explain."

Krieg pursed his lips, then lowered his rifle.

Gideon stepped cautiously into the open—yet ready to dive for cover again. He fiddled with his hat. "I received a telegram. I've had a major financial reversal."

"How tragic."

"I-I need cash—fast! I have to sell my stock. Or I'll be ruined."

Before Gideon could say more, I loped up on horseback, hollering: "Hey! Goldsworthy! I know what you're up to!" I jumped off and grabbed him by the lapels. But he was already so uncommonly disheveled, coat rumpled and hair unkempt, that I momentarily forgot my prepared tirade. "Uhhh . . . Whatever you think you're doing, you can't do it!"

"I most certainly can!"

We knew our scuffle had to appear convincing—not a big stretch for me, considering how much prior trouble Gideon had caused. "We had a deal!"

"Sue me!"

"We will!"

"Ha! You'll never collect a penny!"

Krieg leveled his rifle at Gideon. "Goldsworthy—shut up. Hollister, talk."

I jutted my chin, and my righteous anger rumbled out like thunder. "Hollister and Dodge knows all about his business setbacks. He's not allowed to dump stock to save his sorry ass."

"I'll sell what I want, when I want!"

"No! That violates your agreement with the railroad syndicate!" I turned back toward Krieg. "He bought cheap stock before *anybody* else, with the stipulation he couldn't sell more than ten percent of his holdings in any thirty-day period." I snarled at Gideon again: "That agreement is legally binding. You signed it, you bogus weasel!"

"You mean *this* agreement?" Gideon whipped folded documents out of his inside coat pocket—and ripped them again and again, tossing shredded paper into the air like confetti. "There's your contract, Hollister!"

I yanked a small gun out of my coat pocket. "That's it—you're a dead man!"

"Blanks?" Gideon hissed at me.

"Nope."

"No?!"

"Just selling the illusion."

"Sell less!"

"Where's the fun in playing it safe?" I fired over his shoulder—missing, but not by much.

Gideon dodged behind the buggy. We skittered back and forth. He feinted left, then right, proving surprisingly nimble for a big man—until he tangled his own feet and fell flat on his ass. I fired again. The bullet kicked up dirt barely a foot from his head. His face displayed a mix of bug-eyed terror and impotent fury—amusing from my perspective, if not his.

Our clumsy dance ended the instant Krieg fired a booming rifle blast over our heads. Scared for real, I found myself hugging the ground next to Gideon.

"On my land," Krieg said, "nobody shoots Goldsworthy but me."

Another buggy raced up to the house, carrying Mike Morgan thrashing those reins for all he was worth. When he saw Krieg holding his Winchester, and me and Gideon on the ground, he feared the worst—until he saw us both still moving.

Mike climbed down from the buggy. "Thanks to God nobody's dead!"

"The day is still young," Krieg said.

At Mike's insistence, firearms were set aside, and we reconvened in Krieg's study. After an earful from "Hollister" and "Goldsworthy" on the particulars of our dispute, Mike lectured us. "Senator Flanagan and his associates want this deal completed. They don't care who owns the stock."

Though I was only playing a role, I still took "Herr Richter's" declaration personally. "Then what's the point in a deal? Why even bother with contracts?"

"Mr. Goldsworthy could challenge the initial agreement in court."

"Then Hollister and Dodge'll fight it like Kilkenny cats!"

"And let him tie things up for months? Or years? Is that what your father and his cronies want—to enrich the lawyers?"

"Well . . . no. But there's a principle!"

"Principles're for debating societies. All what matters is seeing to it these railways're built. So let Mr. Goldsworthy sell his stock to Mr. Krieg. These two gents get what they want. And the company secures the money to proceed."

I was outnumbered, and yielded—grudgingly.

"Mr. Goldsworthy," Mike said, "how many shares you lookin' to sell?"

"All of 'em," Gideon said, his voice a dry croak, with a wrenching sigh added for good measure. "Twenty. Five. Thousand. But I'll sell for *no less* than ten dollars per share."

"I will take them all," Krieg said, "for fifty *cents* a share."

Gideon's eyes bulged. "That's larceny!" He threatened, blustered, and begged—and came down to five dollars a share.

"Very well," Krieg said. "*Twenty-five* cents, then."

Gideon's neck veins popped. "That's not how you haggle!"

Mike wagged a finger at the rancher. "Herr Krieg, take care when capitalizin' on another man's calamity. Or the senator might reconsider the arrangement. I suggest two dollars a share."

The gamecocks glowered at each other. Then Gideon knuckled under. "Done. *Mon Dieu.*"

Mike turned to Krieg. "Can you raise the additional fifty thousand?"

"I can."

"Mr. Goldsworthy," Mike said, "you have them stock certificates?"

"In town."

At Mike's behest, both parties consented to a civil transaction, to take place at Krieg's ranch that evening at eight. Mike, Gideon, and me left separately for town.

Krieg wasn't far behind us, headed directly to the bank, where he told Atwood he'd need another interest-free fifty-thousand dollars, this time graciously offering land as collateral. Drained of whatever mettle he might have had, Atwood shuffled back to his vault, opened the safe on the left side, extracted bundles of money, and placed them gently into the carpetbag Krieg held open. He fondled the last remaining clump of cash for a lingering moment, then set it inside the bag.

Atwood hung his head and reached a grasping hand into the safe, hoping he'd find something, *anything*. But it was just a big, empty, armored box. He sighed, and almost laughed, though nothing was remotely funny. "If anything goes wrong, I'm ruined."

"You would have my land."

"Land ain't cash."

"You worry too much, Silas." Krieg buckled up the carpetbag and departed—leaving the bereft banker peering mournfully into a safe as bare as Old Mother Hubbard's cupboard.

That evening, as arranged, Gideon, Mike, and me drove the big surrey back to Krieg's. Wolf brought us into the study, where his father sat behind his desk with the pleased expression of an emperor about to be served a feast. Shoulders bowed, Gideon sat across from him. Acting as master of ceremonies, Mike pushed a folder of stock certificates toward Krieg, then slid the bag of cash to Gideon.

"Herr Krieg," Mike said, "you are now the biggest shareholder in this here railroad."

Despite the money now in his hands, Gabriel Goldsworthy was a beaten man, crushed by his reversal of fortune. "I . . . I never thought it would come to this," he said in a husky whisper. "I thought to take my life instead of demeaning myself this way."

"You have fifty-thousand dollars," Krieg said, without sympathy. "A fortune to most men."

"It all goes to pay debts. I'm a pauper."

"Then you have nothing to lose. If you are a man, you will rise again."

"Or not," I said, as Gideon slumped to his knees and wept. I actually felt a lump of pity in my throat—he was so convincing, I almost gave him a standing ovation.

But the act persuaded Krieg, who regarded Goldsworthy with cold contempt. "Remove this wretch from my sight."

Mike and me pulled Gideon to his feet, and guided him out the door. We left Wilhelm and Wolf Krieg to enjoy their fine brandy, and Angus McDonnell's maps of fanciful railroads that would never exist anywhere but their avaricious imaginations.

We hurried down the steps and into the surrey. As Mike giddyupped the horses and we drove swiftly into the night, I reached over and pried the money bag from Gideon's sticky grip.

He feigned indignation. "You don't trust me? A lesser man than I would feel slandered."

"A lesser man than *I* woulda shot you on the train."

When we returned to the print shop, we found the rest of our gang anxiously waiting to learn whether the scheme had succeeded. I opened the satchel to show them the cash, setting off a round of relieved whooping and cheering.

"Much as it pains me to say this," I said, "even though Gideon Duvall is generally as welcome as a carbuncle . . . as useful as a dry well in a drought . . . as much trouble as—"

"Ride to the point, son," Gideon said.

"Well, we couldn't have done it without him."

Mama took custody of the money bag. "Still, y'all keep an eye on him while I put this away."

She stowed the proceeds in her safe in Salem's back room,

while Cruz uncorked some wine and poured for each of us. Mike hoisted his glass first. "Well, folks, here's to gettin' even."

Jake nodded toward me. "And here's to my little brother, who may be *almost* as smart as he thinks."

As the group traded playful toasts, I huddled with Gideon and held up the promissory note that surrendered his house. And then I tore it up.

But the game was not entirely finished.

30

"How camest thou in this pickle?"
—William Shakespeare, *The Tempest*

Next morning at dawn, Cruz had the surrey waiting to take Mike and Gideon to Waco. From there, they'd catch the first stagecoach to the train depot in Dallas, departing before our final act played out. Mama, Jake, and me were up early to see them off.

I extended a hand to Mike. "Thanks."

He gripped it, and it was more than just a handshake. "Thank *you*."

"For what?"

"Gideon may've done it for the sport. But I done it to see if I still could. You trusted me enough to let me try."

"Bon chance, mes amis," Gideon said, flashing a smile. The two of them climbed aboard, and Cruz drove them away.

Soon after sunrise, Sheriff Huggins rode out to the Krieg ranch. Victoria led him to the veranda out back, where Wilhelm Krieg was midway through a breakfast of bacon, eggs, biscuits, and coffee. "Poppa, sheriff's here to see you."

"Mornin', Mr. Krieg."

Krieg paused between forkfuls, peeved at the interruption. "Sheriff."

"You didn't happen to do business with fellas named Hollister and Dilmore . . . did you?"

Krieg lowered his fork. "Why?"

"Well . . . they're in my jail now." Jawbone showed him two wanted posters with descriptions matching me and Jake. "These came in a couple of days ago. I thought they looked familiar. Caught 'em just as they were leaving town."

Krieg's jaw twitched. He dropped the fork, his appetite expired. He took up the handbills for a closer look. "Wanted, for what?"

Jawbone pointed at the criminal specifics printed on the posters. "Fraud. Railroad stock swindles—stock's worthless. Their company don't exist. I hope that wasn't what you transacted with 'em."

Krieg looked poleaxed. "Fraud . . . ?"

Jawbone somehow kept his expression straight and earnest, trying not to enjoy the moment too much. "Did they take a lotta money?"

"A great deal."

"Hmm. All they had on 'em was pocket change. The rest must be gone with those two older fellas workin' with 'em . . . a short one, and a nickel-plated popinjay." Jawbone gave a low whistle. "Them two had more aliases than hairs on a horse."

Krieg bowed his head. "Who were they, really?"

The sheriff shrugged. "No idea. But they sure weren't who they claimed to be."

Wolf came out on the veranda to join his father for breakfast, took one look at the old man's face, and knew something was very wrong. "Poppa, what's going on?"

Wilhelm's face flushed. "You pushed me into this. You, and your owning the future."

"We will, with that railroad."

"There is . . . *no railroad.*"

Wolf gaped, speechless for once.

"We were swindled."

"I'll . . . I'll kill 'em," Wolf said.

"No, son, you won't," Jawbone said. "Federal marshal's on his way to pick 'em up, and anybody else who might've been involved. Were y'all involved?"

"Yes!" Krieg shouted. "We made a deal! They took my money!"

"Now, take your time and think. Was it all on the square?"

Father and son fell silent.

Without letting on, Jawbone prodded a little more, as if investigating. "Did any bribes change hands? Any shady stock dealings? 'Cuz I got two young fellas in my jail who might have stories to tell. To ease their own way."

"Are you making accusations?" Wilhelm said.

"No, sir. Just, if you go to the law and try to recover your money, you *may* have to admit what you *might've* done, or *could've* been involved with."

Krieg sighed in resignation.

"Unless they confess," Jawbone said, "or somebody catches the other two, I reckon you won't be seeing that money again."

"But I will see your prisoners." Driven by cold fury, Krieg slid his chair back and stood, without bothering to use his cane.

Jake and me occupied one of the three spartan jail cells in the rear of Sheriff Huggins' law enforcement establishment. Still dressed in our business attire, we sat on a cot playing cards to pass the time. We perked up when we heard Jawbone's voice as he entered the office.

"You can talk to 'em," he said. "You just can't kill 'em."

The stout door separating the cells from the office opened, and the sheriff came in, along with Wilhelm Krieg. Jawbone raised a hand to stop Krieg, then confiscated the rancher's gun and knife.

"They're all yours. For now, anyway," Jawbone said. "Marshal should be here to get 'em soon. Anybody needs me, I'll be up front."

Then he left us alone with Krieg. Seeing the murder in Krieg's eyes, I appreciated the bars between us.

"My money may be lost," he said, his jaw clenched, "but I still have my name. If you say a word about my involvement—to the marshal, or anyone else—you will not live to see prison. I will find you. And kill you. Remember this: I never forgive. Or forget."

Then he left. After a mutual sigh of relief, me and Jake exchanged puzzled glances.

"Hey—Sheriff?" Jake called out.

Jawbone came back to the cell, bringing us two cups of his surprisingly excellent coffee.

Jake accepted his cup through the bars. "Not that we mean to bellyache. But there isn't really a marshal coming . . . is there?"

"Naww. Just a little icing I added to the cake."

"Y'know, for a lawman," I said, "you got a real dishonest streak."

Meanwhile, Krieg hobbled into the bank as fast as his gimpy leg could carry him. He barged into Silas Atwood's office and broke the bad news.

Atwood swooned into his big leather chair, slumped forward onto the desk, and buried his face between his arms. With his vault empty, his remaining assets were the furniture, the bank building—and not much else. His voice came out as a muffled whimper. "It comes to this."

Krieg pounded on the desk, bouncing Atwood's head up. "What about me?"

"I'm a founder . . . a pillar here." Atwood fixed Krieg with a contemptuous stare. "You? I told you . . . I *begged* you. This is your fault."

"Do not blame me for your weakness and greed."

"I need money—now! I'm selling your land. Cheap."

"No! I will *never* sell my land!"

"*I'm* selling it. It's collateral—I don't need your permission."

Krieg blinked at the banker. Then he backed toward the wing chair behind him, trying to sit before his knees buckled under the burden of calamitous disgrace. He stumbled and fell to the floor in a daze. Both broken men stared past each other, their anger spent.

"You and me," Atwood said, "we're our own worst enemies."

Back at the jail, even though me and Jake were still a little spooked by Krieg's visit, we settled back to playing cards. As we waited to be released, we chatted idly about where we might lay low for a while, until the local dust settled. "You know what bothers me the most?" I said.

"Yeah—that you can't tell Becky how you singlehandedly saved Serenity Falls." Jake rolled his eyes in good-natured disgust.

"I just don't like her thinking I'm a good-fer-nothin' gambler."

"She's married to Anders Lind. Who cares what she thinks of you? *If* she thinks of you at all."

"Would it kill you to show your own brother a little sympathy?"

"It might."

I saw him sneak a card off the bottom of the deck. "Hey! Stop cheating."

Jake smirked. Then we heard boot heels and jangling spurs approaching from the office. "About time," Jake called out. "Are we finally getting out of here?"

"Well, now, that's a funny question, boys," Jawbone said as he came through the door. But his grim expression instantly convinced us the answer wouldn't be funny at all. "This here's Deputy Marshal Ralph Bell."

Jawbone stepped aside, revealing a man behind him. Blocky and stone-faced, he wore a weather-beaten duster, well-worn hat—and a six-pointed silver star. He carried a big, clanking burlap sack.

"That's nice," I said to Jawbone, "and why's he here?"

Ralph Bell's high-pitched voice didn't match his craggy looks. "Takin' you two desperadoes to state prison at Huntsville. To be held pending trial for felonious fraud."

Jake gripped the bars. "Jawbone! What the hell—?!"

"That's gotta be a mistake," I said.

The sheriff looked genuinely crestfallen. "His warrants and paperwork are good."

"For *what*?" I said.

"Well . . . you boys really did commit fraud."

"Well . . . who the hell wired a marshal?"

"Well, I sure didn't," Jawbone snapped at me. "I'm sorry, boys. There's no choice. I gotta hand you over."

"Can't we at least say goodbye to Mama?"

Jawbone shrugged. "My hands're tied."

"And yours are about to be," Marshal Bell said, serious as a hangman. "I'm taking you to the state prison in Huntsville—"

"Yeah, yeah, yeah," I said, "to be held pending trial for felonious fraud."

Jawbone unlocked the cell. Bell entered, reached into his sack, and took out two sets of irons. We meekly allowed ourselves to be shackled, wrist and ankle. Then we shuffled out to a jail wagon in front of the sheriff's office. Bell helped us climb up into the rear compartment, locked us down, and padlocked the door behind us.

We felt the wagon rock as the marshal climbed up into the driver's seat, shook the reins, and whooped at the mules. As we rolled out of town, me and Jake felt a little like beeves heading for slaughter.

We soon discovered there's not much you can see riding in the belly of a jailer's wagon. There were small barred windows in back and on either side. But between the low roof and our feet chained to the floor, it was hard to stand up and look out anyway. As the wagon jounced along, we sat on the facing benches, in considerable shock, stewing in somber silence.

"Looks like we're fortune's fools," I said after a couple of bleak hours.

With a woebegone sigh, Jake answered my Shakespeare with his own. " 'How camest thou in this pickle?' "

"We're doomed."

"Pretty much."

31

**"So we profess ourselves to be the
slaves of chance."
—William Shakespeare,
*The Winter's Tale***

Speaking of doom, Silas Atwood sat alone at his desk, so pre-occupied by his own impending ruin he barely noticed when Sheriff Huggins appeared in his office doorway. Unencumbered by a sidearm, as usual, Jawbone did carry a dusty potato sack.

Atwood glanced at the empty whiskey bottle on his desk. Though dazed and fuzzy-headed, the banker was peeved that he didn't feel a whole lot drunker. That, after all, had been the point of draining the bottle by himself over the past few hours—to dull the terrifying conviction that he'd burned all his bridges, at both ends. "Shhheriff, I'd offer you a drink. But I am fresh outta whishkey . . . and money."

"Can't help with the whiskey. As for money—well, this might be your lucky day."

"Ha," Atwood said without mirth. "I doubt that very, very . . . very much."

"But I'm here to pay off the mortgages."

The banker blinked. "Whut? Whish . . . *which* mortgages?"

"Well, that'd be all of 'em." Jawbone hefted the sack and set it on the desk. "And a comfortable interval before that eviction deadline."

Atwood opened the drawstrings and peeled the bag down enough to see what was inside—cash. *Lots* of cash. Tied in neat bundles. His eyes bugged out in drunken wonder. It wasn't solely the amount—it was also the windfall's unforeseen arrival in the hands of an unexpected courier. Atwood upended the bag and dumped the contents, forming a money pyramid on his desk. "H-h-h-how much?"

"All told, the folks who held those mortgages owed thirty-two-thousand, eight-hundred and forty-three dollars."

Atwood fanned his face with a bundle of bills. Then he kissed it. "How do I know that's right?"

"Hobie Shroder was kind enough to cipher it for me."

"H-H-Hobie did?"

"Yep. If you'd care to count it, you'll find it's all there."

His mouth agape, Atwood did indeed cut the strings on each bundle, and counted every last bill, setting them in neat piles. No banker worth his salt would take someone's word for that amount, not even the sheriff's. But the tally was correct. "Wh-wh-where did alla this cash come from?"

"Let's just say—from a mysterious benefactor. I hope you didn't have your heart set on all that property belonging to the bank."

"No . . . no . . . no. Money's good." For the first time in days, Atwood dug up a smile. "In fact, money's *grand.*"

With a giddy laugh, he gathered the cash into one big mound of greenbacks. Then he ran his fingers through them, like he was washing his hands clean. While this didn't rectify the matter of *all* the funds he'd been forced to give Krieg, it was enough to avert immediate catastrophe—and more than enough that he'd never *ever* have to reveal this latest flirtation with disaster.

"Now, I need something in return," Jawbone said. "All the mortgage paperwork, marked paid."

Atwood stopped caressing the cash. "B-b-but that could take all night."

"No place I need to be."

"This is highly irregular."

"There's been a lot of that lately. Rather than risk anything happening to you, this here money, or those mortgage papers, there's no time like the present."

Realizing Jawbone had no intention of budging, Atwood told Hobie Shroder to close up. Hobie shooed the last customers out the door, locked up, and drew the shades. Then he and the other three tellers and clerks set to working on the mortgages—with no notice they'd been paid with the very same money Atwood had given Krieg to finance his nonexistent railroad empire.

The bankers finished their accounting by sunrise. A bleary-eyed but sober Atwood found Jawbone napping in a comfy wing chair in the lobby. "Sheriff . . . wake up."

Jawbone opened his eyes. "Y'all done?"

Atwood handed him a leather case containing the processed mortgage papers. "Feel free to verify it's all in good order."

"I can't think of any reason not to trust you, Mr. Atwood. Can you?"

Atwood answered with a wordless, wan smile.

Jawbone tucked the case under his arm and ambled to the door as Hobie unlocked it. "Good day, fellas."

The trip to Huntsville, about a hundred miles away, would take at least four days. That meant me and Jake had plenty of time with little to occupy us, so we went over everything again, and again: *What happened? What did we miss? Who turned us in?*

But no matter how we looked at our fix, every which way, we couldn't puzzle it out. It had never crossed my mind we'd end up in prison. And while the prospect of spending years behind bars was bad enough, I'd also have Jake reminding me—*every single day*—that it was *my* brilliant plan which landed us there.

We were so busy teetering between frustration and fear that it took us into the second day, after making overnight camp and eating miserable grub, before we realized we weren't heading east toward Huntsville—we were heading *north*. But no matter how many times we peppered Marshal Bell with the question of exactly *where* we were going, his answer never wavered: "Where I'm going don't matter. Where you're going is prison."

By the fourth day, even if the marshal had a damned poor sense of direction, we were in the dumps, resigned to our fate and at each other's throats. After bouncing along in silence for a spell, Jake fired a fresh salvo. "This is your fault, y'know."

"*My* fault? Your way, we'd've ended up in pine boxes, six feet under!"

Jake rapped his knuckles against the wagon wall. "We're *in* a box."

"Oak! And above ground!"

"And headed for prison."

"Oh, and *you'd* rather go out in a blaze of glory."

"Damn right I would."

"You and your stupid death wish—"

"Shut up."

"*You* shut up!"

"No—*shhhh!*" Jake held up a shackled hand. "Listen."

That's when I heard the mournful wail of a train whistle. And the hiss of a steam locomotive—and not off in the distance, but close by. We felt the wagon roll to a stop. A minute later, the rear door swung open. Ralph Bell climbed in and unlocked our chains and irons.

"Get out."

"Who," Jake said with a sardonic half-smile, "us desperadoes?"

302

"Out." The marshal didn't appear to enjoy my brother's sense of humor.

I hesitated. "You're not gonna shoot us for escaping, are you?"

"Get. Out."

Following orders, we stretched the cramps out of our legs and hopped down to the ground behind the wagon. It was dark out, but we could see enough: tracks, train, platform, ticket office—and the sign that confirmed we were at the Dallas train depot.

Jake squinted. "What the hell're we doing here?"

"I'm handing you off."

"To who?"

"To me, lads," a familiar voice said. Mississippi Mike Morgan rounded the corner of the wagon, wearing a sly grin and weighed down by three carpetbags.

Jake and me were certainly relieved we would not be taking up residence at the Huntsville hoosegow. But relief gave way to confusion—and vexation, as it dawned on us we'd been hoodwinked. We swarmed Mike and backed him up against the wagon.

"Prison?" Jake said.

Mike shook his head. "Nope."

I nodded toward Bell. "Marshal?"

"Nope."

Jake's anger flared. "Then . . . *what the hell*?!"

"I needed to spirit you lads out of Serenity Falls—without tippin' off that masterful game you ran on Krieg and Atwood. You're new at this. I couldn't risk you'd let slip what we done."

I realized Mike was right. "And if you managed to fool us—"

"—then they're none the wiser." Mike nodded toward the bogus marshal. "This here's Ralph Bell, ol' pal o' mine."

"Very convincing," I said.

Bell shed the grim mask required of his role, chuckled, and shook our hands. "Just doing Mike a favor. When we was young, he tried to save me from a ruinous life of gambling, a pastime at which I was demonically determined, yet remarkably inept."

I gave Mike a hurt look. "How come you never tried to save us?"

"You wasn't inept. You just needed some seasoning."

Jake frowned, still feeling crabby. "Was the sheriff in on it?"

"Yep," Mike said.

"He really *does* have a dishonest streak," I said, disconcerted.

Mike gave us the two traveling bags Mama had packed for us (she was in on it, too), including four thousand dollars she'd set aside to get us going.

"Going where?" Jake said.

"Anywhere but Texas, I expect," I said.

"That'd be wise, for now," Mike said.

A portly conductor strode along the platform, calling, "All *aboooooard*! Bound for St. Looie, and points east!"

"That's us, lads," Mike said. "You're welcome to join us."

Jake shook his head. "Already been."

"Then where to?"

"Well," I said with a peeved scowl, "we hadn't given it much thought, seeing as we'd been led to believe we'd be bunking at the state prison for some time to come."

"And I don't much care," Jake said, "so long as I don't have to ride a horse to get there."

I looked at Jake. "We've never seen an ocean."

"Or the Rockies."

Mike chuckled. "Ahh, to be young and fancy-free."

Jake dug two coins out of his vest pocket and juggled them. "Heads, Denver . . . tails, San Francisco?"

I shrugged. "Sure. Why not?"

Jake caught one and let the other hit the ground, where it

bounced a few times before settling on . . . tails.

"Take 'Frisco by storm, lads," Mike said. At the final call from the conductor, he and Ralph shook our hands and trotted for their train.

We watched them go, grabbed our bags, and headed for the ticket window. "I could get used to trains," Jake said, "and so could you."

"I got a feeling you're not giving me much choice."

"Oh, 'cuz you love trail dust and saddle sores so much."

"I never said that. I'm just sayin' we oughta—"

Whatever I was about to add, the blast of the train whistle drowned me out . . .

32

**"Money may not buy happiness,
but it does let a man choose his own
form of misery."
—Wilhelm Krieg**

Mama's hero Benjamin Franklin once said, "Three can keep a secret, if two of them are dead." Not to dispute Mr. Franklin's wisdom, but the account of how we'd saved our battered, burned little town remained a long-unbroken confidence—and lifelong bond—among our stouthearted band of conspirators. Even for a lawman like Jawbone Huggins, any qualms about ill-gotten gains were outweighed by the principle of well-deserved restitution.

The rebuilding of Serenity Falls began the very morning after the mortgages were settled. That's when Becky Lind drove the first of many wagonloads of board and framing down from the Lind sawmill. Anders kept the mill working overtime for months, producing whatever wood townsfolk needed.

The Linds donated much of that lumber. The rest, and many boxes of nails, hammers, and loads of fire-resistant brick, were paid for by that same mysterious benefactor, whose identity no one ever discovered. And Mama put the remainder of those proceeds to good use as seed money for interest-free loans. Not that he meant to, but Silas Atwood actually did end up helping the town grow.

The town's resurrection included construction of a real schoolhouse, which Juliet happily occupied as the town's first full-time teacher. Mama's bank flourished, while Atwood's shriveled—right up until his final desperate investment in yet another foolish venture, just as the global economic Panic of 1873 struck that September. Atwood lost everything, proving that some people never ever learn from their mistakes, and the sole remaining town founder skulked away in the literal dead of night. No one ever heard of (or from) him again.

To this day, even after considerable study on the matter, I still do not understand the Byzantine tangle that triggered the Panic of '73. As best I can reckon, it involved speculation in railroads, greed, silver prices, greed, coinage, greed, Germany, greed, and a whole lot of other whatnot and greed. In the end, it proved yet again that gamblers—whether they're playing stock markets or poker—think they're a whole lot smarter than they really are.

Not one to let a good building go to waste, Mama took over Atwood's abandoned bank and set up the Serenity Falls Saving & Loan Association—inspired by the Philadelphia Saving Fund Society, established in her hometown back in 1816 as America's first savings bank. Atwood's beleaguered head teller Hobie Shroder came along with the building and was relieved to be working for an honest bank—which he did so well and faithfully that Mama eventually promoted him to vice-president and manager.

Meyer Fein was reelected mayor, several times over. He was so well-liked, nobody ever ran against him. And people continued to like him even after many years in office—a true political rarity, if you ask me.

Our Scottish friend Angus McDonnell did actually finish the job for which he was first sent west. Weeks after his employers had written him off for dead, he reported to them that Serenity Falls was indeed an ideal place for a railroad crossing—and a few years later, an actual railroad company came to call. When they laid tracks right past town and designated Serenity Falls as a primary stop, they generated considerable local prosperity.

And what became of the Kriegs? Well, soon after the railroad swindle, daughter Victoria gathered up her mother's family jewels and slipped away one night on her white stallion, Lucifer. After his excesses drove his father to disown him, Wolf quit Texas altogether to pursue various mercenary schemes, ending up dead broke and dead drunk in Deadwood some years later.

Wilhelm Krieg himself became entangled in the Panic of '73—deep in debt, short on cash, owning too much of what nobody wanted to buy. In the end, the world had told Krieg the word he never thought he'd hear—a resounding "No!" Children scattered, empire in ruins, forced to auction off cattle and land for pennies on the dollar, he'd lost pretty much everything a man could lose, and moved to Mexico to start over. We never heard what became of him after that, and didn't much care.

Still, seeing how Krieg was not a man to forgive and forget, it's just as well me and Jake never did have a burning desire to visit Mexico.

Turned out we found San Francisco a dandy place to hang our hats, so we stayed awhile. And that's where, against all odds, we ran into somebody Jake was hoping he'd see again. There we were, on a Saturday night, engaged in friendly high-stakes poker at the stately Hotel Carlton, when a gloved female hand touched Jake on the shoulder.

"Why, 'Mr. Dilmore,' " she said, "fancy meetin' you here."

We knew that voice, and we both looked up—to see elegant, alluring Victoria Krieg and her sassy smile, a vision in sapphire satin.

With a crooked grin, Jake folded, stood, and took Victoria by the arm. They walked off together, and I didn't see them again until Monday morning. But that's another story for another day.

★　★　★　★　★

We Galloway brothers truly did descend from a long line of gamblers, though they may not have seen themselves as such. The grandparents we never knew could have stayed in Belfast, but they risked everything on a future across a very big ocean, in a new and untamed land.

Their daughter—our mother—carried on their spirit when she fled the familiarity of Philadelphia to wander west, into unknown wilderness. Cara took a gamble when she married Reuben, another when she killed him, and yet another when she kept the saloon and vowed never again to leave her fate in any man's hands.

Fact was, long before Jake and me ever dealt a deck of cards or defied the Kriegs, our destinies were shaped by the bets placed by our forebears. Somehow, they knew we either make our own choices, or others make them for us. Everything's a gamble, one way or another.

But isn't the biggest risk of all leaving your life up to somebody else?

There's a tale about a confidence man and cardsharp known as "Canada Bill" Jones. Famed as a master monte dealer, he could've retired a rich man—but he couldn't resist the urge to imperil his winnings at dishonest faro tables.

One time, Canada Bill found himself spending an idle night in Baton Rouge, with considerable monte money burning a hole in his pocket. So, he searched high and low around town, until he located a faro game in a barbershop back room.

Well, his partner found him there some time later—and immediately noticed Bill's bankroll dwindling, and the dealer cheating. He begged Bill to quit before he'd lost his last cent: "Bill! Can't you see this game is crooked?"

"Sure," Canada Bill said, "but it's the only game in town."

That reminds me of our friend Mike Morgan's first lesson:

"Whatever the game, expect your opponents to cheat."

So, what's a body to do? Here's what I think: Learn what you need to know. Keep your eyes open. Be ready to swallow your pride and walk away. And then, take the gamble.

You might lose . . . but it's the only way to win.

ABOUT THE AUTHOR

New York Times best-selling author **Howard Weinstein** became a professional writer at age 19, when he sold "The Pirates of Orion" episode to NBC's Emmy-winning animated *Star Trek* revival in 1974.

Since his first novel in 1981, Howard's extensive and eclectic writing credits include 16 novels, graphic novels, and nonfiction books (including seven *Star Trek* novels); 65 *Star Trek* comic books; and many newspaper and magazine articles and columns.

His books include *Puppy Kisses Are Good for the Soul,* a heart-warming account of life with Mail Order Annie, his first wonderful Welsh Corgi; and a biography of one of his childhood heroes, New York Yankees baseball star and Hall of Famer Mickey Mantle.

Readers can contact the author at info@howardweinstein books.com and visit him online at www.howardweinsteinbooks .com.

The employees of Five Star Publishing hope you have enjoyed this book.

Our Five Star novels explore little-known chapters from America's history, stories told from unique perspectives that will entertain a broad range of readers.

Other Five Star books are available at your local library, bookstore, all major book distributors, and directly from Five Star/Gale.

Connect with Five Star Publishing

Visit us on Facebook:
    https://www.facebook.com/FiveStarCengage

Email:
    FiveStar@cengage.com

For information about titles and placing orders:
    (800) 223-1244
    gale.orders@cengage.com

To share your comments, write to us:
    Five Star Publishing
    Attn: Publisher
    10 Water St., Suite 310
    Waterville, ME 04901